THE SANTINIS COLLECTION

MELISSA SCHROEDER

Includes the following novellas:

Leonardo

Marco

Gianni

Vicente

When I first came up with the idea for The Santinis, the one person who has always been along for the ride these last few years was Brandy Walker. We share more t han a love of romance and the publishing business. We are both military wives and former brats. She helped me come up with the series and made the most fabulous covers for the books.

More people were very supportive when I came up with the idea. Big thanks to Heather Long for her understanding of my strange sense of humor, Joy Harris because she's Joy and a big thanks to Gina Dewitt for being such a fabulous beta reader, thanks to Mel's Militia for getting the word out about The Santinis, and especially to Noel Varner for her hard work on the edits. And last but not least, thanks to Les and my girls.

LEONARDO

Melissa Schroeder

Dedication

To my parents who showed us that there were good
things about growing up military.

A NOTE FROM MEL

I was born in an Army hospital. I always joke that I was government issued and I know a lot of other brats feel this way. Our lives are not our own but we belong to a huge family, filled with so many different people from various backgrounds that it is quite unique. There is a reason I have found so many military brats-as many of us like to be called- to be some of the most adaptable folks I have met. Still it wasn't something I thought I would do to my own kids. It isn't an easy life. But when my husband Les and I decided that it was best for him to enter the Air Force almost 20 years ago. This coming September, we will come to the end of his active duty military career. To pay homage, I decided to write a series of novellas about a group of extraordinary brothers who all serve in the military. Each book is set in a location we lived for a time.

Leonardo is in San Antonio. We moved there after Hawaii and it was our longest assignment. We lived on base for part of our time there in a house built in 1933 that harbored at least one ghost. We had a rocky time while living in San Antonio but there were good things about living there. We were close to family and back in the land of Tex-Mex. I was living there when my first book, Grace Under Pressure, was released by Liquid Silver Books. I always see our assignment at Randolph AFB (now Joint Base San Antonio) as a transition base. Three of my favorite eating establishments are mentioned in the book: Whataburger, Rudy's,

CHAPTER ONE

The bright sunlight almost blinded Leo Santini the moment he walked into Jeff's hospital room.

"Dammit to hell," he muttered.

"Still a vampire, I see," Jeff said with a chuckle.

Leo squinted at him. "And you're still a sun loving freak from Florida."

As Leo approached the bed, he felt some of his anxiety dissipate. His old boot camp buddy looked better than he expected. After the report he read on Jeff's injuries, Leo hadn't been sure what to expect. Just the fact he wasn't completely medicated meant he was making strides.

"Freak? Please. You're the one who moved to Texas."

He settled in the chair beside the bed. "Please. Not like teaching at Ft Sam was my first choice. Of course, it allows me to see your sorry ass."

Leo glanced around the room. There were four beds but at the moment, only two of them were occupied.

"Smith, this is Leo Santini, an old buddy of mine who is teaching here as a medic. Leo this is Roy Smith."

"Nice to meet you, sir," he said.

"Don't call me sir, I work for a living," Leo said good-naturedly.

"I wonder what Vince would say about that."

Leo stretched out his legs as he thought about his brother who was a Marine Lt Col select.

"Last time I said it to him, he suggested I do something that was anatomically impossible."

Jeff chuckled and closed his eyes. "Santinis never mince words."

"That's definitely true. My mother is ashamed of our manners."

He looked good, almost healthy considering that an IED tried to blow him to hell and back. There were still dark circles under his eyes, but Leo understood that probably had more to do with memories than anything else. "Need me to leave?"

Jeff shook his head and opened his eyes. "I'm resting up for my physical therapy."

Smith laughed.

Jeff frowned in his direction. "That's right. Laugh it up. Me, I have to deal with her today."

"Her?" Leo asked.

"The physical therapist. Johnson. She's...scary."

"That's putting it mildly," Smith said. Leo got a better look at him and realized the soldier was much younger, probably a year or two younger than Leo's youngest brother, Gianni. His red hair and freckles along with the baby face that probably made people think he was younger than he actually was.

"Are you telling me you two are afraid of a woman?"

Jeff laughed. "Spoken like a man who has never been married. But yes, I'm afraid of her. She's tiny, but she's a terror."

"Can't you ask for someone else? It would mean just talking to her commander..."

Leo broke off when the two men started laughing again. They were so loud he doubted either of them would have heard him anyway.

"Yeah, no. That's not going to happen. First of all, she's a civilian. Most of the therapists here are. And, truthfully, I was lucky to get her. She's a battleax but she's the best from what I understand. I just wish she wasn't so mean."

He was going to ask more about the woman, but she'd obviously been eavesdropping.

"So, you brought in someone to bitch to, soldier?"

The voice was strong, southern, and—as the men had said—scary.

He turned expecting to see an older woman built like a Mac truck. Instead, he found a woman who would have been blown away from a hard wind. She was lucky if she hit five-foot-three and she was as tiny as Jeff had said. Small-boned, with long dark hair that she had up in a ponytail, she looked so...well not sweet. Her aquamarine eyes narrowed as she studied Jeff. Her scrubs had some kind of cartoon character on them, but she wasn't smiling. Instead, she settled her petite fists on her waist and frowned.

"Well, are you going to answer me, soldier? Or are you Army guys just too wussy to actually answer a little bitty woman like me."

"You didn't give me a chance," Jeff said.

"Oh, sorry. Forgot what branch of the military you're in. I will allow time for you being slow."

Irritated, Leo rose out of the chair. She looked at him, her gaze traveling the length of him. He ignored the flicker of sensual awareness as she studied him. She had to tip her head back to see his face.

"I think you need to settle down there."

She looked past him to Jeff. "Is he your bodyguard?"

"No, ma'am." Leo heard the amusement in Jeff's voice, but he ignored it.

She looked back at Leo. "I would suggest you take a seat and shut it, soldier. I'm here for Markinson not some overgrown idiot."

He stepped in front of her to stop her. That was a mistake. This close he could see the sprinkle of freckles across the bridge of her cute nose. Her skin wasn't ivory, but golden, as if she spent a lot of time in the sun. Worse, her scent teased his senses. It wasn't anything like perfume, though, just sexy, musky woman.

He shook his head and tried to keep his mind on the problem at hand. "Your attitude needs an adjustment."

She looked up at him. He expected something different than the annoyance he read in her eyes. One perfectly sculpted eyebrow rose.

"Oh, really? Listen, I have two more people to work with today and Markinson here takes the longest because he whines. A lot."

"Aw, come on, Johnson, I don't." Jeff did sound like he was whining but he wasn't about to take the nurse's side in the argument.

"Pftt. You cry more than a cheerleader with a broken fingernail."

Leo was ready to give the woman a piece of his mind but he heard Jeff chuckle. "Santini, you can cool it. Johnson is all bark and no bite."

She looked past Leo again, her attention focusing on Jeff. He could see the slight softening of her gaze. If he hadn't been watching so closely, he would have missed it.

"Don't be lying to these people here or I will make you regret it."

She had lowered her voice, but he heard the change in her tone. It hit him that she was handling Jeff the same way his mother handled him and his brothers.

When she looked back at Leo, her gaze hardened. "Are you going to move, Santini, or do I need to make you cry like a girl, too?"

He wanted to argue with her. She was mean as they said but he realized it might be part of her job. As a medic himself, he understood the position she was in. Sometimes patients needed to be pushed. He nodded and stepped aside.

"Now that the bulldog is going to let me near you I have to say I am ashamed of you. Talking about me behind my back. That's just not right, Markinson."

She motioned behind her and that's when Leo saw the orderly. Leo stepped out of the way and she pulled the curtain closed.

"You didn't have to do that," Jeff said.

"Yeah? What if some sweet little old lady walked by and got a shot of you moving and you showed her some skin. She'd pass out. Can't cause that kind of ruckus."

Leo could tell from her voice she was joking but he knew that she had done it to save his friend the embarrassment of being lifted in front of Leo. His opinion of her went up a notch.

The curtain opened quickly and he found himself face to face with her again. Well, face to chest because she was so much shorter than he was. And in that short minute, he couldn't think. She was looking up at him with those amazing eyes and his brain just stopped functioning. Her mouth opened slightly in surprise and all he could think was that he wanted a taste.

She recovered faster than he did. "Make a hole, Santini."

She barked the order like a drill sergeant. Years of being raised by a Marine and years in the military came raring up and he acted immediately. Once he did, he noticed she let out a slow breath.

"Markinson will be back in about forty five minutes if he isn't too much of a wimp today. Come on," she said and marched out the door.

"You don't have to wait around, Santini," Jeff said. "I'm not that much on company when I get back."

"Do you have any physical therapy tomorrow?"

Jeff chuckled and looked up at the orderly who answered. "No, you can avoid Maryanne tomorrow."

Then, he wheeled Jeff out the door.

"She's not as bad as she seems," Smith said.

Leo nodded, his brain still clouded with the scent of her. What the hell had that been about?

"You need anything?"

Smith smiled and shook his head. "Naw, my mamma lives just outside of San Antonio. She makes sure I have everything I need."

Leo still gave him his cell number and told him to call if there was anything he or Jeff needed. Then, he decided it was time to get back to work. As Leo walked down the hall, his mind went back to the physical therapist. It might seem silly, but he wanted to make sure that she was as good as they said she was. He owed Jeff a lot and he wanted to make sure that he was taken care of. And while his body might be attracted, he couldn't let that get in the way. Jeff was on his own since his divorce. Both his parents were gone and he had been an only child. Someone had to look out for him.

Leo knew he owed the man at least that much for saving his life.

* * * *

"I know you said he's okay, but I wanted to make sure I didn't push him too hard," Maryanne said into her cell phone as she tried to pull a basket free. The little plastic seat was stuck between two carts. She jiggled it a few times before giving up and moving onto another one.

"He's fine, MJ," Freddy, her supervisor said. "He's tired, but you did right by him today. He needed to be pushed. He's getting a little lazy. I have a feeling someone has conflicted feelings about going back in the field."

She had seen it too many times to count these past few years—even with her own brothers. She didn't blame any of them for questioning if they wanted to go back in the field, but the truth was, she couldn't have Markinson get too lazy. He wouldn't be able to recover properly from his surgery if he didn't continue to move forward.

"Okay. Well, I'm going to pick up something for dinner here at HEB and then I am going to head home."

"You need a life, girl," Freddy said. "And a social life."

"Don't I know it, but I work for some pain in the ass at BAMC."

"I will ignore that because I love you. I know a great guy I could set you up with."

"I doubt you know a man who would be interested in me, Freddy."

"No, I promise, I have it on good authority that this one is heterosexual."

Freddy was the sweetest gay man with the worst gaydar. The last setup had been with a man who was more flamboyant than Liberace.

"No. No more setups. Call me if you have any issues with Markinson."

She clicked off the phone before Freddy could retaliate with guilt and pushed her way into the grocery store. It was already dark outside and she wanted to get home. She had stayed late to keep an eye on Markinson. Plus, she'd had a lot of paperwork to do. Before she knew it was after eight on a Friday night. Freddy was right, she thought as she looked around the produce section. She needed a life. She couldn't remember the last time she had a real date, let alone any kind of sex. Maybe that should be her mission for the summer. The mission for booty.

She chuckled to herself. She would settle for a nice night out with an attractive man. If she could find that, Maryanne was pretty sure Freddy would get off her back.

She started going through the oranges and her mind went back to Markinson. He seemed like the perfect soldier but she knew there was something holding him back. If she could figure it out, then she might be able to help him more.

Normally, the first person she would ask would be Santini, but that wasn't an option. The moment she had seen him, her body had reacted. Those wide shoulders, the buzz cut, the bigger than life presence.

She shivered.

From the time she was a teen she had a thing for military men. Military brats often went one way or another. They wanted nothing to do with the military or they were enamored with every sexy military man they could find. She wished she hadn't been in the latter category.

She was not going down that path again. Military men were not for her. Still, when he'd focused those golden brown eyes on her, she had lost all ability to think for a second or two. And that was saying a lot. Hell, she had to fight the urge to fan herself right now thinking about him. All those muscles, that bright smile, and he was tall—at least six feet.

He was in good shape thanks to his job. Markinson had told her Santini was a medic he had served with in Iraq, and that definitely showed in those massive arms. She shivered. They were the kinds of arms that made a woman feel safe.

No. No. No!

She had too many military men in her life. Her father was a marine, her brothers were all marines, and she worked daily with military men. She knew the only thing that would come out of any kind of attraction was heartbreak. It wasn't like he was going to ask her out. From his reaction to her, he probably would have some kind of background check done on her. Not that he would find anything.

She put the bag of oranges in her cart, turning she ran smack dab into a man.

"Whoa, there, Ms. Johnson."

Dammit, she knew that voice. She would probably think about it when she was…never mind thinking about that.

She tipped her head back and found Santini smiling down at her.

"Do you always run around like you're hell bent for leather?" His lips curved into a lopsided smile that had her brain shutting down. "Cat got your tongue?"

She shook her head and tried to step back. It was then that she realized he had those massive hands wrapped around her forearms. His thumbs were caressing her skin ever so slightly. This close she could smell the fresh clean scent of him. All soap and hard, sexy man.

Mother help me.

He looked down at his hands then back up at her. "Oh, sorry. Wanted to make sure you didn't fall down."

He hesitated then released her.

She studied him realizing that he hadn't changed out of his BDUs.

"What are you doing here?" she asked.

"Shopping?" he said with amusement as he tipped his head toward his buggy. She eyed all the fruits and vegetables.

"That's a lot of food for one guy."

He crossed his arms over his chest and she tried to ignore the way his pecs flexed—but she failed. She swallowed—hard—and forced her attention from them to his face.

"I like to eat."

She rolled her eyes and turned to leave. She needed to get away—far away—from the temptation of Santini. If she were lucky he would leave her alone. His footsteps behind her told her she wasn't so lucky.

She stopped and he almost ran his cart into her. With a sigh she turned to face him.

"What?"

His eyes widened and she realized that she had raised her voice. A glance around the department told her she had gained the attention of the few people shopping.

Maryanne slipped around his buggy. "I thought guys like you only shopped on post."

Something that looked like guilt moved over his face before he hid it. Great, now he was coming up with a lie and they weren't even involved. What the hell was wrong with her? This is what she found attractive? The perfectly nice accountant she had dated a few months earlier never lied to her but she just lost interest, mainly because he was perfectly boring.

"I had some work, which I'm sure you did too?" he said, his smile returning.

She did not want him smiling at her. She needed him pissed at her, being mean to her, and staying away from her. When he was smiling like that it just made her want to scream. And kiss him. She really, really wanted to kiss him.

"And you decided to drive all the way over here to Universal City to shop at the HEB? Isn't there one closer to post?"

He nodded. "This one is closer to my apartment."

Oh, so not good.

"Don't tell me you live at the Live Oak Apartments."

"I sure do. Just moved in two weeks ago."

She narrowed her eyes as she studied him. Growing up as the only sister of three older brothers made her very good at detecting bullshit.

He seemed to be telling the truth, but there was that moment before that made her nervous. Worse, she wanted to believe him. Wanted to have him living near her so she could flirt with him, maybe kiss him…

Dammit.

She had no other choice than to chase him away.

"Listen, this might work with a lot of other women, but I don't like stalkers." She practically yelled it. He wore no expression on his face so she decided to get out before he could retort. Grabbing her cart, she hurried away.

Damn, she really did need to get a life.

CHAPTER TWO

"Earth to Leo," Vince said, amusement threading his voice.

Leo had to shake himself free of the thoughts that had been plaguing him for two days now. He glanced at his brother.

"Sorry, got a lot on my mind."

Vince cracked a smile. "Thinking, soldier? I always thought you just reacted without thinking."

It was a common comment from his brother. Controlling his impulses had been hard when he was a teenager, and for the most part, Leo was still that way. Except for work. Instinct ruled his life when he was at work.

"No, just getting settled in the new apartment, starting the new job." He took the exit off 1604. "I saw Jeff yesterday."

"Ah," he said understanding. Vince was the oldest of the Santinis and had seen the most combat, so he knew where Jeff had been. He also knew what it was like to be in Leo's shoes, as he had to watch some of his closest friends struggle with the worst of memories.

"Sorry. I pick you up at the airport and immediately bring you down."

He shook his head as he studied the passing landscape of Universal City. "Nature of the job, Leo."

All four of the Santinis were in the military, and all of them had seen action. They tried their best not to do shop talk when they were together.

"No. We need to hit the Riverwalk tonight. Should be a busy night. Hot weather brings out the hot women."

The moment he said it, the thought of Maryanne Johnson sparked through his mind, leaving a trail of heat behind to tease him. Damn, last night she had smelled so...delicious.

"Dammit, Leo, you drove through that red light."

"What?" He looked up in his rearview mirror and realized he had. Damn, just thinking about the woman was going to get him killed. He shook his head. "Sorry about that."

"I think you have something else on your mind other than Jeff or work."

Vince always had a sixth sense when it came to their lives. He always seemed to know when they needed him to visit, needed a phone call, and he could sniff out any kind of embarrassing situation. It was hell to have an older brother who didn't have a problem rubbing their noses in it.

"It's just this woman. Jeff's physical therapist. She rubbed me the wrong way."

He crossed his arms. "Oh?"

Leo turned into the apartment complex and inwardly cringed. He knew he sounded too defensive and that would intrigue Vince. "Oh, nothing. Just, we got off on the wrong foot and now she might think I am...well, stalking her."

Before Vince could react, Leo spotted her. She was walking, wearing a little pair of exercise shorts and one of those sports bra things. Her hair was up in a ponytail again. It swung from side to side with that sassy little walk of hers. Damn, he would love to see her hair free, flowing over her shoulders. He bet it would feel like silk against his flesh.

He parked in his spot just a few feet from where she was walking. "There she is."

"Why are you whispering?" Vince asked, but Leo's mind was on Johnson.

It still bugged him that she thought he was stalking her and he decided to set the record straight. Without saying anything to his brother, he slipped out of the truck.

"Uh, Leo, I think..."

He missed the rest of what his brother said. Leo walked up behind her, knowing she had to have heard him. "Ms. Johnson."

She didn't acknowledge him—and that was typical of women like her. They were huffing and condescending. And sadly, it made her more fascinating. Wanting her attention, he tapped her shoulder. She screamed. Without turning around, she shoved her bony elbow into his stomach. He doubled over as she came around with her right fist and connected with his eye. Sparks of pain erupted as he fell back. His head hit the pavement with a thunk.

He blinked, trying to focus on her but it was difficult.

"Santini?"

She leaned down looking at him her ponytail falling over her shoulder. It was then he saw the ear buds connected to her mp3 player. She pulled them out of her ears.

"What the hell do you think you're doing?"

He winced at the sound of her voice. "I just wanted to correct your misconception that I was stalking you."

"Oh, well that went over well. Scaring the bloody hell out of me. What is wrong with you?"

The scrape of shoe against the sidewalk had him grimacing. Dammit, he'd forgotten about Vince.

"So, I see you can still charm the ladies, Leo."

She looked up at his brother and her mouth dropped open. "Good God, there's another one of you?"

His brother smiled. "Vincente Santini."

She blinked and Leo was amazed when she blushed. "Maryanne Johnson."

"I'm glad everyone is having fun meeting each other," Leo said rolling up to his feet. Damn his stomach hurt and lord knew he was going to have a damned black eye. Explaining that to the major was going to be fun.

She gave him a disgusted look. "Every time I see you, you whine."

"I didn't whine last night."

"No, you were just stalking me."

He ground his teeth together. "I was not stalking you."

"How long have you two known each other?" Vince asked looking from one to the other.

"Feels like a lifetime," Leo said.

She rolled her eyes, then she zeroed in her attention on Vince. She sniffed in his direction. Vince smiled at her again and she frowned.

"Ugh, not another one. You're not Army though. Marine?"

Vince nodded.

She threw her hands up in the air and released a sound of disgust. "All of you need to just stay away from me. Far away."

She turned and hurried off. Then, she stopped abruptly and spun around. "You need to put some ice or better yet, a steak on that eye."

Then she was off again. He watched her until she turned the corner and sighed.

"Ohhh, so that's the way of it?" Vince asked.

He glanced at his brother. "What?"

"I heard that sigh. Someone has a little crush on the physical therapist."

He didn't. Not really. Okay, a little, but he'd damned if he would admit it. "No. Two days and she's called me more names than I can keep up with. I don't like women who are so damned contrary."

Vince gave him a disbelieving look and headed to the truck to get his bag. Leo looked at the corner she had just turned and shook his head.

"She's the damnedest woman."

* * * *

Maryanne hated to apologize. She hated it with a thousand hot burning suns. In fact, the only thing she hated worse was being wrong. And she wasn't wrong in this case. But, she thought as she walked up the steps to Santini's apartment, she knew she had to do it. After lunch with her grandmother, she had no choice.

She sighed as she reached his landing. She should have never told her about the altercation. Her grandmother, ever the wife, mother and grandmother of military men, told her she had to apologize. It was hard to say no to her grannie, even if it was all because of a soft spot she had for military men.

She slowed down as she reached his door. It was three on a Sunday afternoon and she thought he might be gone, but she had seen his truck in his allotted spot. She had the worst luck lately.

With another heavy sigh, she knocked on his door.

"Coming." One of them yelled out. She wasn't sure which one, but she thought it was Leo.

Stop that. His name is Santini. Not Leo. Leo makes him nice, makes him sexy...makes him irresistible. He was not that. He was Santini.

The door opened and she had been wrong. It was his brother Vince. He was just as tall, just as beautiful. The same physique as his brother and damn, he wasn't wearing his shirt.

Why did guys who looked like that always walk around shirtless? Cuz they look like damned Gods, that's why.

When she looked up at him he was smiling. The one big difference between the brothers was that Vince didn't have a broken nose...and his eyes were dark blue.

"Ms. Johnson?"

"Yes."

"Is there something I can do for you?"

Before she could tell him to put on a damned shirt so her brain would work, the door was pulled open further. Good God, Leo wasn't wearing a shirt either.

She was going to die from lack of blood in her brain.

Leo looked at his brother. "Go away."

"So rude. Mom's not going to like that when I tell her." He smiled at her. "I'm her favorite."

Then he walked away. No, sauntered away. That was the only way she could describe that walk.

"He is not mom's favorite." She blinked at him, her brain starting to work a little. He frowned in return. "Ms. Johnson, was there something you wanted?"

He was wary of her, but she didn't really blame him. The black eye was not extremely pretty. It made him more attractive in a rough and tumble kind of way.

"I came by to apologize for hitting you."

He said nothing, just kept staring at her. It was hard to remain aloof when he was standing there almost naked. Okay, all he was missing was his shirt, but that couldn't be legal in Texas. It would cause a ruckus if he went out like that.

"Seriously, I figured I would just hit you and run away. I never thought I would knock any man out."

"You didn't knock me out."

"Okay, so I knocked you down. I'm sorry."

He just stared at her and she had to fight her compulsion to say something. "Was there something else?"

She sighed. "Okay, see, I have to invite you to dinner as part of my apology."

"Wait, what?"

"I'm inviting you and the other one for dinner."

"His name is Vince."

"Yeah, whatever. So, do you want dinner?"

He leaned up against the doorjamb and acted like he was giving it great thought. Again, she had to keep herself from saying something.

"Does this involve a home cooked meal?"

Irritated she settled her hands on her hips. "Of course it does."

"And for some unknown reason, you have to invite me to your apartment for dinner."

"And the other one."

"Vince."

"Yeah."

He studied her again. She really hated the way he looked at her as if she were some kind of specimen. "What time?"

"Six."

"Okay. Oh, what apartment?"

"Two-fifty-five."

She turned to leave, when he stopped her.

"Are you going tell me why you have to invite me?"

"My grannie said I had to. Of course, I told her she was crazy, but she's my grannie so I have to do it."

Then she stomped down the stairs dreading the night.

CHAPTER THREE

Leo picked up the bottle of wine he'd bought as he headed out of his kitchen. Vince had dressed for dinner, but he still didn't look happy about the situation.

"What?" Leo asked.

Vince sighed. "I told you earlier that I'd stay home."

"It will make me look like a dick. You came here to see me and one of the three nights you're here, I'm going to go to dinner without you."

"I completely understand. She's smoking hot."

Leo rolled his eyes and walked to the door. There was a reason Vince was thirty-five years old and single. He couldn't see that a woman would take offense to that comment. Leo knew he had already started off badly with Maryanne. He wanted to make sure he made a good impression tonight.

"No. She said both of us."

"Actually what she said was you and the other one. I'm not so sure she wants me there."

That would not be good. He was already attracted to her and being alone with a bottle of wine was not a good idea. He needed Vince there to be a buffer. His main objective was to repair the damage and move on.

"So, was last night a little too much for you?"

Vince rolled his eyes. "Yeah. A few beers on the Riverwalk and some hot Tex-Mex food was a little too much for me."

What they had done was spend the night up talking. They were a close family, but he and Vince were less than two years apart in age. They had gone through a lot together growing up and he was the only one who had understood why Leo had opted to go in the Army instead of attending college first. Leo knew he wanted to be a medic for longer than he could remember, and Vince had been the first one he had told.

"Come on. The food might suck, but I have a good wine, and we can always hit fast food later."

"Okay, as long as it's a Whataburger."

"I have no idea how you stay so fit and eat like that. I got the shitty genes apparently."

Vince chuckled as he followed him out of the door and waited for him to lock it. "I could have told you that, Leo. It was evident from an early age I had far superior genes."

It only took a few minutes to get around the apartment complex to where her apartment was located. By the time they were walking up the stairs, his stomach was turning over. Not the kind that told him he was going to be sick. No, these were butterflies...like he was sixteen years old and picking up Sue Martin for his first date.

"Looks different here," Vince commented.

"These are bigger apartments. They didn't have any open when I toured. I wanted one, but another one won't open up for eight months."

Before they reached her door, he could smell the food. Onion, garlic, and basil. She'd cooked Italian for a couple of Italians. He lifted his hand to knock but he didn't get to. It opened with a whoosh. Again, all thought dissolved from his mind.

He had seen her in work and exercise clothes, but it had not prepared him for her in casual clothes. Her hair was down, the soft curls cascading over her shoulders. The hot pink shirt she wore clung to her breasts. And, lord, she had a body that was made for wearing those worn hip hugging jeans. Her feet were bare, but he saw the bright pink polish on her toes. It matched her shirt.

"Hello. Sorry, did I scare you," she said. There was laughter in her voice and it made his heart jerk…along with other body parts.

Vince laughed. "No, but we are stunned by the smell."

She smiled at Vince. Her whole face lighted with happiness. "Thank you. Come on in."

Vince stepped over the threshold, but Leo stood there trying to get his brain to work.

"Santini?"

He shook himself and looked at her. Her brow furrowed as she studied him. Great, she thought there was something wrong with him. He forced himself to smile.

"Sorry."

"No problem. Is that for tonight?"

"What?"

She pointed to the wine in his hand. "Sure." He followed his brother in and didn't miss the smirk on Vince's face. Leo knew he was going to get shit for this.

"Vince is right. Smells delicious."

She gave him a smile over her shoulder. "It is."

"Kind of bold serving red sauce to a couple of Italians."

She laughed and the sound danced over his nerve endings. Damn, he was barely able to control himself when she was mean to him. Smiling and laughing at him…that was going to make her lethal to his libido.

"You two aren't the only Italians around." She started looking through her drawers. "Aha!"

She held up her bottle opener. "Would you mind? I suck at it."

More at ease now, he said, "Sure."

"So, you're Italian, Ms. Johnson?" Vince asked.

"Oh please, call me Maryanne, or MJ. I answer to either."

"And you can just call me the other one."

Her face flushed. "You heard that?"

Of course his brother had heard that. Maryanne wasn't exactly quiet when she spoke.

"Just call us Leo and Vince. One of us will answer."

She laughed as she set a couple glasses on the counter. She rose to her tiptoes to grab another one but Vince walked up behind her.

"Let me get that for you."

She stilled as Vince grabbed the glass and pulled it down.

"There you go," Vince said, his voice even as if he didn't realize he had been that close to her. Hell, if Leo had been, he would have embarrassed himself. When she turned around, her face was pink again.

"Hey, Leo, gonna open that bottle or just break off the bottle opener?" Vince asked as he leaned against her kitchen counter. He looked like he was making himself right at home.

Leo frowned at him, but noticed he was looking at his hand. Leo had the bottle opener in such a tight grip that his knuckles were white. He glanced at Maryanne who was busy at the stove with her back to them. With effort, he loosened his hand and gave his brother a warning look. He uncorked the bottle and set it on the counter to breathe.

"So, you're Italian? Johnson doesn't sound very Italian," Vince said.

She tossed another smile over her shoulder. "My grandmother is Italian. And since she's the one who taught me how to cook, most of my entrees lean that way."

She grabbed a box of spaghetti and dumped the pasta into the boiling pot.

"So, your grandmother lived with you?" Leo asked.

She gave the spaghetti a stir, then turned around. "Yeah. My mom died when I was young, only three. Dad tried for a few years to handle the four of us on his own, but it's hard. Y'all know what it's like with a family of four kids and military obligations. Anyway, there was an incident and basically, he felt he lost control. And you know how Marine fathers are."

Leo snorted. "Losing control is not something any military man likes."

"Of course not. I get it. I mean, you give over so much of your life that you need to control something and when you can't control a five-year-old girl…you feel your life is falling apart. He wouldn't let my grandmother take me away, so she moved in with us. It was the best because my brothers were running amuck and Dad had a lot on his plate. He says he would have never made any of his stars without my grandmother helping out."

"Stars?" Leo asked.

"Don't tell me your father is General Bryan Johnson," Vince said in a strange tone. Leo shot his brother a look, but his brother had his concentration on Maryanne.

"Yeah. Do you know him?"

More than likely Vince did. He'd been Special Forces early in his career, but he had made his rank fast, and he had been to several specialized schools. He was a little young for making Lt Col but he had done his time in the field and his time at the Pentagon.

"Is he still active?" Leo asked.

She nodded. "I wish he would get out and get a life. He also needs a woman."

Vince seemed to recover himself a bit and chuckled. "That's a strange thing for a daughter to say."

She rolled her eyes. "Seriously, it's been a long time since he's had a relationship. I can understand why it's hard for him because, well he's busy. I keep telling him that soon he'll be all alone."

"He always has his daughter to keep him company," Leo said.

She snorted. "Yeah, Dad and I love each other but we usually get in some kind of argument within twenty-four hours. I am the one child of his who is not in the military and he cannot control me at all. It drives him crazy."

Her timer buzzed on the oven and she retrieved some garlic bread. She set the pan on the counter and grabbed a basket.

"What was the incident?" he asked.

"What?"

"The incident. The one you said drove your father to ask your grandmother to move in?"

She sighed. "I was a tomboy."

"No way," Vince said with a chuckle.

"Yeah. Kind of hard to believe with a Marine father and three Marine brothers that I would turn out that way, right? Right now, we don't always get along and they made my life hell in high school, but then, when I was little, they were my whole world. They treated me like one of the guys. So, when I wanted to play t-ball, I expected to get all the same equipment they did for baseball."

Leo frowned. "Yeah, so, why didn't you?"

Her cheeks pickened. "There's one bit of important equipment that boys wear that girls don't."

Then it hit him. "You wanted a cup."

"Well, yeah. They all had one. And from what my grannie tells me, they did anything I wanted up until then. Dad felt guilty because Mom died, not that it was his fault, but still, you know. And he said, even though I was a tomboy, I knew how to work the house of men. I would cry and they would do anything I wanted. But, when I demanded a cup and threw a fit in front of the entire team and their parents because I couldn't get one, Dad decided it was time for some maternal influence in my life."

He smiled, then he found himself laughing out loud. "Seriously, Maryanne, it doesn't surprise me in the least."

She smiled. "It was a good thing though. Having another woman in my house was a godsend. I don't even want to think about talking to my father about puberty."

"Well, I would say that you turned out just fine, in my humble opinion," Vince said sweetly.

She blinked then smiled at him and just like that, Leo was pissed. This was going to be one long night.

* * * *

Maryanne was relieved when the evening came to an end. It had been difficult to sit through the meal and not drool over her companions. Of course, having Vince there made it a little easier. He flirted with her enough to make her feel pretty, but didn't push it. He had no interest in her at all. At least, she didn't think he did. Anyway, the brooding presence of Leo made it hard to be a completely relaxed meal. He added to the conversation, but the dirty looks he kept giving her and Vince made her uncomfortable. It was as if he didn't trust her with his brother.

"Now, here, take this," she said as she offered Vince the plastic container of food.

He took it with that drop-dead gorgeous smile—dimples and all. "No problem. That hardly leaves you any, though."

"Believe me, I don't need that hanging around my house. Once Tuesday hits, I'll be gone so much with work, I will end up throwing it away. Or worse, I will eat it all tomorrow on my day off."

He nodded and headed to the door. Leo said nothing as he followed his brother to the door. Once Vince stepped through the doorway though, Leo shut the door and grabbed her by the wrist pulling her to him, then crowded her up against the door. Before she could tell him to get his hands off her—and she was so totally going to do that, really—he slammed his mouth down on hers.

Her brain fizzled. Just right there, stopped working. She couldn't seem to do anything but to kiss him back. Every other thought dissolved and the primal instinct to connect took over. Heat bloomed within her, pulsing through her veins. In that one instant she went from sort of frustrated to wanting to tear off his clothes. When he pulled back, they were both breathing heavily.

"Just so you know which Santini is really interested." He swooped in for another quick kiss. "God, you taste good."

From the need she heard in his voice, she was sure he would kiss her again, but with a sigh, he stepped back.

"Thank you for dinner." He kept looking at her and she didn't know what to say. That steady gaze had her heart smacking against her chest. What did you say to a man who fizzled your brain like that?

"Maryanne?"

"What?"

He offered her a gentle smile that almost undid her. "I can't open the door with you standing in front of it."

"Oh." Her face heated as she stepped aside. He opened the door and paused.

"I would love to take you out tomorrow." She was formulating her excuses, when he continued. "But, my brother is only here for another day. How about next Friday?"

"You're asking me out?"

She didn't mean to shout the question but this was bad. Worse, she wanted to say yes, Yes, YES.

Oh, god.

"I thought we should explore this...thing."

"Thing?" Great. She sounded like an idiot.

"How about we call it breaking even? You made me dinner. I'll take you out for dinner."

She should say no. A man like Santini had heartbreak written all over him, but she could only say, "Okay."

He smiled as if she had given him some kind of gift.

"Good night, Maryanne."

Then he slipped out the door.

"You need to lock the door, Maryanne," he said through the door.

"You're not my keeper."

But she did lock it.

"Goodnight."

She said nothing and leaned back against the door. The man was dangerous. Big time dangerous. Like get her into all kinds of trouble dangerous. And dammit, that excited her even more.

As a military brat, she had grown up around like men like him, and when she started dating, it was natural to gravitate toward military guys. She knew a lot of her friends went the other way, but she hadn't, mainly because they didn't expect her to be prissy. They accepted the fact that she could take them down like she did with Leo and still see her desirable. She could hunt and fish and be herself. A lot of them liked rough and tumble girls like her.

After awhile though, being treated as their buddy with a side order of sex got boring. They always seemed to think she wanted nothing more than that.

She sighed. Going out with Santini was a mistake. She liked him. He was hot, sexy and that one kiss still had her knees feeling like asphalt on a hot Texas day. She would have to come up with some kind of excuse not to go out with him. And that would be the end of it.

Really.

CHAPTER FOUR

Leo straightened his shoulders before knocking on Maryanne's door. He knew he was in for a battle tonight. She had called and left messages all week. His good sense told him she was trying to break their date. He wasn't about to let that happen. If he had to go in her apartment and dress her, he would do it.

Of course, that brought a whole new set of ideas to the forefront of his mind. Damn, the woman had him hotter than he could ever remember and just from that one little kiss. He hadn't planned on doing that, but something told him he had to at least see what she tasted like. It had been worth getting crap from Vince about it later. Now, he knew she was definitely interested and he wasn't going to let it go.

He knocked on the door. He heard some rustling and then the door opened wide. It wasn't Maryanne. It was a man, as tall as him, with dark hair and a rather pissy look on his face. He had apparently been sleeping.

"What?"

"Jackson Michael Johnson, is that the way you greet someone at the door?" Maryanne asked from behind the man. Of course, he could only hear her. He couldn't see her with the massive roadblock in the door.

"I was sleeping, MJ."

He saw a hand reach up and smack the man on the back of the head.

"Damn, MJ, do you have to hit so hard?" He stepped aside.

"Do you always cry like a little girl?" she asked.

When she stepped up beside the man, he saw the resemblance. Dark hair, blue eyes and that same stubborn chin.

"Leo, I tried to call and cancel because Jack here decided to drop in on me uninvited."

He studied her and realized she was being truthful, but he also noticed that she dressed to go out. The cute little dress she wore wasn't something a girl would wear around the house hanging out with her brother. And, thank the good lord, she wore her hair down again. His fingers had been itching to slip through the silky curls.

"But, you're still going," Jack said.

"Yes, I am. I'm not in the mood to hang around you when you're in such a foul mood. Go back to sleep, loser." She rose to her tiptoes and kissed him on the cheek. "There's beer in the fridge."

Then she stepped out, causing Leo to step back.

"Ready?" he asked.

She nodded and smiled.

"Hey, I didn't get to interrogate him."

She smiled back over her shoulder at Jack. "Yeah, how about that, Marine? He got the drop on you and he's Army."

With that she laughed and started walking down the stairs. He smiled and followed her down.

"Be home by eleven."

"Suck it, Johnson." It was all she said as she waited for Leo to finish walking down.

"So, your brother..."

"Is a pain in the ass. I don't know what he's doing here, but it makes me nervous."

He opened the door and she slid into his truck. She watched him as he rounded the hood.

"He's making you nervous how?" he asked after he joined her.

"Jack has a habit of being involved with women who just tear him to shreds. He usually comes to see me to lick his wounds. And by that, I mean he comes here because I will be the designated driver for him."

"When did he get in?"

"Last night."

"But you tried to cancel earlier than that."

She sighed and looked across the cab of his pickup at him. "I didn't want to want to go out with you."

He blinked. "Wow, that made my head hurt."

She smiled but it didn't reach her eyes. He found himself wanting to make her smile like she had that night at dinner.

"I've been involved with military guys before. It just never ended well."

He could tell she was skittish and he thought it had to do with their initial interaction.

"How about this? We'll do dinner, call it even for you cooking for me like I said, then you can decide if you want to make it...more than platonic?"

She cocked her head to one side. "And if I said no romance you'd be cool with that?"

He thought about it. No he wouldn't be. He wanted her in his bed. He had decided that the night he had kissed her. There was nothing he wanted more in his life at the moment, than this woman beneath him moaning his name. But... he could wait. For now.

"Sure."

She looked out the window. "Okay, let's do dinner."

* * * *

Maryanne tried not to be charmed, but she was. He took her to one of her favorite restaurants, The Alamo Cafe. As they ate he told her stories of growing up with four brothers and they compared what it was like to have an older brother who was a Marine.

"So, all of you got into the military?"

He nodded as he slathered some butter on his fresh tortilla. "Yep."

"But you didn't go into the Marines like your father. What about the other two?"

"Marco's in the Navy. A SEAL. Gianni's Air Force. PJ."

She sat back. "So your entire family represents the armed services."

He offered her one of those smiles that had her heart doing a little tap dance. "Well, we don't have anyone in the Coast Guard, but Mom said she was done after Gianni. And, he was sort of a surprise from what I remember."

"How rude of your mother."

He laughed like she expected and she bit back a sigh. The man had an amazing laugh. There was nothing calculated about it. It did funny things to her insides. Like, having his attention only on her. He wasn't overly flirtatious, but he had asked about her work…and just about her. And, unlike so many men, he had actually listened.

"If my mom can't handle four boys like us, I doubt there's a woman on earth who could."

Okay, that was starting to get to her too. Any other man would sound like a Mama's boy, but Leo didn't. His voice was filled with admiration.

"Where are they all stationed?"

We're scattered all over the place, but at least we're all back in the US, but not the CONUS. Marc's in Hawaii."

She sighed as she indulged in another tortilla. It was one of the things she loved about San Antonio. They brought freshly made tortillas to the table like most restaurants did with bread. It was a huge weakness of hers and she would have to run tomorrow to make up for it.

"All your brothers are Marines?"

She nodded. "Yeah. I'm not sure they thought of anything else, but they are all in different career fields."

"But you never wanted to join?"

"No thank you. I am not good at taking orders."

"Yeah?"

She heard the way his voice dipped and felt her face heat up.

"That is to say, I grew up with three older brothers and a father who had told them it was their duty to watch out for me. I don't think I would have lasted a week in boot. Truth is, I think my father was relieved. He was worried he would have to deal with the aftermath of me making a drill sergeant cry. And, the worry I would end up stationed on the same base as one of my brothers…that did not sit well with me."

"Jack didn't seem to be too bad."

She snorted. "Tell that to my prom date. He showed up and found Jack cleaning his gun. Swear to God I had never been so embarrassed. I didn't even get a kiss good night."

He was staring at her as if she was insane.

"I swear it happened."

"No, I believe you. I just wondered what was wrong with it."

"Please tell me you don't have sisters."

"Nope just the three brothers like I said. My mother said she would never be so mean to a girl and do that."

"Yeah, well, it worked because like I said, I was a tomboy."

"You told me that the other night but I find it almost impossible to believe," he said in mock disbelief.

"No, really. I can even take down a two hundred pound Army dude."

He laughed and she tried to ignore the way his eyes sparkled at her. She was a sucker for a man with a sense of humor. "You didn't take me down. You caught me off guard."

"That's what they all say."

The waitress returned with their entrees. "Another margarita?"

She shook her head. "Nope. I'll stick to water."

Leo ordered water also. It was another thing she liked about him and about his brother. They had a couple of glasses of wine the other night, but they both watched their drinking.

"So, you picked San Antonio, why?"

She shrugged as she chewed her first bite. "I went to UTSA and Grannie was already here at the Air Force Village. I wanted to work at a military hospital. The only other place with so many opportunities was DC and that's where Dad is, and Brett, my oldest brother. He's at the Pentagon, too. So, while I don't mind my Grannie checking up on me, I do mind them. They never understood why I needed space."

He nodded and she did sense he understood.

"I have kind of a personal question and I don't want you to be offended," she said.

"Okay, but I think I can answer the question."

"You do?"

"Yes. And the answer is no, I don't have a problem with you using me as a sexual object."

He said it with such a deadpan expression, she couldn't stop the tickle in her throat bubbling up into giggles.

"No," she said, still chuckling. "Although I do appreciate your sacrifice. What I wanted to know is that you said your father is an officer, and I know Vince is if he's teaching at Quantico, so why didn't you go the college route?"

He cocked his head and studied her for a few seconds, then said, "I wanted to be a medic from the time I was a freshman in high school."

It was another thing that both of them understood. "And you chose the Army because…"

"I wanted to be on the front lines. Other services can get there, but Army has a better chance. Plus, it kept me out of Dad's realm. When I went in, he was still active, and I just didn't want to deal with that."

She nodded. "I don't know how my brothers handle that with my father, but they're freaks."

When he didn't respond, she looked up at him. He was staring at her with the strangest look on his face.

"What?" she asked looking down at her chest to see if she dropped food on herself, then glanced back at him.

"Nothing, just it's nice to see that you're so close to them. We're the same way. People on the outside, they don't understand."

On the outside. Yeah, that was a good way of putting it. Military life for kids could be bad, wonderful and everything in between. Sometimes, the only friend you had was a sibling, and you had to count on each other more than other families, especially in this fast paced world.

She nodded. "We were close. Maybe it was losing Mom when we were all so young, but I know part of it is the brat thing."

Her mind wandered back to Jack and whatever news he had been saving for her. Leo touched her hand and she looked up at him.

"I'm sorry I made you sad."

"Not sad, worried about Jack, but that's okay. It will all work out in the end."

He nodded. "So, how about I tell you horrible stories about my brothers to make me look good."

And just like that, she couldn't help but smile. "Sounds like a plan, Santini."

* * * *

By the time they reached their apartment complex, Leo was ready to scream he was so damned hot. She hadn't flirted, hadn't even tried to. She had been herself, and that was more of an aphrodisiac than anything else. It was the first time in a long time that he had been this attracted to a woman just based on their interaction.

Okay, that sounded bad in his head. More than bad. If his mother could read his thoughts... Whoa, no reason to go down that road. He didn't have time for therapy right now.

After parking the truck, he looked over at Maryanne. "So?"

She glanced at him. "I had a good time, but I'm not sure we should keep going out. First dates can never tell you everything, and it could be an anomaly. Like some kind of freak accident."

"A freak accident is like you hitting me."

She snorted. "No, I meant to do that."

He chuckled. "Okay, why don't we test my theory? You still think we should remain platonic, then I'll agree."

She frowned. "What theory?"

He undid his seatbelt, then hers.

"Leo."

He knew she was warning him, but her voice came out all breathy. The sound of that sweet southern voice slipped beneath his skin. He cupped her face as he leaned closer. She licked her lips and he groaned as he pressed his mouth against hers.

Just like before, she tasted of heaven and sin wrapped in a bundle of need. He slanted his mouth over hers and deepened the kiss, slipping his tongue inside. Sweet and tart, just like the woman. Damn, he could just imagine how her flesh tasted, not to mention other more intriguing places.

His heart beat against his chest, and his cock hardened. Just like the other night he found himself lost in her. Everything around him dissolved into the background as she slipped her hands to his shoulders. He slid his hands down to her waist and pulled her closer. The heat of her body, the taste of her and the sweet scent made for a heady experience. He was contemplating leaning her back against the seat when there was a loud knock on her side of the truck. He ignored it at first, but the knocking got louder. He tore his mouth away from hers and glared at the intrusion. Her brother Jack was giving them both a death stare. Maryanne didn't make it any easier. She slid her hands to the back of his head and tried to pull him down for another kiss.

"Uh, Maryanne, your brother."

Her eyes opened slightly. "What?"

Oh, god, he wanted her. Wanted her like he wanted to breathe, but with her brother standing there looking ready to lob off various appendages, he was pretty sure that it would be a no go tonight.

"Your brother is staring at us."

Her eyes widened as she tipped her head back and looked. The sound that emitted from her was primal and downright scary.

"I'm going to kill him. Dead. First, I will make him cry and then I will kill him."

"I can see you, MJ. If you don't want me to kill your Army guy, you might want to get out here right now."

Regretfully, Leo straightened and pulled her with him.

"I am so sorry."

Leo shook his head. "Don't be. I proved my theory right."

"Are you going to get out of there?" Jack asked.

She turned her head. "You want me to tell Grannie about Vivi Sanders? I didn't think so."

Then she looked at him.

"Vivi?" he asked.

"He snuck her into the house one night when he was fifteen. I think it was… you know his first. Well, I saw it and I have used it as blackmail since."

He watched her brother walk away but only to the sidewalk. "Wow. You're…"

"What?"

"Pretty cool."

She laughed and he responded in kind. He couldn't help it. When she was happy, it made him happy. And that probably made him a sap, but he didn't care at the moment. He had never felt this intrigued by a woman…at least not as long as he could remember. They had a bumpy start, but now they seemed in tune with each other. There was a vibe there between them that had his head buzzing and his body yearning.

"That theory?" she asked.

"I think you can agree there's some sparks there."

She nodded. "Yeah. But…"

"Listen, we'll take it slow. No rushing it."

She sighed. "Okay. I'll be busy with Jack all weekend. There's something going on with him."

"No worries. I understand brothers."

"I bet you do," she said with a smile. Then, she leaned over, cupping his jaw and gave him a kiss. It was sweet, and definitely not as erotic as the one they had just shared but it pulled at him the same way.

"I don't have all night," Jack bellowed outside.

He laughed. "Lord help any daughters your brother has."

She smiled. "Thank you for dinner."

Then she opened the door and stepped out of the truck. She walked up to her brother who was saying something to her and pointing to the truck. She reached up and smacked him in the back of the head again. Then started walking to her apartment. He watched until she opened the door and waved.

He drove to his own parking space, his mood definitely lighter than it had been in a good long while. There was something about her, something that made him think it was more than mere attraction. She was skittish for some reason and mainly because he was military. He would have to be careful about scaring her. He needed a plan.

And, if there was one thing Santinis knew it was how to make a plan. The woman wouldn't know what hit her.

CHAPTER FIVE

Maryanne walked down the hall, her mood getting worse by the moment. She thought coming to work would help, take her mind off things, but nothing seem to be helping. Of course, Jack's news had been bad—worse than she was expecting. She still wasn't ready to accept it. He had stayed for two weeks, leaving late the night before. And he had waited until the last minute to tell her. Well, okay, not the last minute, but pretty damn close.

Inwardly, she sighed. It had taken all her control not to cry. The Johnson boys didn't like any crying. Truth was, they fell apart when she started weeping. She had used it against them for years because she could get just anything she wanted. Now, though, it would not work. A job's a job and the dedication her brothers had to theirs was admirable. Or so people told her. At the moment, she thought it just sucked.

So, she had driven from the San Antonio Airport, barely holding it together until she closed her front door. She had ignored Leo's messages because she didn't want to embarrass herself. In her experience, men, especially ones who had just met her, didn't want to deal with a blubbering mess.

As if conjured out of her thoughts, she saw Leo walking down the hallway. She couldn't fight the little sigh that slipped from her lips. There was nothing like seeing a military man, dressed in his uniform, striding down the hall like he owned the place. Just seeing him made her heart do a little tap dance. The familiar rush of excitement rushed through her, brushing over her nerve endings. She shivered in reaction.

It had been a long two weeks. While they hadn't made it into bed, the heavy petting had left her frustrated. Of course, she hadn't had a choice with Jack around.

"Hey, Johnson. Your brother keep you busy last night?"

His tone told her he was joking but she couldn't really summon a smile for him. "No, he had a late flight."

"Gee, sorry to see him go."

That did make her laugh. Jack had made sure he had either accompanied them or was waiting outside when they got home. Her brother definitely knew how to cock block a fellow serviceman.

"How about lunch?" he asked.

She glanced at the overhead clock. "I have less than thirty minutes to my next appointment."

"That's okay. I brought some with me."

She looked down at his hands then back up at him. "Yeah? Is it imaginary, Santini?"

He chuckled. "Naw. I have it in the lounge."

Maryanne blinked. "You're not supposed to be in there." In fact, it was considered impossible to get the charge nurse to agree.

"I talked to Nurse Samantha and she let me in."

She just bet she did. Samantha ran the floor like a four star general but she had a notorious weak spot for young men in the military. She had two herself serving and with Leo's charm, there was a good chance that Samantha would let him throw a party in the lounge if he wanted.

When they stepped into the lounge, she spied the table covered with the red and white checked cloth. She stopped, but he grabbed her hand and tugged her toward the table. Heat filled her face at the knowing looks her coworkers were tossing in her direction.

He let go of her hand when they reached the table. She really didn't know what to say.

"Leo."

"Maryanne, sit down. I ran out to Rudy's to get you some brisket."

She hesitated and looked up at him. "That's a long way."

He shrugged as he pointed to the seat and waited for her to sit. She did, but not before she saw the little smile curve his lips. He leaned over placing his hand on the back of the chair. When he spoke, she felt his breath against her ear. "You said you liked it, and so I thought I would get it for you."

Then he gave her a quick kiss on the cheek. The Styrofoam containers were sitting there as neat as could be, and there was even a little bud vase in the middle of the table.

"I..."

He laughed as he sat down. "And the quick ride out there was worth it if it left you speechless."

She didn't know how to respond. She'd never really had anyone try to romance her before...and that is what it felt like. They were involved but...they hadn't been to bed and it was nothing serious. Not really.

"You look stunned. It's just lunch, love."

She shook her head and leaned over to keep her coworkers from hearing. "Guys just never do this kind of stuff for me."

He offered her a crooked smile that did funny things to her insides and chucked her on the chin. "Then you've been dating the wrong kind of guys."

She leaned back and even as emotions she didn't want to feel tried to force their way out, she smiled. "Thank you."

"You're welcome. I just thought you needed it. You seemed...upset Saturday and I wanted to do something for you."

It was scary how much he could figure out about her. She hadn't told anyone about Jack's assignment but Leo knew something was bothering her. They had spoken for five minutes on the phone. Her brothers had known her from the day she was born and still couldn't figure that out.

"Jack's being deployed."

He nodded and dished out the food. "Ah. So not nursing a broken heart."

She shook her head. "No."

He glanced at her, his gaze scanning over her. She could see his mind working behind that sexy face of his. "It's his duty, Maryanne."

He didn't try to placate her. He just said the unvarnished truth, which for her was always better to deal with.

"He volunteered. Again. They all do." She shook her head "They piss me off."

Leo laughed. "But you love them."

"Yeah."

"Where's he going?"

She shrugged. "I don't know. He couldn't say."

Which made it worse. Sure, she obsessed whenever she knew where they were, watching every news program and she was insane enough to have a Google alert for whatever country they were in. But...it was better for her that way.

"Hey," he said, his voice lowering and filled with so much concern she felt tears burn the back of her eyes. She looked up at him. "Don't be sad. I bet he'll be back before you know and he'll happily be interrupting my pursuit."

She laughed and sniffed. Then, she leaned in and gave him a kiss on the cheek. "You're sweet."

His cheeks turned ruddy and she smiled. The fact that he was blushing because of her gratitude was kind of cute. And sexy. Why did she find it so appealing that the big Army medic blushed? She was in deep after two weeks if that was getting to her.

"So, no brothers around, yeah?"

She sighed. "I hope not. It would be just like Jack to call them. It would be easy for them to pop in since everyone is CONUS right now. But at the moment, no."

"Good. How about pizza in tonight?"

She smiled. "Trying to fatten me up, Santini?"

He grinned back at her. She felt something clogged her throat. "I have a feeling if I don't feed you, you'll waste away to nothing. So, how about it? I'll bring the pizza."

"No anchovies this time. I can't believe you and Jack did that to me."

"That wasn't my fault. He told me you loved them."

"What woman in her right mind would like anchovies on a pizza?"

He shook his head. "Are you trying to avoid the question?"

A little, but she wouldn't admit it out loud. Having him in her house without her brother playing guardian would be dangerous. Like fall into bed, lose her mind kind of dangerous.

And she really wanted to be dangerous with Leo.

"Just pizza?"

He nodded.

"Yeah. I like that idea, and I'll provide the beer."

Then she dug into her food, feeling better by the moment.

* * * *

"Do not expect anything tonight, Santini," Leo murmured as he made his way to Maryanne's apartment.

It was hard to convince his body to pay attention though. Leo wanted more than a little kiss good night. The cold showers he was taking every day were getting irritating. He hadn't been this frustrated since high school. He found more ways of making out with Maryanne than he ever did during his teenage years and Leo knew he was almost at the end of his rope.

Still, he knew not to push. Granted, Jack had been the main reason they hadn't gotten any further, but something was telling him to go slow. A huge part of him, the one that wasn't listening to his hormones, wanted to take his time. It should scare him, but as his father always said, once a Santini found something he wanted, there was nothing that would stand in his way. The only thing that did, or one of the biggest things, was her experience with men.

She was wary. That was understandable if she had never had a man try to romance her. What kind of idiots had she been dating? Leo had picked up on it the last couple of weeks. The fact that men apparently didn't hold the door open for her, listen to her talk…just pay attention to her had been evident from her reactions. Of course, those other men didn't matter. None of it did because he was in for the long haul.

He stopped in front of her door and just stared at the knocker. What the hell was he thinking? *In for the long haul.* Like forever? He had only known the woman for two weeks. People didn't fall in love in two weeks with someone they barely knew.

Dammit. He was almost all the way in love with the woman.

Santini, what the hell are you thinking?

She's a pain in the ass, prickly as a porcupine and so damned defensive. Just the look on her face today when he brought her lunch…he sighed. He knew she didn't like showing her vulnerability to him, to anyone. But she had for him. That little bit had awakened a need to do things like that more often. And forever.

Before he could work through the feelings, the door whooshed open. She was still in her scrubs. They were blue today, almost the same shade as her eyes.

"Gonna stand out there trying to open the door with your mind, Santini?"

"Uh, no." Oh, that will win her over.

She gave him a saucy smile. "Is that pizza for me or are you just happy to see me?"

The words didn't register. He was in love with her. Leo loved just about everything about her, from the sprinkle of freckles that danced over the bridge of her nose to that smart mouth of hers. Damn. He was pretty sure that she would be pissed when she found out.

Her brows furrowed. "Santini? Are you okay?"

He shook himself, trying to push all those thoughts aside, but his voice was still a little rough when he answered. "Yeah."

"Okay, come on in."

She stepped back and allowed him to pass. After she shut the door behind him she leaned back against it. He turned to face her.

"Are you hungry?" he asked.

Her eyes widened. He didn't blame her for being surprised. Arousal was thrumming through his blood and he heard it in his voice. Leo just couldn't help it. His fingers itched to touch. His mouth wanted to taste. Every bit of his body needed her in a way that should scare the hell out of him.

"Maryanne?" he asked. He would take a step back if she asked. It might kill him, but he would do it.

Then, a small smile curved her lips. "Not really hungry for pizza right now."

Relief coursed through him as he strode toward her. He tossed the box on the table without stopping.

"Thank the Lord," he said as he pulled her away from the door and into his arms. The moment he pressed his lips against hers, he knew he couldn't let her go. Ever.

Now, he just had to convince the woman in his arms.

CHAPTER SIX

Leo stumbled into her bedroom and they fell on the bed with a tangle of limbs. He fell off to the side, bouncing on the mattress to avoid crushing her beneath him. He rose up and rested his weight on his elbow and looked down at her. She was smiling up at him and it struck him then. He wanted to see that smile ever day of his life. He wanted to be the one that made her this happy all the time.

After a few moments, her smile faded. "What?"

He shook his head. He couldn't tell her how he felt. She was skittish as it was. If he told her he was falling in love with her, she would freak out.

"Oh, God, I look horrible, don't I? I didn't sleep last night because I was worried about Jack and then I had a long day today. I must look a mess."

She didn't have much makeup left on her face that was true. But there was a wholesome inner beauty to her, something that had nothing to do with her physical appearance. It would have shone through regardless of her outward appearance.

"No, it isn't that."

It was hard to hold back his true feelings. Leo wasn't a man who ran around singing to the world about private things, but he wanted to for her. Something told him Maryanne wouldn't accept it just yet. He was the kind of guy who planned everything out and he hadn't planned on this. But seeing her now, laying in bed, and feeling her body next to his, he knew that he had come home. For a man who had spent his life in the military, that meant more than anything else.

He couldn't tell her but he could show her.

Leo leaned down and kissed her, softly at first, keeping his eyes open as he brushed his mouth over hers. Her eyes clouded with need then drifted shut and he deepened the kiss. He kissed his way down to her neck as he slipped his fingers beneath her shirt. He pulled it up over her head.

When he saw the simple front closure bar, he sighed with appreciation. There were times he loved fancy lingerie on a woman as much as the next guy, but since his brain wasn't working beyond getting them both naked, simple was best for now. He popped it open and his brain shut down.

God, she was beautiful. Silken skin, pink nipples, and just the right size for his hands. He brushed his fingers over the tip of one, then cupped it. He dipped his head and took a hardened tip into his mouth. That one little sample of her had him wanting more. This wasn't enough. He wanted to taste every inch of her.

He kissed his way down her body, enjoying the curves, the smoothness of her flesh. When he reached her waist, he pulled her pants and panties off easily in one quick motion. Leo knew he was being a little indelicate, but the urgency to see her naked, to touch her bare skin overrode his better instincts. He tossed her clothes on the floor behind him. She lay naked before him, the soft glow of the sunset lighting her skin.

He wondered what he did right in his life to have this moment with her. He skimmed his hand up one of her legs before following the path with his mouth. She shivered as he kissed a path up her legs. When he reached the pussy, he took a deep breath. Musky arousal with a trace of femininity. Her scent drew him in.

The moment he touched his mouth to her sex, he was completely lost. He slipped his tongue inside her wet passage. The taste of her danced over his taste buds. Sweet, tart…intoxicating. Just like the woman. She molded her hands to the back of his head, urging him on. He barely noticed. All that mattered was Maryanne. Her needs. Her pleasure.

He took her clit into his mouth and pulled it between his teeth as he slid a finger inside her. Her muscles clamped down hard on his digit and he hummed against her clit. Leo could just imagine what she would feel like against his cock as he thrust into her. He added another finger and in that next moment she came apart, screaming his name. He wanted that again, he wanted to hear his name as she came again. This time though, he wanted to be with her, to feel all those muscles contracting against him.

Leo rose to his knees, and in the next instant, he realized he forgot to bring a condom.

"Shit."

She laughed and he looked down at her. Her smile was soft and inviting and the joy he recognized caught him unawares. It tugged at his heart.

"In the drawer, soldier."

"What?"

"The condoms, I have some in my drawer."

He leaned down and gave her a large smacking kiss. "Gotta love military brats. They know how to be prepared."

Balancing himself on one hand, as he leaned forward to pull the drawer open. Within seconds he had the condom on. He slipped his hands beneath her back pulling her up and onto his legs, then lifted her and slowly started to enter her. He never took his gaze from hers as he eased his way into her tight passage. When he was finally seated fully inside of her, she leaned down to press her mouth against his. She slipped her tongue between his lips and he sucked on it as he started to move inside her.

It didn't take long before his orgasm rushed through him. She shuddered against him, leaning her head back and moaning his name. The sight of her, and the way her muscles contracted against his cock erased the last of his control.

When he was spent, they fell together on the bed.

* * * *

"Oh, my," was all Maryanne could say. Her brain was still not functioning well.

"I will take that as a compliment."

She laughed and allowed the feeling of contentment to fill her. He rose up to his elbow and looked down at her. He was smiling but there was something behind the serious look in his eyes. She had seen it earlier when they first came into the bedroom. It scared her but it also made her heart warm.

"So, are you hungry now?"

She had expected more, feared it, and now she found herself a little disappointed.

"Yeah, sounds good." She sat up, but he stayed her with his hand.

"No, stay here. I'll grab the pizza."

He gave her nose a kiss and her heart melted. "You don't have to do things like that, Santini."

He frowned. "Like what?"

She motioned with her hands. "Like getting me pizza, bringing me lunch...Wait, are you trying to fatten me up to eat me? Like some kind of sick serial killer thing."

He shook his head and smiled. "Nope. Just like making you smile." Then, completely at ease with his nudity, he slipped out of bed and went to get the pizza.

Her head was still spinning from the lovemaking. How was she supposed to resist sweetness like that? The man had her all messed up. Her first response would be to run. Run far away and try her best not to think about him. But before she could, he was returning with the box in one hand and a couple of waters in the other.

"No wine?" she asked.

He shook his head and dropped the box on the bed. "I want you completely sober tonight."

She frowned.

"And I am staying. Get over it."

He handed her a water and sat on the bed.

"The pizza's a little cold," she said.

"Well, it's been about forty-five minutes since I got here."

Surprised, she glanced at the clock and realized he was right. She shrugged and took a bite of pizza.

"No other complaints?"

She could tell he was joking and she went with it.

"Yeah, you're not very good at that." She motioned with her slice of pizza.

"At pizza?"

"At *sex*. Good lord I don't know why I like you."

He gave her that lopsided smile that always gave her a jolt. "But you do. A lot."

She swallowed, trying to remember to keep it light. "I'm not so sure now."

"Really? Because you screamed my name enough times to make me think it had something to do with liking me."

She wanted to be mad, but she couldn't help it. Laughter bubbled up. "You're an ass."

"But as you pointed out, you like me. You really like me." He finished off his slice of pizza and brushed his hands over the box. He grabbed it, shut the lid and threw it on the floor. She had finished her own slice and he was heading her way.

"Leo..."

"What?" he asked but didn't stop.

"Don't you need a little time?"

"Naw. I need a little Maryanne." He wiggled his eyebrows and slipped over her and pressed her against the bed. "And I aim to show you."

He kissed her then, pulling her lower lip between his teeth.

"And this time, I plan on taking longer than I did last time."

"Yeah?"

"Oh, yeah."

Then he dipped his head and kissed her neck. He started to work his way down her body, but she stopped him.

"No. My turn now, soldier."

He smiled and in that instant, she felt her heart squeeze tight. "Anything to please a woman."

He laid back. She straddled his hips then smiled down at him.

"I think that this time, I like the idea of being in charge."

He settled his hands behind his head. "Yeah?"

She traced a finger down his chest and he shivered. "Yeah. I like it a lot."

"I think I like you in charge too." His voice had deepened.

She chuckled as she wiggled against him. His cock was already hard again against her sex. "I think I can tell that, big boy."

Slipping down she kissed his skin and teased his nipples. She dipped lower, licking her way down to his cock. Taking her time, she enjoyed the way his legs moved restlessly against the bed. She took him in hand, wrapping her fingers around his cock. He moaned and power surged within her. She had never been timid about sex, but she had never acted quite this bold with a man before.

As Maryanne continued to stroke his penis, she bent her head to give his sac a few licks, before moving up to his cock. She twirled her tongue around the crown of it and teased him by only taking the head into her mouth a few times. Then, she took him completely into her mouth.

The taste of his precum rocked her senses as she took him as far as she could without gagging. Soon, he was thrusting in rhythm with her as she started to stroke his sac.

"Enough," he growled as he pulled her up over his body. She grabbed another condom and tore it open, rolling it down his cock.

Inch by inch she took him inside of her. She rose then descended, over and over, but again, Leo took over. He rolled them over on the bed, reversing their positions. He rose slightly, then started to pound into her. The strength of his thrusts had her headboard smacking against the wall, but she barely paid attention.

Instead, she enjoyed the feel of him against her, the weight of his body as he surged into her body again and again. Her orgasm slammed through her, the power of it leaving her breathless once again. He pushed her up and over again, the force of it just as amazing as before. He followed, her name on his lips as he thrust into her one last time. He collapsed on top of her.

The only sound for several minutes was their breathing. She was slick with exertion and her heart was still hammering against her chest. Just like his.

"As I said before, *oh my*."

He chuckled and lifted his head. "I think that's my line this time."

CHAPTER SEVEN

"So you aren't going to tell me where we're going?" Maryanne asked.

Leo hid his smile. He knew she had been going crazy wondering what he had planned. It had been two weeks since they'd had their night together. They had a few nights of quick dinners and then ended up in bed. What he wanted was to spend more time with her outside of bed. Plus, he knew that Jack had shipped out the day before. She had been preoccupied with that so he wanted to do something that would take her mind off that. Planning a date she didn't know anything about had captured her attention and held it. He was pretty sure she hadn't thought of Jack leaving all morning.

"Nope. It's a surprise. Don't you like surprises?"

She frowned at him and he fought the urge to chuckle. He knew he was lost in a woman when her frowns turned him on...not to mention had his heart turning over. She was just so damned cute when she was frustrated. The pout helped too.

"No. Surprises in my house were not fun."

It had been tough, but during the last couple weeks, he'd tugged out details of her childhood. It had been like extracting a rotten tooth out of a grizzly bear.

"Oh? Your dad wasn't big on surprises?"

"The General? No. His kind of surprise was, hey, missing your birthday for a TDY. Those weren't fun. Plus, Jesse was the worst when it came to practical jokes. I really hate that. So you can see why I hate surprises."

"Well, those aren't fun. This will be."

He took the exit off US 281 and took the turns that led them to the zoo. Her eyebrows rose and she smiled at him.

"The zoo, Santini?"

"Yeah, and the botanical gardens. I thought it would be fun just to enjoy the day."

She said nothing for a few minutes as he followed the signs. Then, she sighed. "It is pretty today. I planned on spending the day cleaning the apartment."

An apartment that was hospital clean. She had meant to spend the day dwelling on Jack, checking the news. He had seen her check her phone about five times in the twenty-minute ride from her apartment.

"Well, you can do that tomorrow. It's supposed to rain. It's gorgeous today."

He pulled into the parking lot. It was full of families going to the zoo. She sat there watching them, and he wondered if he'd made a mistake. Maybe being surrounded by laughing families and kids wasn't the thing for them today.

"Maryanne?"

She looked at him and blinked. "You never call me MJ."

Not really a question, just a statement of fact.

"Yeah. You aren't MJ to me. You're Maryanne."

She studied him for a second then her gaze softened. A lump rose in his throat that turned out difficult to swallow. She leaned forward to brush her mouth over his, not closing her eyes the entire time.

"What was that for?" he asked when she finally pulled back.

"For seeing me differently than anyone else does."

There was so much he wanted to say. She was more than the woman at work or the daughter and sister of Marines. It had only been a month since they met but he knew as sure as he knew he was a Santini that this was the woman for him. He couldn't imagine going a day without talking to her. It was a first for him.

Leo knew if he told her, she would freak. Instead, he set those thoughts aside. He gave her a smile and said, "Let's go."

* * * *

By the time they reached the Africa Live section, Maryanne was thoroughly charmed. Again. As she watched him get some feed for the birds, she couldn't help but smile. He was like a big kid truthfully. Granted, he was still a sexy man and the looks he got from some of the women today had proven it if she had any doubts. Still, he had thrown himself into the day with such vigor you would think he had never been to a zoo before.

He came back to her and flashing that smile, which turned her insides to mush.

"What?" he asked when she kept staring at him.

"Nothing. You seem to be enjoying yourself."

He poured a little of the feed into her hands. "What's not to love? Pretty day, beautiful woman, and animals."

Maryanne shook her head. "That sounds wrong."

He laughed and tossed some of the food. "Yeah it does, but it doesn't matter. I'm feeling too good."

"What made you think of bringing me here?"

He shrugged and she thought she noticed his cheeks turning ruddy. "I thought it would be fun."

"It was a good idea. I don't do enough in San Antonio to enjoy it."

"It was one thing Mom insisted on. Dad didn't always get stationed in the best places, but Mom always made sure we got out and enjoyed it."

"I've lived here for three years and never made it back to the zoo. I came with my grandmother when I was in middle school."

"What was it like being raised by your grandmother?"

She hesitated. She was never comfortable talking about her childhood.

"It was different, that's for sure. Dad was there…but not really. You know how that is."

He nodded. "I can just imagine for someone who is on the fast track like your father. I think it's one reason Vince has never settled down."

"Your brother's on the fast track, is he?"

Leo shrugged. "Probably. He made O-5 early. And, well, Vince sort of has some unrequited love thing going on."

She smiled. "Really. Somehow he doesn't look like he's suffering that much."

"Looks can be deceiving."

The tone in his voice caught her attention. She turned to look at him, but he was smiling as if nothing was wrong. For most of her life, Maryanne had shied away from serious personal discussions. In her family, they were frowned upon. As a child, she understood that discussions like that led to lies or arguments. Her father might be a kick ass Marine but he didn't handle messy personal issues very well.

"I understand that."

"Yeah, I bet you can."

Of course, he could see her side of it. Sure, life as a military brat had benefits but there just as many sacrifices.

"Dad always wanted to pretend everything was okay, like we were a normal family." Not wanting to ruin their day, she shook herself free of those thoughts. "But my grandmother was great. She was my salvation in a household of men. Taught me how to cook. She also taught me to stand up for myself, which I am sure you can understand is important in a Marine household."

He smiled. "Well, I like you the way you are, so I'm glad she was around. Especially since she taught you how to cook that red sauce."

Again, she knew there was something behind the words, but she didn't want to worry about that today. She just wanted to enjoy their time together. "So, are you only going to feed the animals, or does your date get some popcorn?"

Leo tossed the rest of the feed out and grabbed her hand. "Never let it be said that Leo Santini doesn't know how to spoil a date."

She followed along, pushing the weird mood aside, intent on enjoying the day and the man.

* * * *

"Dammit," Jeff said as Maryanne and an orderly helped him back into his bed. A month after she started pushing him harder, and she was feeling a lot better about his progress. He was not.

"I feel like an infant after you get done with me."

"That's exactly what I want to invoke in a man. It's probably the reason I'm not married."

He chuckled as she pulled his covers up and over him.

"I just feel like I should be further in my development. I wanted to be further along."

She shook her head as she poured him some water. "No. You are actually further than I thought you would be. You're doing remarkably well."

He smiled. "Does that mean when I get out of here you'll allow me to take you to dinner?"

She handed him the glass. "I don't date my patients."

"I won't be your patient by then."

He was attractive, always had been. But for some reason...she hadn't been attracted enough to even think about the offer. She did have a hard rule about patients. Even after they weren't under her care anymore, she didn't date them. It was not something that she thought would be good for either of them.

"Let me guess. Santini?"

She shook her head. "He has nothing to do with this."

"Damn, I can't believe he stole my woman. I thought we would marry and have ten kids."

She chuckled. "You have got to be kidding me."

"I think we would make a cute couple."

"No, I was talking about the ten kids. What makes you think I want that many kids or any kids at all?"

She had never been sure of marriage or kids. It had been something she didn't want to think about right now, especially since she was pretty sure she was falling for Santini.

"Aw, Johnson." He took her hand and looked around the room to make sure no one was within earshot. "You would make the best mother."

The simple statement and the sincerity of it had a lump rising to her throat. It was possibly the sweetest thing one of her patients had ever said to her.

"Thank you, but I am not ready for that yet, and I can assure you that you aren't either."

He chuckled and released her hand. "If Santini screws it up with you, let me know. I would definitely like to make up his mistakes for you."

"You act like he isn't your friend."

His eyes widened. "He is. It's just...I want to make sure he appreciates you."

Thinking of the lunch he had brought to her she knew he did. "He does."

He smiled. "Thought he might. Of course, you know what they say about Santinis?"

"Uh, no since I don't know the rest of them. I met Vince, but not the rest of the family."

"Ah, well, they are well known for being very loyal, very...hearth and home kind of guys. Once they find a woman they want, nothing will get in their way."

"And just how do you know that? He said all his brothers were single."

"Oh, well, his father and his uncles. My dad and his served together, both Marines. When all the young guys were going out carousing, Santini was either writing letters or coming up with ways to do things for his wife. Dad said he was one of the few of his buddies still married and all his uncles are still married or widowed. They fall hard, or so the legend goes."

She shook her head. "Like your father pays attention to what his friend is doing. He's making that up."

"Nope. Promise. He was Special Forces and they all live in each other's lives while they work. Guys notice when you stop going out, partying, especially with the Santinis. They party as hard as they love...or so says my father."

It was weird hearing a guy talk that way and she didn't like the way it made her feel. Panic welled in her stomach. Leo wasn't in love with her. Sure, they had spent most of their time together in the last few weeks. But...he wasn't in love with her. Hopefully.

"I have another appointment. You make sure you let the on duty nurse know if you have any pain that doesn't feel right."

"Now I know you're the woman for me, Johnson. You know there is a kind of pain that feels right."

She rolled her eyes and resisted the urge to smack him against the back of his head like she would one of her brothers.

As she walked down to her office, what Jeff said started working its way through her. She hoped that Leo didn't think he was in love with her. Sure, she was in love with him, but that didn't mean...

Oh shit.

She was in love with Leo. This was wrong, so wrong. Falling for that idiot wasn't what she wanted. Sure, he was all tough on the outside and all sweet on the inside. Making love with him had taken her to a whole new level.

"Hey, MJ, whatcha doing?" Freddy asked her.

She shook her head. "Nothing. Just tired."

The older man smiled. "More like in looooooove."

"What are you talking about?" she asked, trying to quell the panic that was now blooming in her chest.

"Please, woman, I've never seen you moon over a guy before. This Santini has you wrapped around his finger."

The fact that Freddy noticed was worrisome and she didn't like it one bit. She needed time to think. "Have you been dipping into the meds, Freddy?"

He chuckled. "Just let me know because Dave and I would like to plan your wedding."

"I am not getting married and I am not about to let you and Dave plan the wedding. I've never met two gay men who knew less about style than you and your husband."

With that, she started down the hall again.

"Ohhhh, this is going to be fun, MJ. You can run, but you can't hide."

She slipped into her office and shut the door. Collapsing in her chair, she closed her eyes. Being in love with a Santini was hard on a girl.

CHAPTER EIGHT

Leo glanced at Maryanne, trying to discern the weird mood she'd been in since he'd arrived at the apartment. It wasn't anything she said. In fact, if he had one complaint, she had been a little quiet. She was never that talkative during movies, but there was something definitely eating at her.

"How was your day?"

She gave him a wary look. "Okay. Looks like I'll have a new patient tomorrow."

She went back to biting on her thumbnail and staring blindly at the TV screen. *Not good at all.*

"You haven't heard from Jack, have you?"

"What?" It took her a moment to look at him. She smiled, but it didn't reach her eyes. "Oh, no. I doubt I'll hear anything soon. He'll probably email at some point but I got the idea we won't get to talk often."

Then, she turned her attention back to the screen again. She'd been distant for several days now. He had let it go because he had already learned that Maryanne had her own little moods and he knew her entire world didn't revolve around him. He knew it was best to leave her alone while she worked through it.

Maryanne seemed to be getting worse though. He wasn't happy with the situation but he didn't want to push her. Still, he didn't want her to think that she could use problems outside of their relationship to push him away. And, he could be with her while she worked through it and not be a bother.

He took her hand and stood up. "Come on, love."

She looked down at their joined hands. "What?"

"Let's go," he said. When she raised her gaze he could see the confusion darkening them. "Don't think, Johnson, just come on."

He pulled her up off the couch.

She took her time following him as he tugged her along. "I'm not sure I want to do this."

"I think it will make you feel a whole lot better."

"Guys always say that, but it's always about how they feel."

He kept walking through her room.

"Wait."

He ignored her and led her into the bathroom. He released her hand and started a bath. He knew she didn't like people to know her weakness for something so girly as a bubble bath, but he did and was about to use it against her. He poured some of the bubbles into the bath.

"You might want to get naked because your gonna be uncomfortable in those sweats when they get wet."

"I--"

"Better hurry up, or I'll take up all the space." He could feel her staring at him, but he ignored her. Instead he lit all the candles then pulled off his clothes. He slipped into the tub. He held out his hand. "Come on, Maryanne."

She looked down at his hand then up into his face. The small smile she offered had his heart tumbling down at her feet. The silly woman had no idea just how much he loved her, but soon, she would. She tugged off her clothes and he helped her into the tub. She sat with her back to him, leaning against his chest.

"Now this is nice."

"Yeah, I have agree," he said. "Although, you better not tell any of my students that I did this because there would be hell to pay."

She chuckled as she threaded her fingers though his. He could feel her relaxing against him. "I promise as long as you don't tell anyone at the hospital. I have a reputation to uphold."

"No worries. Your secret is safe with me. No one will know the Battleax of BAMC likes bubble baths and candles."

She sighed. "I have to invoke fear in my patients or they won't push."

He nodded. "I have a question for you."

"No, I don't go for threesomes and I don't have any friends who do. Although, Freddy or Dave would probably be happy to accommodate you."

He chuckled, happy that she was finally relaxing enough to joke around with him. "Yeah, you're enough for me."

The quiet returned. He could see her trying to figure out what that comment meant. It was like when they first started going out. She was weighing everything he said as if waiting for him to say something hurtful. The woman must have dated some shitty men.

"Your question?"

"Oh, I know from your reputation that you could have taken a job at one of the big hospitals or worked as a contractor or at clinics and made a lot more money."

"And?"

"Add in the fact you said you wanted to avoid men like me."

She snorted. "Military men in general."

"Then why are you working at a military hospital?"

The sigh was long and she shrugged. "I don't know. I..."

She said nothing else but he knew what she was thinking.

"You wanted to serve in your own way."

"Don't make me out to be someone who is some kind of wonderful person."

But she was. She worked well past her hours, making sure that her patients were taken care of. In the six weeks he had known her, he had seen it. She stayed late and showed up early. And, she was dedicated to each of her patients. She fretted if they weren't doing well and she celebrated when they accomplished the most simple of feats.

She wouldn't accept his thoughts on that. He knew that. She had this hardened core that made her seem bigger than life, when she was just one woman. It was one of the things that he loved about her.

And he liked that thinking that no longer scared him. The one thing that did scare him was her not being in his life. Less than two months and she had become the most important thing in life to him.

"I understand why you do it." She stiffened. "Oh, let it go, Maryanne. Just because I figured out why you do it isn't bad."

He hadn't meant to sound so pissed but it was a raw nerve with him. He needed the connection to be tighter and she kept trying to pull away. She sat up and looked over her shoulder at him. She was a woman who was made for candlelight. It made her skin glow, her eyes sparkle.

"Why are you mad?"

Because I'm in love with you and you would rather I go away.

He couldn't say it. He knew he was rushing things in his mind. She was there. He knew she was scared of what was going on

"Sorry. Just, I don't understand why it's such a secret."

"It's kind of…well, dorky."

"You think serving your country is dorky?"

"No, wanting to serve your country is dorky."

He could tell from her tone that she was joking and while he wanted to push her more, he knew better than to do that. Instead, he decided to show her. Without warning, he stood, pulling her up in his arms. He had to be careful not to drop her as he stepped out of the tub. He walked over to the small counter and turned her so she could sit on it. He took her face into his hands and kissed her.

Then, he loved her. He might not be able to tell her everything right now, but he knew he could show her. He kissed down her body, teasing her nipples. He settled on his knees in front of her. Then, he set his mouth against her pussy. She was already wet from the bath and from her own arousal. The familiar taste of her exploded in him. Over and over he slipped his tongue between her silken folds. She moved against him, but he never let her go over that edge.

Soon, it wasn't enough. It was never enough. He rose to his feet, grabbed the condom from the drawer. After he rolled it on, he entered her in one, hard thrust. She gasped at the intrusion and he was going to apologize, but she wrapped her legs around his waist to urge him on. He thrust into her, over and over again, pushing them both to the edge. She was close, and he could feel her muscles clenching against his cock.

"Maryanne, look at me." He ground the words out. "Maryanne."

She finally opened her eyes in time for him to watch them go blurry with pleasure as she went over the edge. He slipped his hands beneath her ass to pull her more tightly against him as he allowed ecstasy to take over his actions. He followed her moments later. He was still looking at her when he came.

Moments later, the only sound in the room was their heavy breathing.

He pulled her off the counter and then stumbled into the bedroom, falling on the bed with her. He rose to an elbow and looked at her. The only light in the room came from the candles in the bathroom. Her hair was wet and her mouth was swollen from his kisses.

"I love you, Maryanne."

She stiffened beneath him. "You don't have to say that."

"What?"

"That thing," she said panic coloring her voice. She tried to sit up but he held her steady.

"But I do love you." He didn't regret saying it. He might have rushed it a bit, but now that it was out, he was happy with it.

"That's ridiculous."

He stared at her. Her voice had gone kind of squeaky and all girly. "What?"

"You've only known me for six weeks. You don't know me."

She wiggled and this time he let her go. He figured she needed a little space and he wanted to calm her down. She grabbed her robe, shoving her arms into the sleeves then tying the sash.

He frowned at her. "But I do love you."

"Really? What do you know about me, really?"

"You love your brothers."

She rolled her eyes. "Well, everyone knows that."

"You love your work, love that you are giving back to the military in some way. And you like flowers and romance."

Her face drained of what little color there was. "Take that back."

Leo shook his head trying to understand just what was going on. "What?"

"I do not like romance. I don't really even like flowers."

For a second he didn't seem able to speak. "What do you mean you don't like romance and flowers? They make you go all gooey inside."

"No." She was shaking her head and backing up from him as if she were afraid he would attack her.

"What's wrong with me knowing things like that about you?" he asked, his temper getting the best of him.

"Because, you could use it against me."

She could have taken a knife to his heart and it would hurt less than those words. Did the woman not know him at all? After all their time together these last few weeks, she really thought he would use it to hurt her? Anger and pain surged, but he stuffed them down. If she wanted to fight dirty, he could do it too. One thing he wouldn't do is fight naked. He hurriedly got dressed in silence.

"Where are you going?"

He shook his head. "I don't want to do this right now."

Leo was raised to respect women. He also knew when to step back from a fight that wouldn't solve anything.

"Just like that you're running away? Because I didn't tell you I love you back?"

"No. I am not in the mood to fight with a coward."

The moment he said the words, he wanted to take them back. He didn't normally fight that dirty with a woman. He opened his mouth to apologize but she shook her head. Color rushed back into her face and her eyes narrowed. "I'm not a coward."

"Really? What do you think your abrasive personality tells people?"

"That I'm selective about who I spend time with. And apparently, I made a mistake with you. Just go."

He wanted to argue but she was standing on the opposite side of the room, her arms crossed protectively in front of her. She was not going to talk. Leo knew if he stayed, he would only make things worse.

"You made a mistake? I'm the one who should be pissed, Maryanne."

"What the hell do you have to be pissed about?"

"You think I would use things I know and love about you against you. If you think I would do something like that, then you don't know me at all."

He waited for her to deny it. Instead, she gave him a stony stare.

"I guess I have my answer."

He turned and walked out hoping he hadn't just made a big mistake.

Chapter Nine

Maryanne tried to focus on reading a report, but she felt her attention shift again. It had been that way for two weeks. Two very long agonizing weeks and she was getting worse by the day.

"Are you going to be bitchy for the rest of your life?" Freddy asked.

She gave her friend a nasty look. "If I want."

Okay that was childish and he was her boss, so it probably wasn't a good idea to snap at him. Maryanne just didn't do well on no sleep. She wasn't getting more than two to three hours a night. And dammit, she wasn't eating. Even now she was sitting with a burger made just the way she loved it, and she couldn't get into it. She nibbled.

"If this is the way you are going to treat your gay husband, I might seek a divorce."

She looked up at him and sighed. The worried look he gave her told her he was truly concerned about her behavior. "I'm sorry. I'm just not hungry."

"Yeah, and you've dropped about ten pounds—not that you didn't need it."

"I have not lost that much and bite me."

He set down his burger and looked at her across her desk. "I wouldn't have run all the way to Whataburger if I thought you were going to just stare at the food." He took another bite and chewed it then swallowed. "Tell Freddy what the rat bastard did. Then we can go out and do margaritas and look at all the cute guys on the Riverwalk."

She chuckled, but it sounded more like a sob.

"Oh, dear," he said in true Freddy fashion. "This is bad."

"He told me he loved me."

"I will hunt down the bastard and make him cry...Wait, what?"

"He said he loved me and I freaked. I mean, I didn't think he meant anything because we had just had sex. And so I freaked and I told him he didn't know me. Then he said horrible things about me, like I like flowers."

Freddy tsked. "Disgusting."

"And how I like bubbles and crap."

There was a beat of silence, then a sigh. "Oh, honey, when are you going to accept that a man can love you?"

She felt a sob fighting to get out and pushed it down before she answered. "When I find one who does."

"Really. I think you found one. He's the man for you if he can make you like this."

"Oh, well that's what I want in a man. One who makes me miserable when he leaves." She rubbed her eyes. "I've been through this before."

"No, you haven't."

She opened her eyes and frowned. "How about when I broke up with Richie?"

"You got mad. That is what you do. You get mad, then we party, then you're better. This one...he's different."

She shook her head. She'd known Richie for a year before they started dating. It was true, when he left she barely paid attention. "I hardly know him."

Freddy gave her a knowing look. "I'm assuming you're talking about Leo and you do know him."

"How would you know?" she asked, her voice turning a bit whinier than she would have liked.

"What's his favorite thing to eat?"

"Pasta and red sauce, especially mine."

"And what does it feel like when you're laying in bed without him?"

"Like I'm living in hell," she sobbed out. This was so not like her. She rarely cried and not in front of people. Especially not at work. She was still sniffling when her phone rang. It wasn't a number she knew but she recognized the area code as one of the ones out of the DC area. Fear gripped her. She still hadn't heard from her brother.

"Yes?"

"Is this Maryanne Johnson?" a woman asked on the other side.

She nodded then realized she was on the phone.

"Y-yes."

"Good, I have a bone to pick with you."

Freddy was studying her and then mouthed Jack. She shook her head and he visibly relaxed.

"Uh, okay."

"Listen, I love my sons. Adore them. But I don't want to deal with them here."

She held the phone out and then pulled it back to her ear.

"I might be able to help if I knew who you were."

"This is Joey Santini."

Oh, God.

"And let me tell you, he's been here five days and I can't take it anymore."

"Can I ask how you got my number?" she asked not knowing what else to say.

"I looked at his cell while he was in the shower." She said it as if Maryanne was stupid.

"And you think this is the kind of behavior a mother should display?"

"I don't care. I'm desperate. I want my husband to myself. I love my son, but I know that I can't fix what's wrong. And unless you want me down there with a gun, I would suggest you get here as soon as possible. Tomorrow's Friday. You should be able to catch a flight."

"Excuse me?"

"You need to fly up here and make it right. I'll text you our address. And, don't call him or tell him I did this. He needs to think you came on your own."

Then the line went dead. True to her word, the address popped up in Mary-anne's text.

"Who was that?"

"Joey Santini."

"I didn't know Leo had a brother named Joe."

"What?" She finally focused on Freddy. "Joey is his mom. Or, I'm assuming."

"What did she want?"

"She asked me—ordered me—to come to DC. She said Leo's there and being a pain."

Freddy chuckled. "Tell you what—I'll cover for you tomorrow."

"No. You had a day planned with Dave. It's your anniversary."

"He'll understand."

"I'm not going up there because she ordered me." Irritation burned through her as she thought about Joey Santini. She stood up and started to pace, hoping to work off some of her temper. "The nerve of the woman. Why does she think she can just bellow out orders and I am going to follow them? I hate women who are like that. Just think I'm going to follow her orders because I'm afraid of her."

There was a beat of silence. "Oh my God."

She stopped and looked at Freddy. His wide smile aggravated her even more. "What?"

"You know who she sounds like?"

"Who?"

"Look in the mirror, darling. Leonardo Santini fell for a woman just like his mother."

She settled her hands on her hips. "Are you telling me that I order people around?"

"You get off on it here at the hospital. It's part of what makes you a great physical therapist. You're good at pushing people. That's why we give you some of the worst patients."

"People don't think I'm pushy."

Freddy laughed. "Everyone thinks you're bossy."

She collapsed back into her chair. "Well, that sucks."

Freddy waved that away. "Don't take it that way. People love you the way you are." He smiled. "Especially Leo."

"I don't know how I feel about that."

Freddy walked around her desk and pulled her up out of her chair. "I fell for a man just like my mother too. Go to DC. Do you have the money?"

She thought about her savings account and how happy she had been to build it up. At that instant, she knew it wasn't that important. "Yeah, I can probably swing it."

"Go. Get your medic and then give me babies to spoil." He kissed her on the forehead. "If you don't, then I will never talk to you again."

She smiled as she watched him go out the door. As soon as it closed behind him, she turned to her computer and started searching for flights.

* * * *

"Are you going to sit in here all day?" his mother asked as she leaned against the doorjamb to his room watching him.

"Well, since Dad and Vince told me I couldn't go fishing with them today, I thought I might get some reading done."

She smiled knowingly, and walked in to sit on the bed beside him. It brought back so many memories. His mother had always known when to listen and when to talk to help her sons. It was as if she were born knowing when they needed her, and when they needed their space.

"Maybe you shouldn't have told Vicenti to do something that, as far as I know, is anatomically impossible."

His ears burned when he realized that his mother had heard the argument. He hadn't meant to say it but it was that or punch Vince. He would be in a whole lot of trouble if his mom had caught them in another fistfight.

"Sorry."

She brushed some of his hair away from his forehead. "Considering his situation, he shouldn't tease you about this Maryjane."

"Maryanne."

She nodded and patted his leg. "So, tell me what my son who hates to read is going to read today?"

"Okay, so maybe not read. I might play a few games on my tablet."

"And, you're going back tomorrow."

He nodded. He had finished off his class hoping to see Maryanne at the graduation. He knew then she wouldn't come back to him. It was partially his fault. He'd called his brother names and told him to fuck off when he told Leo he was a coward. It smarted that his brother had accused him of that, especially when he'd done the same to Maryanne. Apparently Vince thought he should have fought harder. It had been a little too much to explain to his older brother he still felt as if he were bleeding. The knife she took to him did more damage than any bullet he would take on the field.

"I have another class coming in week after next. And I have to finish up my reports about the last class."

"You like teaching?"

He thought about it and nodded. "I didn't know if I would, but it's been kind of fun."

"That's good. Too bad it's there in San Antonio since you will always be running into Maryjane."

"Maryanne."

"What?"

"Her name is Maryanne."

He thought he saw her lips twitch. "Oh, okay. I guess it isn't that important though."

Not now that he screwed it up. It had only been six weeks and he should have waited. He could have waited. But there was a little part of him that had wanted more and telling her he loved her had slipped out. When she had freaked, he had reacted. Badly. She was in the wrong just as much as him, but he hadn't made things any better. He admitted that now and he was pretty sure she wouldn't accept the apology.

Leo heard the car outside and paid no attention. He was sitting in his room in a foul mood. Okay, he'd been in a bad mood since fourteen days ago, but he had gotten into an argument with his father. And his brother. The only one who had been understanding was his mother. She was the only one he could count on.

His mother walked over to the window and peered through the slit in the blinds.

"Is that Vince?"

"Uh…yes. I'll take care of it."

"I didn't know he had a car."

Vince usually rode his Harley everywhere.

"Of course he has a car. He lives in Virginia. You can't ride on a motorcycle in the middle of winter. You stay here and I'll tell him to leave you alone."

She turned to leave then stopped to look back at him. "I love you, Leonardo."

He smiled. "Love you too, Mom."

She shut his door and left him to his thoughts. He was going to have to make up with his brother before he left, but he was still mad about earlier. Considering Vince had been mooning over the same girl since high school, it seemed kind of hypocritical of him to call Leo a coward. Still, they rarely let a fight get between them like this for more than a few days. And, it didn't feel right going back to Texas without apologizing.

He just needed to get that woman out of his head. And at some point, he might be able to get her out of his heart.

There was a knock at the door.

"Not in the mood, Vince."

There was a beat of silence. "It's not Vince."

He knew that voice, had hoped she would call, but when a week passed, then two, he realized she didn't want him. The fact that she was there in his parents' house in Warrenton, Virginia was a little too much to comprehend.

"What are you doing here?"

"Wondering why I flew up here to see you if you're too much like a little boy to open the door."

Dammit. He was trapped. Irritated and still hurting, he rose from the bed. "It's unlocked."

"Oh for the love of God."

She opened it and stepped in. It took all of his control not to drop to his knees in front of her and beg for her to take him back. Bruises marred the delicate skin beneath her eyes, she was pale, and she looked like she'd been traveling through hell to get there. He had to fight the need to comfort. Especially when she was wearing such a mean frown. Then, she slammed the door shut behind her.

"My mother will think you're rude."

Maryanne snorted. "I think you don't know the first thing about your mother. Do you know what I had to do to get here?"

His heart was in his throat and this woman was griping at him as if he were some naughty boy she had to discipline. If she could be defensive, so could he. "No, why don't you tell me?"

"Freddy is working on his anniversary, which made Dave mad at me. I cleared out a chunk of my savings to get the last seat on a horrible flight next to a man I'm sure used his hair to floss his teeth, and you can't even open the door for me?"

The last word came out as a sob. For a second, he didn't know what to say. He wasn't accustomed to seeing her like this. Other women, sure, but Maryanne never cried. She just wasn't the type.

"Sure, it's okay for you to go running off, ignoring me."

As she talked, the tears flowed. What little makeup she had on was smeared all over her face. It hurt to see her in pain, but there was a little ray of hope lighting his heart. It made him feel like a bit of a bastard but he couldn't really help it. If she was miserable, she had been missing him.

She wiped her face with the backs of her hands smearing her makeup even more. "And I have to come here, like you're the girl or something."

"You said to leave you alone."

"Well, I didn't mean it," she screamed. His ears were ringing from the volume. "Fine, that's what you want. I'm gone. I'll go back to Texas tomorrow."

But even as she said it, she didn't move.

"What are you here for?"

"Because I love you, you idiot. I swear I've never met such a stupid man before. Do you think I would fly all this way and cry in front of you if I didn't love you?"

"Fine."

She sniffed. "Fine."

"I love you too."

"I think we covered that. And how I'm a coward," she said and this time she wailed it. He really didn't know how to react. The worse she got the more awkward he felt. He rarely dated women who were overly emotional. It was tiring and he really didn't know how to react.

In the end, he did the one thing he knew would work. He reached out and grabbed her. He thought she might fight him, but she didn't. When he pulled her against him, he thought the feel of her body against his made everything right in his world.

"I'm so sorry. I didn't mean to hurt you, Leo."

He kissed the top of her head so happy he didn't care what happened now. "I shouldn't have called you a coward."

"But it's true."

He leaned back and looked down at her. Her nose was red and the little bit of makeup she wore was smeared over her face, but she was the most beautiful woman in the world to him.

"No. You're not."

She pushed away from him and he panicked. "No, give me a second. I had to do a lot of thinking and I realized you were right. Everything was happening so fast, but then, it never happened like that for me."

"You've never been in love."

"No. Well, that too. I mean, I would date guys a lot longer than we did and didn't allow them to infiltrate my space."

He chuckled. "You say the sexiest things. Infiltrate your space."

Her face flamed pink and he laughed louder.

"I didn't mean it like that. Oh my God, why do men make everything about sex?"

"I haven't touched you in two weeks, it's about all I can think of right now."

He stepped forward and she held her hand out. "No, wait, let me say this. Never before had I allowed a guy into my life like you. I dated one guy for six months before I would let him come into my apartment and stay for more than an hour. I thought all of them were walking away from me, but I realized that I was already gone before they did. But you...you wouldn't allow that. You just busted your way in by being nice and sweet."

"That's because I raised him right," his mother said through the door. "And he knows the rules about closed doors and girls in his room."

He rolled his eyes. "Good Lord, Mom, I'm over thirty."

"You do not take that name in vain. You have exactly one minute."

Maryanne's eyes widened. "Is she serious?"

"Yeah. Mom never jokes about that. Says it like it is."

"Yeah, tell me about it," she murmured. But before he could ask her about it, she said, "What I was trying to say is that you let me be who I am and love me for it."

He pulled her closer. "Of course I do."

"Most men don't think women like me are keepers."

He looked down at her as she tipped her head back to look at him. "Well, those guys are wimps. I'm made of tougher stuff than that. I'm a Santini."

He bent his head and did the one thing he had wanted to do since she had opened the door. She rose to her tiptoes and returned the kiss. Everything in him said to take her then, lay her down on his bed and show her how much he loved her. But his mother had other plans.

"You're a Santini who's about to get your ears boxed if you don't open that door in the next ten seconds."

EPILOGUE

Leo leaned against the doorjamb and watched Maryanne. She was looking out their hotel window at the Riverwalk. The soft glow of the shops below the only light against her skin.

"Hey, there, Mrs. Santini, might want to be careful who sees you in that towel."

Maryanne looked back over her shoulder at him with a smile.

"I doubt they can see me from the Riverwalk all the way up here."

"I don't know about that," He said as he made his way across the room to her. He pulled her into his arms. "I know if I saw you from down there I would find a way to meet you."

She slipped her hands up his bare chest. "Yeah?"

"It's bad enough I had to wait four months to marry you."

"You know I couldn't marry you with Jack deployed."

He nodded thinking of his brother-in-law. Jack had some ghosts to contend with. It was pretty clear he had seen some nasty action, but Leo was happy to have him back, mainly because it made Maryanne happy.

"And, we had to let Dave and Freddy think they planned the whole thing."

He shook his head and sighed. "None of it matters, love. You're mine now and that's the important thing."

"Oh, Leo, I was yours the minute you brought me lunch at the hospital."

"You mean the way to your heart was through your stomach."

She laughed. "No. It was that you sort of made it romantic. I told you. Guys never tried to romance me before. I didn't accept it, but that's when I knew I was falling for you. The fact that you made our wedding even more romantic was wonderful."

He had known that no matter how far she had come in accepting her soft side, Maryanne still wasn't ready to admit she had wanted a big romantic wedding. It hadn't been huge, but he had made sure it had been something she should never forget. They'd married outside, just as the sun was starting to set over the Riverwalk.

"Oh. Okay."

She laid a hand on his chest. "Now wait. We're married now. Tell me when you fell for me."

"Seriously?"

She nodded.

"When you punched me."

She snorted. "Oh, come on."

"No, really. I knew a woman with that much punch had a passion I wanted to taste."

"So you wanted me."

"No, I wanted you the moment I saw you. Marching into the room all sassy, giving orders. It's the way to my heart."

She smiled. "Yeah?"

"But, when you hit me, well…I guess it was sort of like being hit by cupid's arrow."

She laughed and rose to her tiptoes. "It's a good thing it was you and not Vince."

He laughed, lifting her off the floor and carrying her back into the king-sized canopy bed.

"I would have had to kill my brother."

"Leo," she said, shaking her head. "You would never kill your brother."

"Okay, maim him. But, there isn't much I wouldn't do for you, Mrs. Santini."

She smiled. "And that's why I love you."

"Yeah?" He laid her on the bed. "Well, just let me show you how much I love you."

Then he joined her on the bed and showed her.

MARCO

Melissa Schroeder

Dedication

To my sister, for all the years
we shared together as official brats and beyond.

A NOTE FROM MEL

Ah, Hawaii. It was a dream come true for many people to be stationed there, but we had a rough time. We moved there just months before 9/11. We went from Aloha Fridays, with Les coming home an hour or so early, to lock down on the base. Our world was turned upside down. I was also pregnant, our surprise. Living in a two bedroom with two kids that were seven years apart in age wasn't easy. But I will always love Hawaii for the culture and for inspiring my most successful series, Harmless. Since Marco is a SEAL, I had to have in Hawaii and I needed to give him a Hawaiian woman. For some reason, I just did. There are a few Hawaiian words I throw about in the book:

Ha'ole-newcomer, not Hawaiian

Kama'aina- a local, an Hawaiian

Tutu- grandmother

Ko'u ipo – my sweetheart or sweetheart

I hope you enjoy Marco and Alana's story.

Chapter One

Marco Santini jogged up the stairs to his cottage, enjoying the loose feelings in his muscles. It had been a few days since he had been able to hit the beach to run in the morning. He'd been so busy with work lately he hadn't had the time to make it out. He did his PT but his morning run started his day off right.

As he stepped up to his tiny lanai, he noticed his landlady walking in his direction. Although, every time he thought of her that way, it felt wrong. For most of his life, Marco had always thought of a landlady to be older. Alana was young and beautiful and always had a smile for him.

"Good morning, Lieutenant Santini," she said.

Marco resisted the urge to tell her she didn't have to use his rank, but he knew it was useless. He knew she did it out of respect and there was a part of him that found it kind of cute.

Now, the rest of her, he found downright gorgeous. She was wearing a blue t-shirt that hid most of her curves, but she had on a pair of black spandex shorts that she regularly wore for her walks. They clung to the sleek muscle and emphasized her long legs.

"Good morning."

"Your brothers are getting in today, right?"

He nodded. "Yeah. Sort of an after the fact bachelor party for Leo."

"That'll be fun. You have the keys to the SUV, yeah?"

"Yes. I really appreciate you switching cars with me."

"No problem. I couldn't pass up a chance to drive your convertible."

When he had asked her about renting an SUV she had been more than willing to switch cars for the weekend. The truth is, she had to be one of the most accommodating people he knew.

"We'll try not to disturb you too much. I appreciate you letting me have them stay here."

Her eyes widened. "Of course I would. There's nothing as important as family. Make sure to let me know if you need anything else."

Before he could respond to that, she waved and headed down to the path to have her morning walk. He watched until she disappeared around the hedge then started to his house.

He had found the rental through his commander who told him Alana liked to rent to military folks because her father had been an Army ranger. It had been a godsend. Marco wasn't in the mood for apartment living.

He walked up the steps and unlocked his front door. His cell played the Air Force song before he could close the door.

"Hey, Gee, shouldn't you be on your way?"

"There's a delay here, but we should be taking off within the hour."

"I'll be picking you up at Hickam so just call like I said."

"We were going to rent a car. I don't think that little convertible of yours can fit us all."

"No, it can't. My landlady has an SUV she's letting me borrow."

There was a beat of silence. "Don't tell me you're letting her drive your car."

All his brothers thought he was fanatical about his car. Sure he didn't let Gee or Leo drive it, but if anyone saw their driving skills, they would understand. Vince was the only one he allowed in the driver's seat. Sometimes.

"Yes. Well, sort of. I'm leaving it here for her today."

There was a sigh on the other side of the line. "I wouldn't want to think about some little old lady driving Sally."

"Stop calling my car Sally. It's weird."

"A man that in love with his car should at least have a name for it. What?" There was some mumbling in the background. "Vicente said you should at least buy her a drink or two considering you're using it to fulfill your lack of a sexual relationship with a woman."

"Oh, shove it down your pie hole, Gee."

"Mom wouldn't like that kind of talk."

He chuckled. "Mom taught me the phrase. What time are you set to land?"

"They're saying we'll be landing at fourteen hundred."

"I'll be there before that. I'm only working half a day."

After getting a few more things cleared up, complete with name calling, Marco hung up and decided to grab a bite to eat. As he poured cereal into a bowl, his mind drifted back to his landlady.

Alana.

Even thinking her name made his heart skip a beat. It was corny to even think of it in those terms, but it was the truth. It was understandable he would be attracted to her. She was tall and curvy, but there was also a sweetness about her that drew him in. He wondered about the family she often referenced but never saw visit. She seemed like such a happy person, always wearing a smile, those blue eyes sparkling at him...

He drew in his breath and ordered his body to take a rest. It had been a long time since he had been this interested in a woman. She was just his type, but she was off limits. He wasn't ready to get tangled up with his landlady. No matter how much he wanted to.

* * * *

Alana was cutting up the pineapple she bought the day before for the Santini brothers when she heard the car in her driveway. She knew the sound of that engine, knew the way the person parked.

Colin.

She wiped off her hands as the front door opened and closed. Not many people had access to her house, but Colin always had a key. A girl had to have a best friend and basically, he was hers. From the time they were in kindergarten they had been fast friends. Usually, she didn't have a problem with him dropping by unannounced. Today, though, she wasn't in the mood, especially since she had a bad feeling why he had decided to come over.

"Alana, love?"

"In the kitchen, Colin."

He turned the corner and she inwardly cringed. He looked like he had been run over by a truck.

"So, I guess you and Sara are broken up, again."

He sighed and walked into the kitchen. She knew it was hard on him. Being the boyfriend to a woman who didn't want to acknowledge your relationship because of her conservative Chinese family couldn't be easy. Sara came from a very wealthy family and for some reason she didn't think they would approve of Colin. She used Colin for a lot of things, mainly sex and to make herself feel better. It tore Colin to shreds emotionally and Alana was stuck picking up the pieces every time. She ached for her best friend. Alana hated Sara and that was saying a lot. Alana didn't use that term to describe her feelings that often.

"This time, I think we are really through."

She would be happy if it were true. But she knew it wasn't. It was a mantra she'd heard so many times before.

"Whatcha doing there?" he asked.

She looked down at the knife and pineapple. "Playing bridge."

He chuckled, although it didn't sound happy. "Did I ever tell you you're a little sarcastic for your own good?"

"Many times, but I have also told you that I only do it with you and other people I love. Let me finish this up and then we can decide what to do tonight."

"I didn't say I was spending tonight with you."

"It's five on a Friday, you're in a rotten mood and I'm not letting you hit any damned clubs in Honolulu tonight. You'll do something you'll regret. Then, I will have to deal with that. I don't have time for that. How about we do dinner in?"

He smiled. "That sounds good."

"And you can drink as much as you want and stay over."

She packaged up the fruit while Colin made himself coffee.

"I might want some of that," he said without turning around.

"Too bad. It's for the Santinis."

"Santinis? There are more of them?"

Before she could answer, she heard her SUV pull into the drive and then over to the cottage she rented Marco.

"Yes. They're here to visit."

She picked up the container and headed to the door. She felt him on her heels and turned around and put her hand on his chest. If Colin saw her with the lieutenant, he would know she was interested in him.

"No. You stay here. I'm not going to deal with you and them."

He frowned but there was a bit of sparkle in his eyes. She sighed and headed out to catch the brothers before they left. She could have slipped in earlier and left the fruit for them but she didn't. She knew the lieutenant wouldn't have minded but for some reason, that had felt wrong. Unless there was a good reason, she didn't like to invade a tenant's privacy.

As she neared the cottage, the noise level rose. There was laughing and she was sure insults. She smiled. It reminded her a lot of her brothers when they were younger. Kai and Mikala always seemed to have their volume set to twenty on a scale of ten. She knocked on the door, then had to do it again because apparently she couldn't be heard over the discussion.

The door opened with a whoosh and she came face to face with a younger version of Santini. Except, this one was blond and had golden brown eyes. He blinked, then, his lips curved. Two dimples appeared.

Oh, my.

"Well, hello. Can I help you?" he asked.

"Who is it, Gee?" a man asked loudly from somewhere in the cottage. She wasn't sure if it was Lieutenant Santini though.

"I have no idea but I think I'm in love," the aforementioned Gee said.

"Lieutenant Santini, it's just me."

She thought she heard him curse, then he came to the door with a frown. Oh, no, he was irritated with her. She always tried her best to stay out of her tenants' way but she wanted to make sure his brothers were welcomed properly to the island.

"I just brought some pineapple by for your brothers."

"You can move now, Gee," the lieutenant said.

"I think Mom would be embarrassed by your manners." He didn't stop staring at her and something tickled the back of her throat as she felt her face heat up. He took her hand in his. "My name is Gianni, but everyone calls me Gee. Will you marry me?"

Before she could answer, another of the brothers showed up. This one was older and if possible, bigger. Dark haired and blue-eyed, he was just a gorgeous as the others. Goodness.

"And you can call me, Vince."

"Go away. I found her first," Gee said playfully. "If you won't marry me, how about just dating me?"

Vince bumped his brother in the back but Gee ignored him. The older brother sighed. "How many times do I have to tell the rest of you? Finders are not keepers, especially when there's a Marine around."

"She's mine," Marco said.

Both brothers broke their attention from her and looked at him. She did the same and thought his cheeks were turning pink. It was actually very cute. He was such a big man and to see him blush...well it made her like him even more.

"Sorry, I didn't mean it that way. I meant this is my landlady, Alana Kailikea. These are two of my idiot brothers. The third is on the phone with his wife."

She couldn't say anything. There was just too much male beauty to form a coherent thought. Two of them were smiling at her and one was frowning, but it didn't matter. Any heterosexual woman would have problems speaking around them. Lord, Honolulu wouldn't know what hit them.

"Guys, you're making her nervous. And, Gee, it's going to be hard to be a PJ missing a hand."

Gee raised her hand to his lips, kissed it, then winked before letting it go. After the brothers shuffled back in the house, Santini sighed.

"I'm sorry about that. They can be pains in the a...butt."

She smiled. "No worries. My brothers were the same way. Here's the pineapple. I don't want to intrude on your weekend, but seeing that you're men, I have a feeling you won't make it to a good produce stand before they leave. Everyone needs to have fresh pineapple when they come to the islands. It's a rule."

Good lord, she was rambling on about fruit and Hawaii. She blamed it on the Santinis but it was one reason she avoided long conversations with the lieutenant. She babbled when she was confronted by a gorgeous man.

He took the fruit and smiled. "That sounds fantastic. But we might have some decent food since Vince likes to cook."

"I'm not cooking for you, Marco," his brother yelled from the other room.

"I'll let you get back to your brothers. Make sure you let me know if you need anything."

He nodded and just kept staring at her. He was so quiet at times, it was hard to be in his presence. For a few moments, she just stood there and stared. When she realized what she was doing, she stepped back.

"Have a good time."

"Thank you for the pineapple."

She nodded and turned to walk. She was hoping he went into the house, but she had a feeling he was standing there staring at her. He did that a lot. He always seemed to want to make sure she was in the house or on her way before he broke his attention from her. It had to be a SEAL thing.

When she walked around the corner she found Colin waiting for her. "You're supposed to be in the house."

He rocked back on his heels and smiled. "I have to look out for my girl."

She snorted. Colin had never been interested in her and the feeling was mutual, but he did feel it was his duty to watch out over her now that she was alone. "I don't think you need to worry about that."

"I'm not so sure about that. They all seemed to be interested, *very* interested. Especially the tenant."

She rolled her eyes and walked past him into the house. She didn't need to get all excited about how that made her feel. She had a little crush on the SEAL since he moved in a couple months earlier, but she had learned early in her life men like him would be interested only in her for her money. Otherwise, they were just nice to her. Like a brother. A really hot brother.

God, she needed to get her mind on something else.

"I think you've gone mental," she said as Colin shut the door behind him.

"I think you have a blind spot. And, I think you need to take a chance again."

She didn't want to talk about Pete or the mistake she had made. It had been five years and she still felt like a fool. Her romantic life had been desperately barren since the episode, but it was better that way. A woman in her position couldn't take a chance on a man, not when every one of them knew how much money she had. The thought that Pete would have gotten ahold of the money for the charity still haunted her. Thankfully, she had found out what a scum he was before.

"I don't want to talk about it. Tonight is only for happy discussions. Unless you want to bash Sara."

He wanted to say more, she could tell from the expression on his face. He rarely held back when it came to her love life, but thankfully he refrained.

"I'll make the drinks, you get out the carbos that will kill my waistline," he said with a smile.

"You got it."

And maybe, just maybe, she wouldn't go to sleep thinking about one sexy lieutenant just yards away from her bed.

CHAPTER TWO

"So, she's not a senior citizen," Vince said conversationally.

Marco wasn't fooled. Vince wanted to take a few jabs at him. He said nothing as he grabbed up his keys to drive for the night trying to ignore Vince's amusement. He was still trying to deal with his feelings about watching his brothers flirt with Alana. One thing he knew, any kind of discussion would lead to a fight that would definitely turn physical. Santinis didn't mind mixing it up a bit, but he wasn't in the mood. He didn't want Alana finding out. He had been attracted to her from the start, but it didn't explain the urge to beat the hell out of Vince and especially Gee.

He glanced at Vince. "No."

That had been one thing he had felt guilty about. He let his brothers assume she was older because he was sure they wouldn't see her. It had nothing to do with the fact that he knew both of them would want to get to know her better.

Of course, Vince wouldn't let it go. "And, she's hot."

Why did he invite them over for a visit? Why didn't he just keep her to himself? Dammit. He had to remember she wasn't his.

He noticed that Vince was looking at him in that way that made the three younger Santinis nervous. He liked to know what was going on in their lives just like some little old woman.

"Don't talk about her that way."

Gee came walking out. "That's right. Don't talk about my future wife that way." He closed his eyes and hummed. "That voice of hers about drove me crazy."

Marco knew what his brother was talking about. The Hawaiian lilt was something he'd gotten accustomed to, but there was something about the way she talked, the roll over her voice as she spoke made him lose his thoughts. He wanted to hear her say his first name, against his skin, in the dark.

Shit.

He ignored his brothers, saying nothing because he knew they would make more out of it than it was.

"Are you ready, yet? Can someone tell Leo this is his bachelor party...or *at least not a bachelor any more* party?"

Gee nodded. "Leo, stop talking to my girlfriend and let's roll."

Leo was walking down the hallway. "So, what did I miss?"

Vince smiled. "Marco here almost beat the hell out of us for flirting with is landlady."

"And I found the woman I'm going to marry," Gee said.

"You're going to marry some old woman with a lot of money in Hawaii?" Leo asked as he slipped on his shoes.

"No. Who cares about her money? She's not old," Gee said, wiggling his eyebrows.

"Yeah?" Leo said as they headed out the door. "How old?"

"Not old. Very young," Gee said.

Leo grunted. "Like could get thrown out of the military young?"

"No."

Marco tried to ignore the byplay of his brothers but it was hard.

"I would say twenty-eight," Vince said.

"No, I would say about twenty-one. Or maybe twenty-two," Gee responded.

"Twenty-five. She's twenty-five," Marco growled. He hated rising to their bait but they would just keep going on. Proving his point, Gee continued.

"And gorgeous."

Marco snorted. "You only like her because she brought you food."

"No. That's not it. She has some meat on her bones and I do like a curvy woman. She's got hair all the way down to the middle of her back. Also, she told me she loved me."

Marco shook his head. "She did not."

"Yes, she did. With her eyes. And, as you said, she brought me food. That makes her a fifty on a scale of one to ten."

"Air Force math never adds up," Vince said laughing.

"I don't care. She wants me. She loves me. That's all that matters," Gee said.

This time Marco wasn't so irritated when he said, "Shut your pie hole."

"What's on the agenda tonight?" Vince asked, apparently realizing they needed to switch subjects. There was always a chance the brothers would end up fighting for no other reason than to fight if they didn't.

"I suggest Honolulu. There are a few clubs we can hit."

"Any on the list?" Leo asked.

Being military, there were a lot of places restricted to them, depending on where they were stationed. Marco almost rolled his eyes but didn't. Leo acted like he was the mother hen of the group now that he was married. Marco had been in the military long enough to know the rules, but Leo seemed to feel the need to check on them.

"None of the ones I go to. The ones on the list are there for a reason. Especially here. There are some bad parts of downtown Honolulu. Besides, there are plenty of Honolulu clubs that can handle us."

"Not sure any of them can handle the Santinis but I'm willing to give them a try," Gee said. "Let's get this show on the road."

* * * *

"So, I think that possibly we should go over to Maui for a week," Colin said.

She sighed. When he drank after a breakup with Sara, he was always planning trips for the two of them.

"And why should we do that?"

"We could go all wingman for each other and find some hot loving."

She giggled as she took a healthy sip of her lava flow. "I don't think that's going to work in my case. You know how I am."

"I know what you need to do. You need to be a slut, as least for one night."

"And why would I do that?"

"Then, you might not feel so badly about what happened with Pete."

"So, according to you, I need to loosen up my morals and sleep with a man I don't know for an evening—"

"Men."

"As in more than one?"

"Yes."

"Now I know you're drunk. The man who always threatens my dates wants me to have a gangbang to get over my mistake."

He frowned. "I didn't say that I would approve, but it might help you."

She cast her gaze to the heavens but found no help. When she looked at him, he was studying her. His eyes were glazed over from the amount of alcohol he had consumed but he was thinking. When Colin thought, it was a bad thing.

"What?"

"You like Santini."

Damn. If Colin sniffed out her attraction, he would make the lieutenant's life miserable.

"I don't care what you suggest, I will not have a night with all the Santini men."

He stared at her for a moment, then he laughed. "That would be awkward, yeah?"

"Want another drink?"

He shook his head then rested it on her shoulder. The gentle lap of water soothed her, soothed both of them. They were born and bred Kama'aina, or locals, and they never thought of living anywhere else for long. They had both done their time off the island, and they enjoyed travel, but Hawaii would always be home in the end.

"I think I just want to sit here."

"That sounds like a plan."

"You know I love you, Alana."

"I love you too, even if you offer warped advice."

"And that's why you love me. Too bad the thought of kissing you disgusts me."

She laughed. "Right back at ya, Colin."

And they sat there, watching the stars and listening to the ocean. Alana wouldn't have it any other way.

* * * *

"Hey, your landlady had company last night," Leo said as he came through the front door. It was barely seven in the morning and he had already been out on the beach running. Sadly, he had been the designated driver at his own *after the fact* bachelor party.

"What do you mean?" Marco asked.

"She's in the driveway talking to some guy."

"So, he could have stopped by."

Leo shrugged. "If he did, it was early. She's still in her robe."

Marco stood and walked to the window. Sure enough, he saw Alana talking to some guy in a slick sports car. She was wearing a kimono. His irritation grew as she leaned in and kissed the guy.

"Oh, that will just not do," Gee said. "I'll put up with a lot but not her being with a schmuck with a sports car."

Marco frowned. "Hey, I have one."

"Exactly," he said sipping his coffee. "What kind of coffee did you say this was?"

"Kona," he said without taking his gaze away from the scene in the driveway. She laughed at something the dickhead in the car said and he felt a growl rumble in his chest.

"Oh, I think someone is very, very angry," Gee said.

He glanced at his brother. "What do you mean?"

"Uh, you growled, Marco."

Shit. "I did not."

"Yeah, you did, I heard it too," Leo said.

"Screw this," Marco said and walked out the door. He had been on his way for a run and now he definitely needed it.

He heard the car driving away and changed directions. It was against his better instincts, but he did it anyway.

"Alana," he said, catching her before she walked into the house. She turned to face him, her face a little pink from embarrassment.

"Did you need something Lieutenant Santini?"

He shook his head. "What I mean is that I wanted to thank you again for the pineapple. My brothers really liked it."

She smiled and he felt his heart leap into his throat. All because she smiled at him. Maybe he was still drunk from the night before. Of course, he hadn't been drunk but there had to be some kind of explanation for the way his head was spinning.

"That's good. I hope you had a fun time last night. Did you need anything else?"

"I don't think I've ever seen your friend from this morning around before."

Her face turned even pinker. "Excuse me?"

"Well, in the few months I've lived here, I don't think I've ever seen a man leave." When he said it, it sounded like an accusation.

"You don't come home every night, lieutenant."

"Oh, I just never thought…" then he trailed off when he realized he was about to stick his foot in his mouth. It was already too late. Her smile faded.

Shit.

"I might not be the type of woman you are interested in, but it doesn't mean that men aren't interested in me. Is there anything else?"

He wanted to apologize, but he knew that it wouldn't work, not right now. He shook his head. She said nothing else as she slipped through her door and shut the door, locking it loudly.

"Oh, way to go, bro," Gee said from behind him.

Great. Exactly what he needed. Gee would never let him get away with this without giving him a hard time.

He said nothing to his brother as he turned and headed down the path. He needed that jog. Unfortunately, Gee came with him.

"You know, I don't understand why you haven't asked her out."

He shrugged. "She's not my type."

"A woman like that is every man's type, and I hate to tell you bro, she so is your type. You always went for the exotic looking women. And Alana is definitely that."

For once he wished he had unhealthy brothers. He could try and outrun Gee but he was younger and he was a PJ. He'd done the training Marco had for SEALS. He was as fit as any SEAL because as a combat paramedic he had to carry men on his back.

"She's my landlady. What happens if we go out and the break is bad?"

"Well, let's be honest, it would be your fault."

"That's stupid. What makes you say it would be my fault? She could turn into some kind of crazy woman with men she dates."

"Come on. Alana is the epitome of sweet. What woman—especially a woman with her kind of money—picks up a pineapple and cuts it herself for guests she's never met."

"Lots of women would."

"Not a lot of women I know."

"You know the wrong women, Gee."

"Can't help it. The dating pool is kind of small in Valdosta."

Marco snorted. "Yeah, I can imagine. Gotta have a few sexy coeds at the university."

He shrugged. "I have to deal with the questions about why I'm not an officer."

Marco knew that could be an issue with some people. Out of the Santinis, he and Vince went to Annapolis. Leo and Gee both opted to enter as enlisted. Both had wanted to have jobs that were either closed to officers or had very few of them in the field. They might give each other shit, but all of them respected their chosen career paths.

"Screw them, then."

Gee laughed. "That's the problem. They don't want that."

Marco chuckled as he lengthened his strides. Gee responded in kind without a word.

"So, back to Alana. I think you should ask her out."

"And I say, none of your business."

"Just saying, bro, you get that pissed with us and that one guy who was leaving—and I'll bet the dude was gay—you might want to work through those feelings."

"You think the guy was gay?"

"Just a hunch. That or a friend. If they spent the night in bed together, it couldn't have been that great if all he gave her was a kiss on the cheek, so I am saying nothing happened."

The knot in his stomach loosened. "Doesn't matter."

"Just one thing to think about. If she comes home with a guy again, are you going to be an ass? Because, if that's the case, you might want to just go ahead and date her. I could see her tossing your ass out if you keep acting like you have this weekend. Race ya' to the steps."

And just like that, the little ass took off. Marco didn't speed up. Instead, he let his brother's suggestion infiltrate his thoughts. There was a chance that over the next two years, he would have more interactions with Alana when she was with men. There was a good chance that he would make an ass of himself again. He couldn't help it.

All his life he was known as the quiet Santini. He could be loud around his brothers, but in groups and especially with women, he was often the quietest person in any gathering. His mother had always made the joke it had been the reason he had long-term girlfriends in high school. She was convinced all the girls thought he was actually listening to them as they jabbered on.

He smiled. His mother knew them all so well. For a woman surrounded by men, she gave as good as she got. And she always knew just what to say.

What would she say to him now? She would probably tell him to get his head out of his ass and go apologize. He sighed and looked over at her house as he slowed to a walk. He would, but he needed to wait until his brothers were gone.

By then, he might have just figured out what to say to her.

CHAPTER THREE

Alana was standing on a chair rearranging her cupboard when her home phone rang. There was a good chance it was someone from the charity so she ignored it. It was the weekend and if it was an emergency, she would handle it. Board members didn't accept her boundaries and their idea of an emergency was remarkably different than hers. So, she didn't give them her cell phone and she dealt with them through landlines.

She sighed as she set another platter on the top shelf. She rarely used it, but it was her mother's and there were things she just couldn't let go after the accident. She glanced around her kitchen. It was still a disaster but it was shaping up. She'd spent more than two hours cleaning and rearranging her house, mainly out of irritation. It needed it, but she needed to work off her mad—not to mention her embarrassment. She knew men looked at her differently than say a super model… or a cheerleader. Still, she didn't like to have it thrown in her face, especially by Marco Santini. It seemed worse somehow.

After her message, a woman with a thick Texas accent spoke. "Hello. This is Maryanne Santini and I am looking for my idiot husband and his idiot brothers."

Alana jumped off the chair almost killing herself in the process but she figured it was worth it. She didn't know where the Santinis were that afternoon, but if a wife was calling, there was a good chance something bad had happened.

She grabbed the phone, breathless. "Hello, are you still there?"

"Yes. Sorry to bother you, but no one is answering their cells. Do you know where they are?"

Alana looked out the front window. "The car is still there, hold on. Maybe they're on the beach."

"Thank you. I'm assuming your Alana, the landlady?" She continued on without waiting for an answer. "I really need to talk to Leo. Are they behaving themselves?"

"Yes. I mean, they're adults."

"That's true, but when the four of them get together, there always seems to be a problem. Last time we were all together, Gee and Marco got in a fight about which career field was tougher, being a PJ or a SEAL. They settled it with arm wrestling."

"Uh, that seems civilized," she said, trying to keep up with the other woman's thought process.

"It was after they rolled around in the backyard and their mother had to cool them off with the hose."

Alana stepped out on her deck looking towards the beach. She squinted against the bright afternoon sun. The beach was packed, mainly because of the great waves and mild temperatures. Being Saturday, there were a lot of families enjoying time together. She scanned the beach thinking she might be wrong. Then, she saw them.

Good God, they were walking up from the beach, without shirts, wet…her mind went blank.

"Hello?"

She let loose a little breath trying to calm her heart. "Sorry, they are on their way back from the beach. Hold on."

She moved the phone away. "Leo? Your wife is on the phone."

He took off in a sprint toward her. "What's wrong?"

She laughed and handed him the phone. "Sounds like nothing but she couldn't get ahold of any of you."

He took the phone. "Hey, babe, what's up?"

He was quiet for a few minutes. "No I'm not by myself. I'm on Alana's phone, so she's standing right here. Why do I need to sit down?"

He shot a smile at Alana as he listened. Then, the grin dissolved and he went white. It happened so fast, she was afraid he would pass out.

"Lieutenant," she yelled out as she reached out for Leo.

"What's the matter?" Marco asked.

She had a hold of Leo's arm. "I don't know, I think its bad news."

Marco looked at his brother. "Leo?"

"How far?" Leo asked. He laughed. "Of course I'm happy. Why wouldn't I be happy?"

"Have you called your father and my parents?"

Silence again.

"Okay. Wow. I mean, shouldn't you be in bed resting."

She shared a look with Marco and shrugged as the other two brothers joined them.

"I'll call you in the morning. Call your dad and I'll call Mom. She will flip out."

He hung up the phone handed it to Alana, then grabbed her by her upper arms and gave her a loud, smacking kiss.

"Hey," Marco said.

"Can't help it. Had to kiss a pretty woman because I am going to be a father."

There was a moment of stunned silence then they all started talking at once. Questions and pats on the back from the others, but apparently Marco wasn't as happy as the others. He was frowning at Leo.

"You can let go of her, Leo," Marco said.

"Oh, sorry," he said with a sheepish smile.

She smiled and patted his arm. "No problem, Leo. Congratulations, daddy."

He went white again. "Daddy."

She laughed and gave him a kiss on the cheek.

"This calls for a celebration," Vince said. "Know a good place to eat, Alana?"

"Sure, what are you looking for? Dressy or just hanging out?"

"I think a hanging out kind of place. How about one of the shrimp trucks we passed?"

"Yeah, that will be good. I can give you directions if you can't remember how to get there. Let me get a pad of paper to write on."

"Why would you do that?" Vince asked.

"So that you can find your way."

"Vince means he expects you to go with us," Gee said. "You can sit in the backseat with me."

"She'll be sitting with me up front to give me directions."

She glanced at Marco and wondered about his tone. "Maybe since it's my SUV and I know where I'm going, I should drive."

"Give us a chance to wash up and we'll meet up with you out front in about twenty," Vince said.

"I would make that thirty if I were you, Vince, there's only one shower," Marco said.

"I call shower first," Gee yelled and took off running.

"Damn," Vince muttered. He and Leo tore off after their brother.

"You don't have to go with us if you don't want to," Marco said after a few moments.

"I don't mind, unless you do."

"No."

Another long moment of silence.

"I guess I should go get ready."

She nodded and he kept staring at her.

"What?" she asked.

"Are we cool?"

For a second she didn't know what he was talking about, then it hit her. His comments from this morning still bothered her, but she wouldn't let him know that. Her pride wouldn't allow for that.

"Yeah, we're cool, lieutenant. You might want to hurry because I have a feeling your brothers will have no trouble leaving without you."

He sighed. "See you in a few."

She watched him walk away, her gaze slipping down his body. When he turned the corner she sighed. She couldn't seem to keep her mind or her attention off his body. Seriously, what woman could? And she had just agreed to have dinner with all four of them.

She had to be insane.

* * * *

"You should really ask her out," Leo said as he took a sip of beer. They had returned hours before. Dinner had been…nice. Alana had been a bit reluctant to join into the chatting until Leo had loosened her up.

"She seemed more comfortable with you."

He chuckled. "Yeah, because I'm not a threat."

"What does that mean?"

"She's shy around guys. The Santinis aren't that easy to take even for the most outgoing woman. And with all of us there at once, we are kind of loud. I have a feeling that your lady is accustomed to quiet times."

He grunted but said nothing as he took another sip of beer. He knew she was shy, but she hadn't been so quiet with him. Their interactions had always been pleasant until that morning when he made an ass out of himself.

Leo apparently wasn't ready to let it go. "Make sure not to wait too long. That's one woman who won't last long."

"She doesn't date much."

"Could be that the right guy hasn't asked her out."

He thought about that for a moment or two then nodded. "You're probably right."

"Maryanne isn't a woman who would be considered shy, but I did have to convince her to go out with me."

Marco snorted as he thought about his larger than life but petite sister-in-law. "After she punched you in the nose."

"No, she hit me in the eye." He sighed. "It's when I started falling for her."

He chuckled. "You're warped."

"And I'm gonna be a daddy. Lord." He shook his head. "We wanted to try right off, because you know we don't know how long I'll last at teaching. They might put me back out in the field and that will mean more deployments. Still it happened fast."

"You're getting kind of old, so good decision."

"Yeah, at least I'm not old and cranky, like Vince."

"I heard that, jackass," Vince yelled out the window.

Leo ignored Vince because once he got going on a subject he would not shut up. "Still, I think you should take a chance. She's a sweetie and since you're so hung up on her, it might be a good idea."

He opened his mouth but Vince interrupted him. "I now know why I'm not married. Apparently it turns you into someone who talks about feelings and babies and shit. Can you two shut up or go somewhere. I need sleep."

He shared a smile with Leo who nodded. Marco counted off with his fingers then they both banged on the wall. The sofa was located against the wall. Vince fell on the floor with a thump then a string of curse words filled the air. Both of them started laughing.

Then, they heard him stomping down the hall at them. He appeared in the doorway in his boxers and T-shirt. He'd had to put on his glasses and damn he looked pissed. It made them laugh even harder. He looked like some kind of deranged serial killer. Even with his hair as short as it was, it was already smushed upside his head.

"I'm going to kill you both."

He came after them and they took off on a run.

"You're getting old, Vince, so I am pretty sure you won't be able to catch them," Gianni yelled after them.

He had just reached Marco and leapt at him, taking them both down so they were rolling over the grass in front of Alana's house. Vince straddled him and had his arm lifted to smack him against the head when the lights came on. Both of them blinked against the brightness trying to focus. Then the door opened.

Shit.

"What is going on?" Alana asked, concern lacing her voice.

Marco looked over and his tongue stuck to the top of his mouth. Damn, the woman was almost naked. She was wearing a soft t-shirt that stopped at her waist and some low riding shorts. It gave him enough of a view of her belly to make his brain go blank.

"My brothers are making fools of themselves," Leo said with a smile.

Vince rolled to his feet and offered a hand for Marco. He took it and stood beside him.

"That still doesn't tell me what's going on."

Now she didn't sound concerned. She sounded irritated.

"I'm sorry about that, Alana. Vince decided to chase us in the yard and tackle me."

"Oh," she said, but the tone in her voice told him she didn't understand. "Okay. I just wanted to make sure you were okay. Good night."

She slipped inside and shut her door.

"Well, that impressed her," Leo said with a chuckle.

Marco glanced at the door one more time before following his brothers to his house. It would be one more thing he would have to apologize for when his brothers headed back to the mainland.

And sadly, he was looking forward to it because it meant time with Alana.

He just hoped she was still talking to him by then.

CHAPTER FOUR

Alana sat by the pool and tried to keep her mind on the figures she was looking at on her laptop. It was getting close to her quarterly meeting for the charity she headed up and she hated it. The charity, she loved. But, this…well, numbers should be illegal. And spreadsheets.

She shut the top of her laptop and frowned. She had been in a bad mood for two days and she knew it had to do with Santini. They had seemed to come to an understanding but there was still something there. She didn't know if it was her embarrassment or his, or something else. If she hadn't known better, she would say that it was sexual tension, but that would mean he was attracted to her also.

With a sigh she leaned her head back on the lounger and closed her eyes. She shouldn't be surprised that he thought of her like that. Most hot men did. They would tell her she was pretty in the same tone they would tell their sister…and that was all she would ever be to them. A sister figure. And it wouldn't hurt so much if she hadn't been letting Colin's comments get to her.

She knew she could lay the blame of all of this at Pete's feet. He had made her believe that a hot man like that would be interested in her. The romance had been fabricated, as was any kind of feelings he had for her. He had only been interested in her money and in the money she raised for the charity.

The sad thing is, she would have given it to him. Hell, to have a real family again, she would give up her money, the house…and she would do it to get her parents and brothers back. How many times had she thought about that phone call to her dorm room in the middle of night that had changed her life forever?

"Alana?"

She shook herself out her sour mood and looked up. It was Marco and he was alone. She hadn't heard him. And he was standing there looking glorious, and she was in her bathing suit. Damn.

"Is there something you needed, lieutenant?"

"No, I just wanted to thank you for being so nice to my brothers. They can be a bit overwhelming."

She nodded. "They've already left?"

He slipped his hands into the pockets of his jeans. "Yeah."

"That's too bad. To really appreciate Hawaii you need to be here at least two weeks."

"Well, Leo used up most of his leave on his honeymoon."

He said it with enough confusion she smiled. Nothing like a man who's never been in love enough to want to use his leave on a woman.

"Was there anything else you needed? I have some work to do."

He glanced at her closed laptop. Then, he looked at her for a minute. "I wanted to apologize for my behavior Saturday."

She said nothing. She had been down this road before with men. Somehow it all turned out worse than when they were an ass to her. Apologizing for not being attracted to her always hurt. She knew they thought they were being nice, but it was always very painful for her.

"Accepted."

"I don't know why I behaved that way, and part of it is I don't know much about your personal life. I know you do volunteer work, but I don't know what you do."

"Are you going to keep standing there making me look up at you or are you going to sit down?"

He gave her one of those little smiles he rarely offered and took the lounge chair next to hers. She wanted to sigh. Why she had invited him to sit was beyond her. She knew why. She was sick enough to want him to stay and be pissed because he did.

"Are you going to tell me what you do?"

She cocked her head to the side. "Why do you want to know?"

He shrugged. "I think I should know more about you."

She nodded and looked out over the pool. "I do a lot of volunteer work, but the main thing I do is head up an organization in my family's name. Which is what I was doing when you showed up. I have a meeting tomorrow and it has to do with the budget."

She hoped he would take the hint that she had work to do. Okay, she really didn't want to do it, but then, he didn't know that. Instead, he leaned back on the lounger. Being subtle with a Santini apparently didn't work.

"Are you going to tell me more or are you going to make me pull the information out of you?"

She smiled. "Our main purpose is handling several homes on the islands for battered women and their children. We are talking about expanding to raise funds for scholarships."

"And you took it over at such a young age?"

She shook her head. "I established it."

She said nothing else because she didn't know what to say. Most people in her personal life knew about her work, and most people on the islands where familiar with her story. The whole situation was odd. She never had her tenants out on her back patio. They were permitted to use it, but she mostly stayed out of the way then. And other than a cordial greeting here and there, she didn't really get to know them. She probably knew more about Santini than any of the others.

"So, you're not going to tell me more." He said it as if he were thinking some great decision over. Then she realized he had made one. "I would like to take you to dinner. You know, to make up for being an ass."

She sighed. "Lieutenant—"

"Please call me Marco."

That wasn't good. It was more intimate but from the look on his face, he wouldn't let it go. "Marco, you really don't have to do that. I understand."

"I don't think you do."

She gave him a smile. "I do, and that's okay."

And if she sat there any longer arguing with him, she would get mad...or worse, cry. She stood and turned to grab her laptop, but he stopped her. He had risen too but so quietly she had not heard him. He was like that, but then, he was a SEAL.

"No, I really don't think you understand."

He was so close she could smell the clean scent of the soap he had used that morning. She could imagine him in the shower, water dripping from his flesh....

Alana stopped that thought. It would only cause her more sleepless nights. She raised her eyes to his face and shivered at the look he was giving her.

Marco slipped his hands up to her face, cupping her jaw gently. She tried to swallow, but couldn't. Her body was hot, so hot and he hadn't really done anything. He dipped his head, brushing his mouth against hers. All the while, he continued to look into her eyes.

When he pulled back her lips were tingling.

He hesitated, then stepped back from her.

"I think that will dispel the myth you've concocted in your head."

She raised her hand and touched her mouth. "I guess."

"So, dinner, Friday night. Seven okay?"

"Seven?"

His lips curved again and she felt her heart dance a little. He didn't smile often. Not that he was dour, she just assumed it took a lot to catch his fancy.

"Yeah, as long as Mr. Stay Over doesn't mind."

"Stay over? Oh, you mean Colin. No, he won't mind."

"Just so you know, if I was in his shoes, I would. See you at seven on Friday."

He turned and walked away. She stood there on shaking legs and then collapsed on the chair.

"Oh, my."

* * * *

Marco was almost ready for his date when his cell phone started playing his mother's ringtone.

"So, did my boys behave in Hawaii?"

He chuckled. "Yes. In fact, with Leo not into women anymore of course, and Vince has turned into some old man who can't stay up past nine at night, it was kind of quiet."

"Good. I didn't call you for several days after because I know how you are. So, I deserve points."

He smiled. His mother understood his need for solitude. It was hard in a family of four boys to get it but his mom had always known when he needed it.

"It's kind of late over there, isn't it?"

There was a pause and he got worried.

"I'm just wondering if Vince said anything to you about Jules being back in the area?"

Ah, that was the way of it. In high school, his brother had a major crush on the woman, but she had been his best friend's girl...then wife.

"No."

"Okay. He's been avoiding her for some reason."

"Mom, we all know that he has feelings for her."

His mother tsked. "That's no reason to avoid her now. She's single. No kids."

"And you want him married. Let it go." He stopped walking toward the front door. "I take it that Dad told you to drop it too?"

"Your father doesn't know what his sons need."

The disgust in her voice made him laugh. "Mom, believe me, if you push Vince, he will push back. Or worse, act out. You know how he is."

"Okay."

Then she said nothing for a second or two.

"Anything else?" he asked and instantly regretted it. The Armed Forces could learn a thing or two about gaining information from Joey Santini. He was pretty sure she had taught his father interrogation tactics.

"I understand you have a very cute landlady."

Shit. He was going to kick Vince's ass next time he saw him.

"Yes, she is. Your sons were a bit rude to her while they were here."

"Really? I understood Gianni wanted to ask her out."

And Marco had explained to Gee just what appendage he would remove if he thought of doing that, but his mother probably wouldn't look kindly on that.

"They were here less than seventy-two hours. I think that he didn't have time to romance her."

"Vince said you're hung up on her."

Again, he was definitely going to beat the shit out of his brother next time he saw him.

"I am not hung up on her."

"Attracted."

"Yes. And that's why I asked her out and I'm about to be late to my first date. It's not going to look good to the woman if I am late, especially since I live twenty yards from her front door. I can't tell her I'm on the phone with my mommy, because, ya' know, women get funny about a man so attached to his mother."

"Okay. I love you Marco."

He couldn't help but smile. His mom was one of the toughest women he knew, but she never failed to tell them she loved them.

"Love you too."

He clicked the phone off and slipped it into his pocket. He would rather turn the ringer off, but with his job, he couldn't do that. Twenty-four, seven he was on duty, although he would love to disappear with Alana tonight. Just go somewhere private and do all kinds of things to her.

Not a good idea, Santini. Keep your mind on your mission.

He had to mend some fences with Alana. As he walked to her house he realized he had never had such a bad start to a possible romance—ever. Maybe that was why for the first time in years, he felt butterflies in his stomach. It wasn't like him to get nervous over a date, but something about her pulled at him. And while it may never amount to anything, he really hoped it would.

He stopped and shoved his hands into his pockets. Damn, he was kind of hung up on her. It had been years since he'd thought about getting serious with a woman.

"Lost your nerve, lieutenant?"

He looked toward her front door and felt those butterflies go crazy. Good God. The woman did know how to dress for a date. She was wearing a dark blue sundress that matched her eyes. The fabric clung to her body leaving no doubt she was a woman with curves. His fingers itched to explore them. His gaze slipped down her body. The dress stopped just short of her knees and she was wearing strappy high-heeled sandals. Her red toenails intrigued him.

"Marco?"

He allowed his gaze to travel back up her body. "Wow. I'm glad you didn't dress like that around Gee."

She chuckled and shut the door behind her. "Really, you don't have to keep exaggerating."

"Actually, I'm not. In fact, there had been a discussion of how much I would hurt him if he came over here."

Her eyes widened. "Why on earth would you hurt him?"

"I didn't want him moving in on what I saw as my territory." The moment he said it, he regretted it. "Sorry, that was..."

She laughed. "No, don't. I actually like to be thought of as territory. Not sure I've ever been thought of like that."

"Well, I guess we should go."

She nodded and stepped down to him. With the heels, she was almost level with him.

"Okay, I just have to get this out of the way."

She opened her mouth to say something, but he ignored her. Instead he leaned in and kissed her. Unlike the kiss before, he put everything he was feeling for the past three months into this one. He skimmed the seam of her lips first, then slid inside for a taste. He wanted more. Wanted it all.

By the time he pulled back, they were both breathing heavy.

"Wow," she said.

"Yeah, wow. Okay, we have to go or we will never make it out of here."

She shook herself and then followed him to the car. "You know, I do have some ability to resist your charms, Marco."

He smiled at her as he held the passenger side door open. "I'm trained to break through the enemy's front line."

"So you think of me as the enemy?"

"No, not really. Just as someone I need to conquer."

She shook her head and slipped into the car but not before he saw the curve of her lips. He shut the door and tried his best not to dance around the hood of his car. Tonight was going to be great.

Chapter Five

Marco chose a local place to eat that was one of her favorites on her side of the island. They weren't too fancy but they had an extensive menu. It was always amusing seeing what a haole would pick. She should have known he wouldn't go to one of the brand name places, but a small local place on the North Shore. In the short time she had known him, Marco had acclimated himself to the area. Most military people did. She had never seen a group of people who could settle into a different culture so easily, but she knew that was just part of their lives.

The restaurant was set off a side street, just a block from Kam Highway. It was only a few minutes from her house. The menu featured so many different cuisines, she could usually find something to suit her mood. She was there so often, they knew her by name.

"Hey, Alana, how you doing, cuz," Jaime the night manager asked as he showed them to their table.

"Not too bad."

"I heard you might be doing a scholarship with that charity of yours."

She forced herself not to grit her teeth. She loved her islands and her Hawaii heritage. The only problem she had was with the gossip.

There might be close to a million people on the island of Oahu, but everyone seemed to know everyone else—or their cousin. And, in her world, most people knew her, even if she didn't know them.

"Yeah, looking into it. Trying to set up the parameters."

Once they were seated Marco stared at her.

"What?"

He shook his head. "I guess I should pay more attention."

"To what?"

"Your charity. You."

She shrugged and opened the menu; although, she knew what she would order. She'd been here so many times, she knew the menu backwards and forwards.

"Alana?"

She glanced up at him and he was still staring at her with that solemn expression on his face.

"I guess I just thought you were independently wealthy," he said.

"None of us are independent. At least not in Hawaii. We are all part of the whole."

His lips twitched. "You sound like you're talking about a SEAL team."

She laughed. "That's something I have never been accused of."

Before he could comment, the waitress stepped up to the table.

"Hey, Alana, how you doing, cuz?"

She smiled. "Pretty good."

After getting their orders, the waitress left them alone.

"So, tell me how someone so young is in charge of such a big charity."

She shook her head and sipped her water. "First, I'm not all that young. Secondly, the charity isn't that big."

Marco frowned at her as the waitress brought his beer to the table. He waited until she left.

"What do you mean by that? That host knew who you were."

She laughed. "I forget you've only been here for a little while. If you live here for any amount of time, especially if you're Hawaiian or married to a Hawaiian, you get to know a lot of people."

"And so everyone knows you."

She realized he didn't know her story. Alana was accustomed to having people know about what brought her to this point in her life. Explaining herself wasn't normal. From the expectant look on his face, she decided there would be no getting around it.

"When I was eighteen, I was at UCLA my freshman year of school. My parents and brothers were killed in an accident. It was kind of a big thing here on the islands, so people know me and they know my charity."

He nodded. She could tell he was disappointed that she didn't reveal more but she couldn't right now. She normally didn't even have to tell people about it. Explaining the horror of that incident still made her cry and she refused to do that on a first date in front of her SEAL.

Dammit. Not her SEAL. A SEAL.

"Did you ever go back to college?" he asked.

"Yeah, but I stayed on the islands. I went to UH. It was just easier." She wanted to get away from the discussion of her family. "So, your brothers had a good time, yeah?"

To this he frowned. "Yes."

She had hit a nerve with that one. "What?"

"I just...okay, I'm not happy with Gianni or Vince—especially Vince at the moment."

She shook her head. "Brothers."

"What do you mean by that?"

"It's been a few years, but I remember the rivalry. It's probably good you didn't go into the same service."

He took a sip of beer and nodded. "It wouldn't have been too hard on Gee or me. We are young enough not to have to compete with the others. Plus, we are far enough apart in age it doesn't really matter. Now, Leo and Vince, they are really close in age. Less than two years. So, it would have been hard. Leo didn't want to go into the Marines though."

"And your father is okay with this. He was a Marine too, right?"

He nodded. "He's happy we all wanted to serve. It's a Santini tradition."

"My father was an only child, but I think he would have liked to have my brothers serve."

"Neither of them did?"

"No, they were only in middle school when they were killed."

Damn. He opened his mouth but was interrupted by Ashton Martin, a local politician.

"Alana, darling, I didn't know you would be here tonight."

She sighed and turned her attention to him. If she hadn't been so interested in talking to Marco, she would have noticed Ashton coming in. He had more hair gel and teeth than sense, but he did help her with fundraisers.

He leaned down and kissed her cheeks. There was an odd sound from the other side of the table. She glanced at Marco who was giving Ashton the death glare.

"I'm not making an appearance, Ashton. I'm on a date."

He turned to Marco. "I see."

She could tell his feelings on the subject. Ashton was only an eighth Hawaiian, much less than she was, but he was kind of stuck up about it. He didn't like mixing with haoles. She truly thought it had more to do with the fact that they couldn't vote for him.

"Ashton, this is Marco Santini. He's stationed here with the military." That changed Ashton's demeanor quite a bit. "Marco, this Ashton Martin, one of our local politicians."

Marco smiled and was pleasant enough. They were lucky enough that their entrees came and she could shoo Ashton away. When he left them alone, Alana dug into her mahi mahi. She had missed lunch and was starving.

"So, did you ever date Ashton?" Marco asked casually.

She choked on a bit of fish. She grabbed her water and took a gulp.

"I'm sorry, but no. He's much too old for me."

"He doesn't think so."

She frowned at Marco. "I can promise you that he doesn't. Ashton has never looked at anyone that way. Even his last wife. He is all about his career. He thinks he will make it to DC at some point."

"You don't like him."

"I wouldn't say that."

He gave her one of those toe-curling smiles. "You can't even be mean about someone you don't like."

"I don't approve, something completely different than not liking."

"What don't you approve of?"

She could have just shied away from the question. Most people wouldn't want to talk about things like that on a first date. Marco was different. He didn't talk much so she found that when he did question her, it was important to pay attention.

"He uses his Hawaiian heritage to get ahead and to exclude people. That just seems wrong to me."

Something shifted in his eyes and then his lips curved again. Oh, god, her heart started beating and her body heat shot up a thousand degrees.

"I agree," he said. Then, he shifted the talk to other things. She figured it was just a moment in time, but she would cherish the moment Marco Santini looked at her as if she were the most special woman on earth.

* * * *

Marco pulled through the gate at the house and was kind of disappointed he couldn't come up with something else to do. He hadn't planned on a long date, mainly because he knew his limits. All SEALS did. Being alone with Alana for hours on end was hard on him...especially certain body parts.

He parked in front of her house.

"I had a really good time tonight, Marco."

He loved hearing his name in her accent. She drew out the name a little and the Hawaiian lilt in her voice made it sound magical. Everything she said sounded magical.

"I'm glad."

Lame, Santini. Really lame.

She reached across the console and patted his hand on the steering wheel. "And I forgive you."

He frowned and looked at her. "What did I do now?"

"I understand this was something you were doing to prove you weren't a complete jerk. It's fine. I enjoyed it and I enjoyed dinner."

She leaned toward him and brushed her mouth over his cheek.

"I have an early morning tomorrow, so I'm going to head in."

For a second he sat dumbfounded. He couldn't seem to respond. She slipped out of the car and he couldn't come up with anything to say. She thought he did the date out of pity. Why would she think that?

He looked at her walking away. There was a light mist of rain that always seemed to cling to this side of the island falling around her. The glow of her porch light created an almost mystical scene. She was already at the door by the time he reacted.

He opened his door and marched toward the door. She didn't hear him until he reached her. He grabbed her arm and turned her fully around.

"Marco?"

He didn't say anything. He cupped her face and slammed his mouth down on hers. For months now he had resisted her out of respect. He poured all those feelings into the kiss, thrusting his tongue between her lips. She didn't respond immediately, but the next instant, she slipped her hands up to his shoulders and pressed all those wonderful curves against him.

His body reacted immediately. It had been a long time since he'd had a woman...really wanted a woman. Now, he had one that made everything in his body sizzle, his brain shut down. Without breaking the kiss, he backed her up against the door. God, she tasted so good.

He slanted his mouth over hers again and again. He was already fully erect. She shivered against him and it was enough to bring him back to reality. With much regret, he pulled away from the kiss.

"I just wanted to clear that up."

He untangled himself and then walked back to his car.

It was going to be one long fucking night.

CHAPTER SIX

Alana shifted in her chair trying to enjoy the late afternoon breeze, but it didn't help her mood. All week she had been growing more agitated by the day. She was known for her even temper but just yesterday she hung up on a board member. It was that or tell him to shove it. That would have definitely raised a few concerns.

"Are you going to tell me why you're being a raving bitch?" Colin asked.

She frowned at him. He had dragged her out trying to get her out of her funk but it was getting worse by the minute. Right now, she wanted to dump her drink on Colin.

She shook herself from that thought and took a sip of her drink, then set it down on the table.

"That's a dirty mouth you have on you. Does your Tutu know you talk like that?"

"You know her. She taught me the words. So, are you going to tell me what's going on?"

She sighed. "I'm frustrated because of Marco."

"What did he do?"

She glanced out at the passing traffic on Kam Highway and tried her best not to sigh again. "Kissed me."

He frowned at her. "What's wrong with that?"

"Nothing." Not really. Except that she hadn't had a decent night's sleep since he did it. Her lack of sleep had definitely added a layer of that bitchiness Colin had pointed out.

"I thought he kissed you before."

She shook her head. "No. He gave me a kiss. This was a *kiss*."

"Ah."

He had one of those condescending looks that irritated her. Okay, most of the time they amused her. This time she wanted to punch him in the face.

"What does that mean?" she asked.

"Well, it's been awhile for you."

She frowned into her drink. "I had a date a couple months ago."

He shook his head. "First of all, we have to talk about you admitting that as if it is a good thing. Secondly, I meant sex. It's been awhile."

"I don't know why I share things with you. You always say horrible things about me. And not trying to be the raving bitch you accused me of, but you are hardly someone who should be talking."

"I have sex fairly regularly."

She snorted. "Besides, it wasn't sex. Just a kiss."

"Tell me this. Did you forget your last name?"

That kiss was seared in her memory. The feelings filtered through her just as they did every time she thought of that moment. She had never had a man kiss her like it meant more to him than his next breath. There was a pretty good chance she would remember it on her deathbed before she remembered any sex she'd had.

"Yeah."

"Being the man that I am, I'll give a little advice. Men like Santini do not kiss like that on a whim."

"I think that he might just be a better kisser than you. In fact, from my experience with you, I would say he is definitely better."

"There's that bitchiness again."

Dammit. She hated when Colin was right. He rarely was. It was probably the reason he was so damned smug about it when he was.

When she didn't respond to his taunt, he apparently decided to continue on. "He wouldn't do that to his landlady."

She snorted. "Sure, whatever. He hasn't touched me since."

He stopped with his fork midway to his mouth. "You've been out again?"

"No. I was going down to the beach a few days ago and he showed up. Then, I was potting some impatiens on my lanai and he helped. I got a little kiss."

He chewed his food as if coming up with some great advice. God, she hated when he got like this. Colin was her best friend, but he was horrible at advice. He gave it to her even if she didn't ask for it. "A little kiss?"

"Like a peck."

Colin studied her for a moment or two. "Have you made any advances?"

"No."

She had never been that sexually aggressive, and she hated to admit it, but her time with Pete made it tough to take the chance again. He had been laughing at her behind her back all the time.

"I want to beat the hell out of that bastard."

She snorted again. "I think you would end up with...how do people say it? Oh, you would end up with your ass handed to you. I wouldn't mess with Marco if I were you."

"I wasn't talking about him. I was talking about Pete. I should have done it before he was chased off the islands by his creditors."

"You're so sweet. Why didn't we end up together?"

"Because the last time we tried to kiss like boyfriend and girlfriend it felt like I was kissing my sister."

She laughed. "That's true. It was...kind of gross."

"I think you're going to have to make your move."

"On Marco?" She shook her head. "No way. I can't do that."

"Why not?"

"He's a SEAL for crying out loud. He should be the one to launch a maneuver."

Colin laughed as he sat back and studied her. Then, he sobered. "You haven't told him about your family, have you?"

She shrugged. Other than the brief discussion on their date, she hadn't said anything else and he hadn't asked.

"He's waiting because you aren't open with him."

"First of all, men don't care if you are going to tell them your background."

"They do if they are serious."

She waved that away. "Marco Santini isn't serious about me." Colin opened his mouth but she shook her head. "No. He's not. And, I don't know much about him other than the fact that he's a SEAL, his family all serve in the military, and he will be an uncle in less than a year. That's about it."

"Well, you need to quit tiptoeing around it. I might die an old man without children to spoil if you don't hurry up."

She rolled her eyes. "I guess you haven't heard from Sara?"

"Nope. She called. I ignored her."

"Hmm."

In a moment of rare seriousness, he said, "I couldn't go on like that any more. I'm sick of her treating me like a dirty little secret."

Alana leaned forward and studied him for a second. "You mean it."

"Yes, I do."

"Good. You need to get away from her."

"And you need to make a move on Santini. He kissed you, now you need to up the ante."

"I don't know about that."

"Tell you what. You go talk to him tonight. I'll pick you up for breakfast in celebration or as a pick me up."

She smiled. "You were always the best friend I ever had."

"Well?"

She drew in a deep breath and nodded. "I'll try my best."

Alana figured at this point it would be better to know than to be wondering if he was still interested.

* * * *

Marco was having a crappy day. A long crappy day at that. He had been late for PT in the morning, and that had pissed the commander off. It went downhill from there. Now, dealing with his brother on the phone was starting to piss him off.

"How is my future wife?" Gee asked.

Marco ground his teeth. He hadn't told any of them he was going on a date with Alana, but apparently his mother did and Gee wouldn't let it go.

"Alana is not your future wife."

He was so fucking frustrated being a nice guy with her. He got the idea that she didn't want to rush things and he knew she was a little inexperienced. Being the situation they were in, it was probably best that he didn't push her. If he screwed this up, living there would be horrible.

"You don't know that."

He glanced out the window and noticed that her car was back. "Yeah I do. I have to go, Gee. Shouldn't you be in bed?"

"It's only ten here on a Friday night. I'm young enough to stay up later, old man."

"So, a single man, one who claims to be full of vigor, is sitting at home on a Friday night talking to his brother on the phone. Sad, Gee, really sad."

There was an ominous beat of silence, then he said, "I'm being deployed. Nothing huge, but I'm going over to Afghanistan for the next few months."

That stopped Marco's pacing. "You were there not too long ago. I thought they gave you more time between deployments."

He sighed. "One of the guys has a mother who is pretty sick. They needed a volunteer."

"When?"

"Not sure. Within the next two weeks. Haven't told anyone else."

It was common for the two of them. Gee was the youngest and Marco was the closest to his age. From the time they were little, Gee followed him around like a lost puppy dog. It had been aggravating at first, but since they had matured, they had grown closer. "But at least you'll be back soon with the drawdown."

"That's the way I looked at it. I'm one of the few single guys around right now."

Even though many people would peg Gee as shallow, he wasn't. He understood what military families went through, and he knew what volunteering to go meant also. It wasn't something everyone would do. Sure, he would earn a little more money, but to help a fellow PJ because of family was more important. Joey Santini had raised them right.

"Mom won't take it easy, that's for sure."

Gee sighed. "I thought maybe you could call her and tell her."

Marco laughed. "Yeah, no. Not unless you're going to tell her when I get called up next time."

"Well, damn. Maybe I should let Leo do it. He's giving her a grandchild, so she's all happy with him."

"I bet he won't want to lose that buzz he has going with her."

"He owes us. Mom is all over me about Alana and you, just so you know. Ever since Leo found MJ she's been crazy for more women in the family. I can't believe we're going to be uncles."

Marco laughed. "Yeah. Even harder is to believe that Leo is going to be a father. His kids will be crazy."

"Not too crazy. MJ will make sure they're raised right. Like Mom did with us."

He knew that Gee was in the mood to talk, but he saw Alana walking his way. His heart was suddenly in his throat and his palms started to sweat. She was wearing a pair of board shorts and a T-shirt. He was so used to seeing her in a dress, every time he saw her dressed casually, his brain shut down. The fabric of her top clung to her breasts. He'd spent the last week imagining just what they looked like. He sighed as his gaze moved lower. He had more than one daydream about having her long legs wrapped around his waist as he thrust—

"Marco?" Gee said.

He shook his head trying to get it back to the conversation, but he kept his attention on Alana. "Sorry, what did you say?"

"Nothing. I'm going to go. I have to get enough sleep to get the nerve to call Mom tomorrow."

"You're in the US military and you're afraid of one little woman."

"And you're not? You're a SEAL and I'm pretty sure you wouldn't want to call Mom."

"Point taken. Night, bra."

Gee chuckled. "Listen to you getting Hawaiian with me. Night."

He hung up the phone just as Alana knocked on the door. He set his phone down on the counter and slowly walked to the door. He had to fight every instinct to run to answer it. He couldn't help it. He wanted to spend every free moment he had with her. Every day he found himself hurrying home to see if she was free. It was worse than when he had his first crush.

He opened the door and lost his train of thought. She'd picked up a flower along the way and slipped it behind her ear. He noticed she did that a lot. Just like he could imagine the way it would feel to have her beneath him.

"Hey," she said, her lips curving. "I didn't know if you were busy tonight or not."

He shook his head and said nothing else. He was still trying to get his head wrapped around the idea that she had walked to his house. With barely any clothes on. For Hawaii, it wasn't that strange, but…

"Uh…Marco?"

"Oh, no, not doing anything. Do you want to come in?"

The smile she offered hit him harder than a ton of bricks. "Sure."

He stepped back ordering his body that this meant nothing. She was just stopping by to chat, just like they had been doing for the last week. She walked past him and he caught the light scent of flowers and sensual woman. It was something he would always associate with Alana for as long as he lived. He shut the door and watched as she walked into his kitchen.

He followed her in. "Gee says hi."

She leaned against the counter. "That's nice. Wait, he's home on a Friday night? For some reason, that seems odd. It's odd that any single Santini man is home on Friday night."

"I'm home."

"Yeah, I find that strange. As I have for the last few months."

He shrugged. It was hard to admit that the dating scene had been boring him for the last year. It made him sound like Vince, and he didn't like that. Vince *was* old.

"We went out last Friday night."

She tilted her head to the side and studied him. "We did. But, then you backed off."

"No I haven't."

"Yes, you have. You haven't…you know."

He couldn't seem to follow the line of questioning. It was probably because all the blood had moved from his brain southward. Just being in the same vicinity as the woman had him rock hard. "No, I don't know."

"You haven't really kissed me since Friday night and I want to know why."

He could only stare at her. Right now his fingers itched to touch and his mouth was dry at the thought of tasting her. Did she really not understand how attracted he was?

From the blank stare on her face, she didn't.

"I didn't want to rush you."

She snorted and rolled her eyes. "Okay, Marco. I've got some work to do, so I'll see you around."

This was wrong. Very wrong. He knew women didn't like to be rushed, especially women like Alana. Plus, there was a part of him that wanted to take it slow because something felt very different with Alana. She was already walking past him when he grabbed her wrist. She stopped and looked down at their hands, then back up at his face. Confusion and pain darkened her green eyes.

"I told you before you have the wrong idea about me."

She gave him a smile that didn't reach her eyes. "No. I had the wrong idea. It's just best if we let it go. I have lots of guy friends."

He didn't like the sound of that. He didn't know what bugged him more: The fact that she put him in a category of friend already or the fact that she had a lot of male friends.

"Does this have to do with the guy who was here a couple weeks ago?"

He hated to think she had been involved with both of them, especially after he had specifically told her his feelings on the subject. She shook her head.

"Colin and I have known each other since kindergarten."

"That's it. No one in the way. No other man?"

She shook her head.

"Good."

Then, without a word, he let go of her wrist, sliding his hand up to cup her face. He didn't hesitate as he leaned in to brush his mouth over hers, then deepened the kiss. He poured everything he could into that kiss. Every feeling—anticipation, frustration, infatuation—he had for the last few weeks as he had realized how attracted her was to her. She sighed and leaned against him. Something squeezed tight in his chest

When he pulled back, she was smiling.

"So, whatcha waiting for SEAL?"

He couldn't let the challenge go. He bent at the waist, and lifted her up and over his shoulder. She squealed. He smacked her on the ass, leaving his hand there. Gee had been right. Marco liked a curvy woman, and Alana was definitely that.

"Just what do you think you're doing, Marco," she said, laughing.

"You should know better than to mess with a SEAL, Alana. You gave me a challenge. This is my acceptance."

He said nothing else but dumped her on the bed. Her hair was a mess now, but it was spread out over his pillows. He realized he wanted her there. Not just now. Not just for the time he had left in Hawaii. He wanted her in his bed every night. Forever.

"Marco?"

Touching her tonight, sharing with her in his bed, he knew what that meant to him. Now he just had to convince the woman he was in love with.

"Time to pay up," he said, before jumping on the bed ready to rise to the challenge.

CHAPTER SEVEN

Marco had to fight the primal urge to plunder. It beat in his blood to take, to taste, to lose himself in the woman. But he wanted this to be memorable. He wanted her to understand just what this meant to him.

He leaned into her and brushed some of the hair out of her face.

"Marco." Her voice was barely a whisper and if he hadn't been paying attention to her, he would have missed it. The sound of it sung through his blood. Her arousal was easy to hear. Another surge of need rushed through him, but he fought it back.

He leaned his head down and kissed her. Slowly, keeping his eyes open as he slipped his tongue into her mouth. He lost himself in the simplicity of it. Her tongue slid against his and she hummed. Tiny little vibrations shook him to the core.

He broke away from the kiss and kissed a path down her jaw to her slender neck. The woman smelled of the ocean and flowers.

He slipped further down her body and pushed her top up. He kissed the golden flesh he exposed. When he reached her breasts, he thanked god for front bra closures. With a quick click, he undid the bra. He didn't hesitate. He pulled her shirt all the way off as he took one nipple into his mouth. She moaned, her legs moving restlessly against him.

He pulled back and blew on the nipple.

She moaned his name. The sound of it on her sweet lips had his body singing. He couldn't wait. He should. He wanted to take this slowly. It just wasn't going to happen. He slid her board shorts and panties off and kneeled between her legs. Damn she was beautiful. The sun seemed to kiss every bit of her skin, leaving a golden sheen to it.

"Marco," she said, her voice telling him she was embarrassed.

She moved to cover herself, but he stopped her.

"Don't." The request came out more like a growl. He grabbed on to what little control he had left. "Please."

"I'm just not..."

"What? Not used to being naked that much?"

Her face turned pink as she nodded.

"You better get used to it around me, Alana. I plan on having you naked as much as I can."

He didn't wait for a response. Instead, he settled himself between her legs and kissed her right thigh. She shivered and he took that as a good sign. His kissed and licked his way up to the curls at the apex of her thighs. First, he breathed in the scent of her—flowers, ocean and aroused woman. No liquor in the world could intoxicate him this way. He wanted to stay drunk on it, on her.

He didn't hesitate. He pressed his mouth against her pussy, slipping his tongue inside her. The taste of her exploded over his taste buds. Soon, she was pressing up against his mouth as she slipped her hands through his hair. It didn't take long for her to go up and over the edge. She screamed his name as she jolted against his mouth.

The need to share that moment with her as she came again urged him on. He slipped out of bed and tore his clothes off, throwing them behind him, not caring where they fell. He grabbed a condom and joined her back on the bed. When he opened the packet, his hands were shaking. Damn, he hadn't been this overwhelmed since his first time. Before he could slip it on, Alana sat up and surprised him by taking the condom out of his hands. She placed it on the tip and in no apparent hurry, rolled it down his cock. He had never seen something so sensual. Her long fingers slid against his flesh and the condom and he almost came right there. Marco shivered.

By the time she had it on him, he could barely remember his own name. She looked up at him with one of those little smiles that struck him dumb. She cupped his face and pulled him down for a wet, open mouth kiss.

He gained his bearings then and pressed her against the bed. He slipped his hands down to her waist, rose to his knees, and entered her in one fast thrust. She gasped at the intrusion.

"Sorry," he said.

She wrapped her legs around him. "Don't be sorry."

He laughed and leaned down to kiss her. Then, he moved. His fingers dug into her skin as he continued thrusting in and out of her. Soon, though, he knew he could not hold back any longer. Still, he wanted to feel her orgasm as he came. He wanted her there with him.

"Come again, baby, do it for me," he ordered in a growl. She opened her eyes slightly and looked at him. In the next instant, he watched as another orgasm lanced through her. Her eyes went blurry with satisfaction before she closed them. It was the single most erotic sight he had witnessed in his life, it pulled his own orgasm from him. With one more thrust, he let pleasure take control as he lost himself in her.

* * * *

"Well, that was interesting," she said a few moments later.

He laughed and a warm feeling that had nothing to do with the sex stole through her. Rising up, he rested his weight on his elbow. "That's a helluva way to describe making love."

Her heart lurched at the words he used. She wanted it to be love, but Alana didn't know if she would recognize the emotion. Her one dip into that pool had proven she didn't know much about it.

"I couldn't come up with any other words. My brain melted the second you touched me."

His eyes softened and again she felt that suspicious warmth. She didn't want that. She *couldn't* want that. Falling for him would be a big mistake. She lusted after him, that's for sure, but she couldn't let herself fall into that deep pool again.

"Well, it was kind of fast, so I promise to take longer next time."

Her eyes widened at that comment. She glanced at the clock then back to the man to see if he was joking. He wasn't.

"Really? Longer?"

He smiled. "I plan on feasting on you, so I hope you're up to it."

Just the way Marco said it had her body tingling. She was definitely lost if he was getting her hot with sex talk. Usually it embarrassed her but when Marco said it, her body reacted. Maybe it was because she was positive he meant it.

"I'm not sure you could top what you just did."

His smile turned devious. "If you think that was good, just watch this."

Before she could react to that statement, he had her on her stomach and he was straddling her hips. His cock was already hard against her buttocks.

"You have the most amazing skin. All golden brown everywhere." He brushed her hair aside. Leaning down he kissed her earlobe.

"It makes me wonder if you've been naked over there at the pool. And just how I would love to see you out in the sun, nude."

His voice had deepened and she hated to admit how wet it made her. Marco was a man of few words and when he spoke to her like that, she couldn't seem to think of anything but giving him what he wanted.

He took her earlobe between his teeth, then he sucked on it. Marco continued to tease her like that. His mouth against her flesh, his tongue sliding along until she was a quivering mess by the time he pulled her up to her knees. He entered her from behind. It only took him a few thrusts until she was screaming his name. He took her up and over so many times she lost count before he finally followed her.

He collapsed on the bed next to her, their breathing the only sound in the room. He slipped his hand beneath her body and pulled her closer.

"Now, give me a few, and I'll see if I can top that."

She laughed and looked up at him. His mouth curved.

"If you top that, you might just kill me, Santini."

Marco opened his eyes and cupped her face with his free hand. "I have a powerful need for you, Alana. I've been ignoring it for months."

"Months, you say?"

He nodded as he started to play with her hair. "I've wanted you since the first time I saw you."

"Really?"

"You tested my control, but I'll say seeing my brothers flirting with you was what sent me over the edge. I hope I don't scare you off."

She smiled and leaned up to kiss him. "Don't worry, bra, I'm made from hearty Hawaiian stock."

"I like the sound of that," he said.

His eyelids were already drooping and she herself yawned then settled her head against his chest. There was something so soothing about having his body heat surround her as she listened to his heartbeat. It was her last thought before she drifted off to sleep.

CHAPTER EIGHT

Alana woke to the sound of birds the next morning. She was accustomed to nature waking her in the mornings, but usually it was to the sound of waves. She opened her eyes and looked around.

Marco's room.

She smiled and closed her eyes, letting the memories of the night before wash over her. Then, she realized he wasn't there. She opened her eyes again and sat up holding the sheet to her chest. She wasn't that modest of a woman but she didn't sleep naked all the time. Okay, never.

She found the bed empty beside her but saw a note. She picked it up.

Out for a run. Rest up. M

She smiled. He was such a creature of habit. It was one of the things she could handle. Her father had been military and ran her family like his own battalion. They had set hours for everything from when they were supposed to eat breakfast to bedtime.

She realized she had a pressing concern to visit the bathroom. She spied one of his t-shirts on the chair beside the bed. She grabbed it, hoping he didn't mind that she wore it and then found her panties that were lying unceremoniously on the floor. She slipped them on and went into the bathroom.

Like the man, it was neat as a pin. Sparse like the rest of his house, but not truly lacking. She looked at herself in the mirror and stopped. The woman staring back at her was not someone she recognized. Her hair was a mess, her lips were still a little swollen and there was razor burn on her along her jaw line.

"I look like I've been ravished."

She smiled. She had been, more times than she could count. Part of her wanted to know how long it would last. But, there was a bigger part of her that didn't want to know. She had planned so much of her life out for herself. Every time, life seemed to throw her a curveball. For once, she decided to live in the moment.

After the trip to the bathroom, she couldn't go back to bed, so she wandered to the kitchen. He kept it neat for a bachelor. That military training again. She knew it had to be that because she had been to Colin's place and it was a mess. And, she thought as she opened the fridge, he never had food. Marco's fridge was well stocked and put Colin's to shame. Last time she had been there he had half a bottle of champagne and caviar to eat. That was it.

She pulled out the carton of eggs, the milk and some cheese and got to work. There was one thing she knew about a man with Marco's stamina was that he would need food when he returned.

* * * *

Marco was humming when he walked up the path to his cottage—nothing like a bout of healthy sex to loosen him up. It had been one of the best nights of his life, if not the best. Making love with Alana had been sexy, sweet and it had blown his world apart. Maybe that's why he'd been avoiding it with her. He had known before they had even gone out for their first date that she could mean so much to him.

He had wanted to wake her up this morning and make love to her again, but he had forced himself out the door for a run. They had gotten very little sleep the night before and he was pretty sure she was exhausted. As he headed for his front door, he spotted that red sports car in the driveway. He stopped and watched the blond-headed man head to the door. The polo shirt and khaki shorts weren't formal, but Marco was damned sure there wasn't a wrinkle in them.

Marco could have told him that Alana wasn't there, but he took some kind of satisfaction out of watching him walk to the door and ring the bell. Then to

Marco's irritation, the bastard used a damned key. *A key.* How did he rate a key? After a few seconds, pretty boy stepped out of the house and spied Marco and headed in his direction. Worry etched his features.

"Santini?"

He nodded.

"Have you seen Alana? We were supposed to go to breakfast this morning but she's not in her house."

"She's in mine."

He expected the guy to get upset, but he didn't. Instead, relief smoothed out his features. When the man smiled, there was something familiar about it, something from Marco's memory he couldn't seem to grasp.

"Thank goodness. Alana has a habit of taking in strays and I'm always worried that someone will take advantage of her."

"Marco?" Alana called out. She had opened the door and was walking down the front steps of his house. She was wearing one of his shirts. The sight of it transfixed him for a moment or two then he realized she was walking out there with Colin looking on.

"Colin's here, Alana."

"Oh." Then she frowned. "Oh, no. I forgot about breakfast."

She stepped in full view of Colin and Marco tried his best not to get irritated. It was Hawaii and people tended to be very lax about the way they dressed, but he didn't like the idea of his woman being looked at by another man, especially one who spent the night at her house just a few weeks ago.

"Alana, love, I can't believe you threw me over for another man."

She rolled her eyes. "Come on in. There's enough for everyone."

Marco was nonplussed for a second then he smelled the eggs cooking.

"As long as Navy man doesn't rip my arms off, I'll be fine."

She snorted. "Come on."

She turned and left them standing there. Colin leaned in and said, "A bit of advice for someone who has known Alana since she was five. Just go with the flow. Alana gets what she wants."

Then he walked away, following Alana into his house. For a moment, Marco couldn't think. His brain was just not functioning. The woman stood there in his shirt after one of the best nights of his life and invited another man to breakfast. And he hadn't done a thing to stop it.

"Marco?" She called out. He looked and saw her looking out the window. "Come on, or your food will get cold."

And, as Colin said, he just went along with Alana. But they would have a discussion about her relationship with the other man, and soon.

Alana knew that Marco was irritated, especially when he grumbled that he was going to take a shower before eating. He was polite to a fault on occasion, but today he had been rude. At least now she could make his omelet the way he liked it.

"Methinks lover boy is jealous."

She gave Colin the stink eye but said nothing.

"Well, I guess you moved past your problems in the bedroom."

"Colin Fergus McKenna, I will tell your Tutu if you don't stop saying things like that."

He smiled then took a sip of coffee.

"I have the worst luck. I can't believe I forgot to call you."

"I think that's a good thing."

She sprinkled a little grated cheese onto Marco's omelet. "What do you mean?"

"You never forget anything, but I think we all need someone who makes us forget our obligations for a little while."

She frowned at him. "Don't tell me you've been back with Sara."

"No."

She sighed. "Good."

"Yeah." But he didn't sound convinced.

"Colin, you know it's a good thing for you to stay away from that woman."

He smiled, although it didn't reach his eyes. "I should have known to stay away from her. You never liked her."

"She's a user."

"Very true."

"And you deserve someone better."

"I agree with you there."

She stopped her arguments after that because he had surprised her. "Yeah?"

"Yes. Seeing you with Marco this last week made me realize I wanted more than to be someone's booty call."

She chuckled. "You're showing your age there, Colin. They don't call it that anymore."

"It's neither here nor there. We are done. Which I told her last night. She wasn't very happy."

"Oh, I wished you had called me."

"I did, but someone was busy."

Her face heated.

"And since you're cooking him breakfast while wearing his t-shirt, I'll assume you were really, really busy."

She rolled her eyes. "I am not giving you details."

"Good because that would completely gross me out. It would be like hearing about my sister." He studied her over the rim of his coffee cup. "I'm just glad he makes you happy, not like Pete. Have you told him about your family?"

She shook her head. She hated telling people about it. Most everyone knew about the accident and the scandal that followed. They definitely knew about the money she had been rewarded by the state. But she didn't want to talk about that, not yet.

"He knows they died in a wreck, but that's about it."

"Well, I think it's still a good thing, especially if you are going to cook omelets every weekend."

* * * *

Marco showed no reaction to the conversation he'd overheard. He had a feeling Alana hid a little bit of herself from him, and he felt justified listening. Okay, not really justified. His mother would smack him if she knew he had been listening, but Marco had wanted to make sure of the relationship between McKenna and Alana.

He stepped into the room and he couldn't help but smile. She was cooking at the stove, humming a little tune and tapping her foot. He had thought she would get dressed but she didn't. True, his shirt covered her, but he had thought with another man around, she would. Although, there was a part of him that was thrilled she wore something of his.

"Your omelet's ready, Marco."

She hadn't turned around, she just knew he was there.

"Smells good," he said as he grabbed a cup and filled it with coffee. She set the plate on his small kitchen table but before she could return to the stove, he grabbed her and gave her a large smacking kiss. Partially for his benefit, but also for McKenna.

She was blushing when she turned back to the stove.

"So, McKenna, what do you do for a living?"

The younger man didn't answer him for a moment and Marco looked up.

McKenna shook his head. "Sorry, I'm used to most people knowing what I do."

Alana laughed as she rinsed out the pan. "There's that big head of yours, Colin. He does the news for one of the local stations here in the morning."

Then it clicked. "Oh, yeah, that's why I recognized you."

He gave Marco a self-depreciating smile. "They like the 'hometown boy does good' angle here."

"Yeah. I don't watch much television, especially in the morning."

"I'm going to wash up," Alana said, leaning over his shoulder and giving him a kiss.

"Aren't you going to eat?" he asked.

She laughed. "I did. I don't believe in waiting for food."

Then she walked out of the room and he watched her go. Damn she had the sweetest walk, and those legs. They were long and muscular...

He looked back at McKenna who was giving him a narrowed look.

"I would suggest you mind your own business," Marco said.

"Yeah? Why is that, Santini?"

"She might have been yours at one time, but now she's mine."

Marco said nothing else as he dug into his omelet. Heaven was more like it. The woman could cook.

"Tell me something. Are you telling me you're planning on making it a permanent arrangement?"

Marco's first response was yes. From the moment he gave her that one little kiss he had known she was the woman for him. Getting to know her over the last few weeks had given him insight into her character and he knew he wanted to spend his life with her.

"I'm planning on the long term for right now."

A few more seconds ticked by as the man watched Marco. "But you don't want to tell Alana. Smart man."

Marco chewed on another bit of omelet as he studied the man across the table. He and Alana were the same age and there was an intimacy there that he hadn't liked before. But, now he was thinking there was something else going on. It wasn't sexual intimacy, but more like familial intimacy.

"You're not a former lover."

"Eww. No. We have never been lovers, although, we did share our first kiss and second. It might explain why neither of us has been lucky in love before now. It ruined us."

"Really? You aren't attracted in the least?"

McKenna smiled. "No. Do you have sisters?"

He shook his head. "No, just three brothers."

"Well, I look at Alana as a sister and she thinks of me as a brother. I was raised by my Tutu and Alana's family sort of adopted me. Tutu worked a lot of hours and they filled that time. So, it is kind of gross to me to think of her as more than a sister."

Then McKenna's smile faded and his eyes narrowed again. He might appear affable, but his next words let Marco know he wasn't as harmless as he appeared.

"Just so you know. She might not have her brothers around, but I won't think twice about making you disappear if you hurt her."

It wasn't every day he received a real threat. Most people would look at him and turn the other way, especially the ones who knew he was a SEAL.

"You know what I do for a living?"

McKenna nodded. "Yeah, and before Alana's father found out, I was running with a really nasty crowd in high school. If he hadn't found out, I probably would be in prison right now for theft...or worse. I know how to do more things with a knife than you do, SEAL, so just remember that."

He stared at McKenna. He wanted to tell the bastard to take a fucking jump, but there was love there for Alana. He couldn't fault the man on that, so Marco nodded.

"Good. Now I would suggest you don't tell Alana we had this chat. Last guy I did that with was a real bastard who hasn't been back on the island since he hurt her. If he does come back..." He shrugged.

"I'm impressed. I'm not sure anyone has threatened me like that other than my brothers."

"Can't help it. I love the girl like a sister and I can't have her hurt again."

"Again?" Marco asked. The man was talking in riddles and Marco wasn't in the mood.

"I think you need to ask her about that."

He heard the floor creak in the hallway telling him she was on her way in. "Are you through disparaging my character, Colin?"

His facial features softened when he looked at her. "Oh, don't even get me started on that. I could tell you some stories about this woman. She got me in more trouble than you could dream up."

"Oh, please," she rolled her eyes, and as if she had been doing it for years, pulled her chair next to Marco's and sat down next to him. "You're the one who convinced me to drive your Tutu's car when we were thirteen."

Marco relaxed, listening to the conversation between McKenna and Alana knowing that at one point, he would have to deal with her need to hide part of her past from him. But now, with the morning sun lighting the kitchen and her laughter filling the room, he did what his mother said was important for every military person. Live in the happy moment and worry about all that stuff tomorrow.

CHAPTER NINE

A month later Marco was still waiting. It irritated him on some level that Alana would not open up to him, but there wasn't much he could do about it. Pushing her might just push her away. He knew what he was about to do was wrong but he couldn't help it.

McKenna had hinted it was something more than just a regular wreck. He couldn't ask her friend about that. He would never betray her trust and it was something that Marco admired about the man.

It only took a few clicks on a search engine and he found the first reports of the accident that changed her life.

Local Hero Killed by Drunken Cop.

He read through the article that spoke of the repeated violations of the policeman and how he had blood alcohol over twice the limit. In fact, the bastard had used his authority and threatened a patrolman's career earlier that night when he'd been stopped.

The uproar that followed filled the paper for weeks. The cop had been white. With Alana's father being Hawaiian and a decorated Marine, the anger exploded. There were pictures of Alana. Lord, she had been young. Just eighteen. He recognized McKenna and an older woman in the pictures. His chest tightened when he saw the haunted expression on her face.

There were reports of a settlement and the scandal disappeared from the papers.

He was about to close out the browser when he saw an engagement announcement for Alana Kailikea and Peter Messinger.

He read through it realizing it had only been months after the settlement had been announced. Then, nothing. There was no mention why they broke it off, why he wasn't part of her life anymore.

Frustrated, he sat back in his chair and stared at the screen. He was irritated he hadn't known she'd been engaged, but his mind kept going back to that picture of her in the airport. He pulled it back up again.

His family was a pain. They were Italian so that meant they were loud and meddled in each other's business a little too much. Still, he couldn't imagine life without them. He knew that no matter what, he could call on one of them or all of them for support. Alana had no one. No aunts or uncles, no cousins. The only person she had in the world was McKenna and his Tutu. That was until now.

He heard her SUV in the driveway. He glanced out the window and watched her hop down.

How did someone recover from that? From losing almost everyone she cared for, and still be so happy. She smiled as she walked to her front door and he was sure she was humming one of those Hawaiian songs she always seemed to have in her head.

He had loved her before, admired her even, but now...he was stunned.

He walked over to her house trying his best to come up with a way to talk to her about what he had discovered. But when she opened the door his brain went blank. She was wearing a long sundress that hugged her curves. Her feet were bare and her red toenails peeked out from beneath the skirt of her dress.

"Hey, Marco, I didn't know you were going to be home."

"Took the afternoon off." He stopped on the top step. "Hey, babe."

Her smile widened. "Hey, yourself."

Marco couldn't say what he wanted. He admired the fact she hadn't wasted her money. That she had spent the last few years building a charity that helped others to honor her parents. She would be upset if she found out that he had been snooping. So, instead he decided to show her.

He kissed her. Cupping her face, he deepened the kiss. He backed her into the house and closed the door behind him. Then, without breaking the kiss, he picked her up and walked her into her bedroom. He broke the kiss only to set her on the bed.

She leaned back, the smile on her face touching something primitive in him. He thought he knew what it was to love someone. For growing up in a house dominated by men, their mother had made sure they all knew they were loved and emotions were regularly talked about.

Now he found himself speechless. Knowing what she had overcome and just how much more beautiful she was for having survived it humbled him. She had done it with the support of only a few people.

"Marco?"

He shook his head, but he couldn't say anything. There was a lump in his throat and his chest was tight. So, instead, he decided to show her. He slipped onto the bed. He slid her dress off her, leaving her completely nude.

"If I had known you were naked under there, I don't think I would have made it to your bedroom."

She chuckled and there was no blushing. He had done his damnedest to get her to leave her inhibitions behind. It hadn't been that hard.

"Yeah, well, SEAL, I'm kind of waiting for you to reciprocate there."

He smiled and took off his clothes. He laid on top of her. Tasting every inch of her. She was a delight of curves that he could explore endlessly. Soon, though it was too much for them. Once he had the condom on, he rolled them over the bed. She gasped as she tried to steady herself, her long, lean legs straddling his hips. His cock twitched, eager to plunder, but in this, he wanted her in control. He wanted her to take what she wanted.

"Take me in."

She lifted herself up to her knees, and she slid down his shaft. Damn she was hot, wet and tight. She rode him then, slowly at first, but soon her movements grew more frantic. She had her head thrown back, her long hair tickling his legs and she moaned his name. The sight of her in the throes of her orgasm sent him over the edge. He thrust up into her one more time and followed her.

She collapsed on top of him, hugging her body against him.

"That was definitely a wonderful homecoming."

He tried to smile, but since he knew she could see him, he said nothing. Within moments, her breathing was even, telling him she had fallen asleep.

Marco stared at the ceiling wondering just how he was ever going to get her to open up to him.

* * * *

Alana was in her kitchen watching the ocean surf out her window the next morning when the phone rang. It was Colin.

"This must be a record for you to be up at sunrise on the weekend."

"I have bad news."

She wanted to joke, but there was something in his voice.

"What is it?"

He sighed. "Pete's been arrested."

"Oh, thank goodness. I thought it was your Tutu."

"No, but the word on the street is they found out he'd weaseled himself into some rich woman's bed."

"It is his pattern."

"There are going to be questions. There already is, in fact."

"About what?"

"What kind of information did he have for the Kailikea Foundation?"

She set her cup down. "I gave him no access. None. You know that."

"I'm sorry, love, but there are going to be questions. Just be ready for them."

"Okay."

"Feel like spending the day together?"

"Marco's off for the day."

"Good, at least you won't be worrying about it, then."

"I won't worry another day about that bastard."

"What bastard?"

Marco's quiet question startled her. Just like always, he had slipped into her house and she hadn't heard him.

She turned around and looked at him. He was wearing his workout clothes but held no expression on his face.

"I gotta go, Colin. I'll talk to you later."

After hanging up, she said, "No one really. Just a guy I used to know."

He said something under his breath and turned to walk down the hall to her bedroom.

"Marco?" she asked. She was getting up to follow him when he came back in with his clothes from the day before.

She looked at the bag then back up to his face. "I thought we were spending the day together."

"I don't know if I can be around you right now."

"You've heard the news about Pete?"

"No. Why don't I know about him? Why have you never told me about him?"

His anger lashed out at her. Alana was used to his cool demeanor. She didn't know what to say to him when he was like this.

"Why can't you open up to me?" he asked, frustration lacing his voice.

"What do you mean?"

"You think I don't know that your family was killed by a drunk driver? A cop with a history of drinking and driving and that you were rewarded money for it?"

She was stunned. "Were you spying on me?"

"No. Yes. Not really."

She would have been amused if she wasn't so pissed. And scared. She was damned scared and she didn't know why.

"Which is it?"

"You said they died, in a wreck. I looked it up. And you didn't tell me about your fiancé either."

He spat it out as if accusing her.

Panic twisted her gut. She had learned long ago that men used what they knew about you.

Marco wouldn't.

She shook that thought away. She might want that to be true, but the news of Pete's arrest brought back everything. The lies, the embarrassment.

"Listen, Marco, if you want to end this, you don't have to fabricate a fight."

His eyes narrowed. "What do you mean?"

"I understood when we got together that it wouldn't last. You're going to be gone soon, or some time and you were just passing the time."

For a few moments, he said nothing. He studied her as if she were a puzzle he wanted to figure out. He walked up to her, grabbed her and slammed his mouth down on hers. "I was not just passing the time."

Then he marched out of her house. Drained, she collapsed on the couch. Her phone rang with Colin's ringer. She wasn't in the mood, but she knew he would just keep calling until she answered.

"What do you want?"

"Oh, that doesn't sound good. I guess I can wait on the news."

"Great, more news. What now?"

He sighed. "That's not important. What happened now? You sound like you've been crying."

"I had a fight with Marco."

"About what?"

"He said that I had been hiding things from him."

"And? Have you?"

She closed her eyes. "No. Yes. Maybe."

"Honey, I know that you think you need to protect yourself from him, but you don't. That man wouldn't hurt you."

She felt a tear trickle down her cheek and she brushed it away refusing to give in. The fear that she had from the time she was eighteen bubbled up.

"He'll leave. Everyone leaves."

"No, they don't. I'm still here."

"But…"

"I think I need to make a trip to the mainland and kill that bastard. At least I know where he is."

"Colin, really. Stop talking about beating Pete up. He's going to have enough worries now that he's the pretty man in prison."

He chuckled. "Still. I want to kick his ass for making you doubt someone like Santini."

"That's not what I'm talking about."

"What then?"

She sighed. "When Pete left, I was hurt, but it was my pride more than anything else. It wasn't my heart. I realize that now. But, with my folks…" She took a moment to gather herself. Otherwise she would be crying on the phone to Colin. "Everyone leaves sometime."

He sighed. "You have to take a risk, Alana."

"But, I could get hurt."

She hated to admit she was afraid. Afraid of being so in love with a man who risked his life for a living. One who would never give it up. And she couldn't ask him to do that because it was so much a part of him. It was one of the things she admired about him.

"Part of the reason you love the man is because he is so committed to what he sees as his duty."

"I know that. Don't you think that I know that?" She shouted into the phone. "It's what makes him so wonderful."

"He's a good man, Alana. And I'm pretty sure he loves you."

"He's never said it."

"Have you told him you love him?"

She said nothing.

"Pot meet kettle. Take a risk, tell him, love. Don't let him get away."

She hung up and stared out the window again. She did love him. From the beginning she had known she would fall hard and she had tried her best to resist that. It was more than the sex. It was the way he made her laugh. And every now and then, he would look at her, just a look. It made her heart feel like it was turning over in her chest.

With a sigh, she decided to take that chance Colin talked about. When she thought of never seeing Marco again...of being a stranger to him...that hurt worse than even thinking he wouldn't be there all the time.

A few minutes later she was frowning. His car was gone. He had run off. Damn him. If he didn't come soon, she might lose her nerve and it would be all his fault. When she realized she was crying again, she closed her eyes and took a deep breath. She opened her eyes. If he was going to be like that she would use different tactics. She marched back to her house. She had a plan and when that man got home he would have to answer to her.

CHAPTER TEN

Marco was pissed. Beyond pissed. He wanted to smash something, to beat people up. But, he couldn't. Part of the reason was because it was his own fault for upsetting Alana. Part of the blame was hers, but he shouldn't have pushed her. He pulled into the driveway and forced himself not to look at her house. When he parked in front of his cottage, he saw a light on. He thought he had turned it off, but then, he wasn't in the best frame of mind.

Marco walked up the stairs to the front door, but it was unlocked. He frowned and opened the door. She was sitting there in his kitchen. Just seeing her there made his heart ache.

"I don't think you're allowed in my kitchen without my permission."

She gave him a nasty look. "I own the house."

Oh, so that's how it was now. "What are you doing here?"

"I came to talk to you, but you had ran away like a little girl afraid to fight."

"And so you decided to break the lease and come into my house without my permission?"

"Maybe for my next tenant I'll add a clause for when he acts like a coward."

For a second, he didn't know what to say. First, she was yelling at him. And she was pissed. He didn't think he had ever seen her pissed before this. Where was the sweet woman he fell in love with?

"I did not."

She stood up then poked him in the chest. "Yes. You. Did."

Damn, that hurt. He rubbed his chest. She had some damn strong fingers for a woman.

"And another thing, Santini, I am not in the mood for you to be telling me I'm holding things back from you. Do you realize how much you hide from me?"

"There are things I can't tell you."

She rolled her eyes. "Or what? You'll have to kill me?"

He said nothing. His head still couldn't function. She was yelling at him like he had done something wrong.

"You know what? When you get the nerve to be truthful with me, you get back to me, okay?"

With that, she brushed past him and stomped out of his house. He stood there stunned, trying to figure out just what happened. He had been the one mad because she had been mean to him. Not mean, but secretive. Okay not that. But... shit, he had no idea why he was mad now.

One thing he did know was that she had no right to be mad at him. Wasn't that just like a woman? Irritated he strode out of his house and made his way to hers. Then, he heard her walking down to the beach. He should probably wait until she got back, but he was too irritated to listen to his better judgments. He followed her and found her with her arms crossed and frowning out at the ocean.

"I have a bone to pick with you, woman."

He ignored the interested looks from bystanders. People in the area knew Alana, and there looked to be a few locals hanging around. He didn't care.

"Go away."

"No. I don't feel like it. I want to have this out. You think I hide things from you. What? You know my family, you know me."

"You don't talk about work, ever. You don't tell me what's going on, or that you might have to deploy at sometime. You act like I can't know anything."

He hadn't talked about work because he had worried that she would run the other direction. Women weren't always comfortable knowing what being involved with him would be like. For a lot of spouses, men and women, it was a bit too much to take. So, to protect himself, he had kept it from her. And now, he realized she was right. He had been as bad as she.

"Alana."

"No, I don't want to talk right now."

She still sounded mad, so he was completely undone when he stepped in front of her and found her face soaked with tears.

"Oh, baby, I'm sorry."

"I said, go away. I don't want you to apologize because you feel sorry for me."

He stared at her. The woman had no idea what he saw in her. "Feel sorry for you?"

"Yes," she said. "I won't have it."

"Why should I feel sorry for a woman who lives in a multimillion dollar home, fills her life with things that make her happy?"

She looked away from him.

"Not gonna touch that, are you?"

She still said nothing. He hated the silent treatment, especially when it was done on him. He had always been the master of the silent treatment growing up, but it was pretty shitty to have someone use it back on him.

"So, you're feeling sorry for yourself because we had a fight."

"You said I hid things."

"You do." She gave him what she called her stink eye and he had to fight the urge to laugh. Her eyes were swollen, her face was smeared with tears and dammit she was the most beautiful woman in the world to him. "But, I know I do too. I'll be honest with you."

"That would be nice."

"I'm not used to sharing things with other people. With a family like mine…I love them but there were times when they could be overbearing. Add in my job and I am just used to observing. But it's who I am and I can't change some aspects of it."

She must have picked up on what he had been talking about. "I would never ask you to give up your job, Marco. It's who you are, and one of the reasons I love you."

Happiness exploded. "Yeah."

She smiled. "Yeah."

He stepped closer. "You know what that means, don't you?"

She shook her head.

"You're gonna have to marry me, woman."

For a few long seconds she studied him. Then, she grinned. "Name the time and place, SEAL."

He pulled her into his arms and kissed her. She opened her mouth willingly and pressed her body against his. For a moment, everything faded away and it was just the two of them.

They were interrupted by a cheer. When he pulled back, he noticed the crowd had watched the whole argument and his proposal. He glanced at Alana and found her blushing.

He leaned down, lifting her into his arms.

"Marco." She giggled and he realized that as long as he could make her laugh, everything was going to be okay.

He turned toward their audience and said, "Next show's in about five minutes, folks, but it's just for private viewing."

Then, he turned to walk back to her house.

"I love you, Marco," she said as she laid her head on his shoulder.

"I love you too, Alana."

And he planned on making sure she knew that every day of their lives.

EPILOGUE

Marco's phone rang in the middle of the night with his mother's ringtone. He shot up in bed and answered it immediately. If his mother was calling at this time during the night, there was trouble.

"Marco?" Alana asked.

He looked at her, shaking his head and turning on his phone.

"What's wrong?" he asked.

Only one of them was deployed and that was Gee.

"It's your brother. He's okay, so don't freak out."

His mother's voice was thin as if it had been a long night.

"It doesn't sound like it."

She sighed. "Gee is okay. They had to set down hard and so he has a concussion. Luckily, he only has two weeks left so they are sending him home. He's coming here."

Oh, that didn't sound good. Not that he doubted his mother's recitation of the facts. That he believed. For a PJ, there were a lot worse injuries he could have sustained. They dropped into war zones to save lives. Some of them ended up fighting for their own in the end.

The fact that Gee was now going to be subjected to his mother's care…that couldn't be good for Gee.

"What is it?' Alana asked.

"Gee, he got a concussion."

"Oh, no. Do we need to get back to the mainland?"

He smiled. "No."

"Is that Alana?" his mother asked. His mom knew she raised a bunch of healthy men, but she did not like to be confronted with the fact he and Alana were living together until the wedding.

"Yes."

"Let me talk to her."

"I don't think Alana—"

His fiancé grabbed the phone out of his hand. "Joey, is everything okay? Do you need us there for Gee?"

He watched her nod taking orders from her mother. It was amazing how both of the newest members of the family had aligned with his mother on every issue.

"Of course. But you will call if it is worse than what he says it is? You know these Santini men. None of them are hurt, ever."

She laughed.

"Yeah, Vince is the worse, but it's hard to say which one comes in second. Do you want to speak to Marco again?"

She waited, listening to his mother.

"Okay, well, goodbye."

She clicked off his phone and handed it to him.

"What the hell, Alana?"

"Everything is fine. When Gee makes it back, she'll have him call us. Vince and your father are there to help if she needs it. Also, there is a pressing reason for him to return to Georgia."

She settled back in bed and snuggled under the covers.

"What?"

"Your mom's not sure, but apparently, MJ thinks it's a woman."

There it was again. The women were ganging up and talking with his mom behind all their backs. They were doomed.

"Marco, is there something wrong?"

He looked down at her. There was nothing but moonlight filling the room but he could see her. How did a man get so lucky? A beautiful woman with such a kind heart and she was all his.

"No, love. But, since my mother decided to wake us up…"

One eyebrow rose. "Yes?"

He slipped over on top of her. "I thought maybe we could find something to fill our time."

"Really? And just what would that be, SEAL?"

They both slept in the nude, so he was pretty sure she knew exactly what he had in mind. He was already hard.

"Well, how about I just show you, Ko'u ipo," he said as he started to kiss his way down her body.

GIANNI

Melissa Schroeder

Dedication

To the other brats I have met along the way. Jan, Darla, Tamilya, Lara,
and Brandy. Only those who have lived it know
exactly what being a brat is all about.

A NOTE FROM MEL

We had good and bad in Georgia. It was where I made the final decision to definitely start writing seriously. We had a lot of fun with the squadron Les worked in, and well, I was really involved on base. It was also our first encounter with a rescue squadron. I admire their abilities and their dedication to the job.

I won't forget those Monday Margarita nights with my next-door neighbor Kathy, and all the crazy women I met at the OWC. And I will never forget the gay ducks that came to my door every day for bread. Gators, snakes, and stories of escapee pigs—it was definitely an experience.

Just a little note. Each chapter begins with a quote from either Kianna or Gee. They were taken from the emails the two shared while he was deployed. I hope you love their story as much as I loved writing it.

CHAPTER ONE

It wasn't expected that we would serve, but none of the Santini boys would have it any other way. -Gee

Gianni Santini stepped into his favorite sweet shop and was granted a view that every heterosexual man should dream of. A woman was bent at the waist picking up change off the floor. The fabric of her red skirt stretched across her full rounded ass.

He sighed and gave a grateful glance up to the heavens. When he returned to his gaze to the woman, he noticed she had stepped up to order. He sighed. There was a God.

In the eighteen months he had been stationed in Valdosta, Georgia, he hadn't seen her in Anna's shop. Of course, he rarely made it in on a Saturday morning.

He didn't realize he had been standing there staring at her until someone bumped into him from behind.

"Excuse me," a little voice said from behind him. He turned to find an old woman about five feet tall, giving him a suspicious look. Considering the way he had been ogling the woman in front of him, there was good reason for it.

"Sorry."

Then stepped out of the way and turned his attention back to the woman. She had straightened and was at the counter chatting with Anna, the owner.

He moved closer and tried to remember if he had seen her before. Okay, he knew for a fact he hadn't seen her before—but he still hadn't seen her face.

She wasn't tall, maybe about five-foot-five, and she had curly light brown hair. Her skin looked like the finest cocoa powder. When he inched closer, he could hear her voice. Deep Georgia threaded her tone telling him that she was from the area.

"I think I'll go for one of your malasadas today. I can't tell you how super happy I am you have friends in Hawaii who taught you how to make those. Although, I have to say, my hips aren't that happy."

Anna laughed. "Well, figuring my condition, I will refrain from feeling sorry for you."

Gianni smiled. Anna was about eight months pregnant and huge. For such a tiny woman, she carried a massive package in her stomach.

She gave the woman her total and Gianni said, "I'll pay for that."

The woman turned to look at him, a questioning smile on her mouth. Right there and then, his brain stopped functioning. She was amazing. A heart-shaped face surrounded by all those springy curls and the most amazing skin. Her eyes, lord, they were golden. It was the only way he could describe them. His gaze dipped down to her mouth. Holy mother of God, she had a mouth that would tempt a saint to sin—full with just the tiniest of overbites.

"Why would you do that?"

It took him a second to realize she was talking. To him.

"What?"

He heard the snickers behind him but ignored them.

"Sorry," he said, his face heating up. Good God, he was blushing. He just thanked God his brothers weren't there.

Her smile faded a bit. "I asked why would you do that."

"Watch yourself here with Santini. He buys all the pretty girls sweet treats," Anna said with a laugh.

He gave Anna a dirty look but then turned his attention back to the woman. "I would just like to buy you. A treat."

Jesus, he sounded like a fifteen-year-old trying to flirt.

She shrugged. "Oh, well, if you want to pay, soldier, you go right ahead."

"Airman."

She shook her head. "What?"

"Airman. We're called airmen. Or, PJs to be specific."

She sighed. He would swear he felt it shiver through his blood. "Oh. I have to admit that I know very little about the military. Well, other than what my students tell me."

"Students."

"Yes, I teach at the university."

"Here you go, Kianna," Anna said handing the woman a little paper sack.

"Thanks again," she said then turned to find a seat.

He watched her walk through the cafe, his brain fizzling at that moment. He couldn't help but appreciate they way her hips swung. There was something so sensual.

"Earth to Santini," Anna said breaking into his thoughts.

He turned and felt his face get hotter. The suspicious look she sent him was enough for that. In fact, it looked like his mother when she caught him doing that to the general's daughter when he was in high school.

"What are you doing in here on a weekend?" she asked.

"I'm shipping out tomorrow."

Something he couldn't discern moved over her face. "Are you pcsing?"

He shook his head. That was how much Anna knew about the military. She was in tune with what was going on over in Valdosta at Moody like someone with family in the military; although, he knew she was a local girl married to a local guy.

"Nope, just heading out to Afghanistan."

She frowned at him. It made him think of a grumpy little elf. A very pregnant grumpy elf.

"By yourself? Don't you usually go with a whole group?"

"Yeah, this is a special circumstance. I'll be home in two months."

She didn't say anything and he looked up to find tears in here eyes. Panic set in. Santini men were known for being cool under fire. Three generations had served in the military. But, show him a woman who was crying, he couldn't deal with it. He was saved by her husband.

Max clapped him on the shoulder. "Don't look so scared, son. Anna is a hot mess these days. The hormones."

She sniffed. "Be nice or I'll name our daughter Gertrude."

"So, do you have any of those malasadas left?"

She nodded. "Want the cinnamon one?"

He shook his head. "If I have to go two months without any sweets, I think I'll go for the one with cream in it."

She packaged it up and he waited for a total. "Anna?"

Her watery smile sent another fission of panic through him. "On the house today. Come back in one piece."

"Thank you."

At that, he turned in search of the woman. He saw her sitting by herself at a table for two. Her attention was on the tablet on the table so he felt safe studying her for a moment. He watched as she picked a piece off her malasada and slipped it between her lips.

He sighed. He just had to get the woman's number. With that thought in his head, he made his way over to her. He had less than twenty-four hours before he headed out and one thing Gee Santini understood was making sure you lived with no regrets.

* * * *

Kianna was trying to concentrate on the book she'd just downloaded, but it was hard. The encounter with the military guy had her brain frozen a bit.

"Excuse me."

She looked up and found him standing beside the table. Kianna knew she should be better prepared, but it was hard to think ahead. He was standing there holding a coffee cup and a little white bag. She smiled and tried to hide her nerves. The man was gorgeous and gorgeous men made her stutter.

"Yes?"

"I was wondering if you would share your table with me."

She glanced around the shop. There were plenty of open tables. "Why?"

He chuckled. "Well, you put me in my place."

She frowned. "What I meant was there are plenty of tables open."

Cocking his head to the side, he studied her for a moment. "You're not trying to play hard to get."

She shook her head trying to follow the conversation. "Hard to get? Why would I do that with you?"

"I am trying to sit with you because I'm interested in you," he said shaking his head.

"Oh." It took a few seconds for it to hit her. "You're interested in me?"

She said it so loud several people glanced over.

"I don't think this is going the way I thought it would. I must be losing my touch."

"Hmm."

He sighed. "So, can I sit with you?"

"Sure."

He took his seat and smiled at her. Damn he was fine. Blond hair and golden brown eyes. Where did they make men like him? He was so handsome he made her eyes hurt.

"I'm Gianni, but you can call me Gee."

"Why would I do that?"

He stared at her for a moment then laughed. "It's my nickname."

"I just wondered why you wouldn't want to be called such a fabulous name."

"Well, it's not half as pretty as Kianna."

She tried not to smile but she couldn't help it. "Thank you. I take it that your nickname came from family?"

"I'm the youngest in the family so they started calling me that when I was barely walking."

"Ah." Okay that showed all her intelligence. A borderline IQ and all she could say was a one-syllable acknowledgement. "Big family?"

He shrugged as he watched her. God, he was pretty. Not too pretty, but he had blond hair, milk chocolate eyes, and the cutest smirk. He was bigger than most men his age—which she pegged for mid-twenties. She inwardly sighed.

"There are four of us. All boys."

"Oh, wow, we had three girls. Not sure how I would handle that many men."

He stopped in mid sip. "Really?"

"Yes." Then she realized the double entendre. Her face heated. "I mean I was raised in a mainly female household, so boys are a foreign unknown."

He nodded.

"So, you buy lots of girls sweets?"

"Yeah. Well, not a lot, but every now and then."

She nodded and played with the paper beneath her half eaten malasada.

"Are you going to eat that?"

"Okay, I'll admit it. I am a bit of a freak and you're making me nervous so it's hard to eat."

He blinked at her, and his lips curved. "No reason to be nervous. Wanted to spend my last day in Georgia with a pretty Georgia woman."

"Oh? You're moving?"

Figures. Just her luck that an attractive man who would buy her food was leaving. Not that it was anything but him being nice, and apparently some kind of thing that he did all the time.

"No. Just heading out for a two-month deployment."

"I didn't know they had a squadron going out from the forty first."

"You didn't know that we are airmen but you know that?"

She could tell he was teasing by the tone in his voice. The man was so sweet she could get a toothache just from talking to him.

"Yes. Some of my students are connected to the military. I also have a few spouses and a few active duty in my night classes."

He nodded. "What do you teach?"

"English."

"Just English?" When she didn't answer right away, he said, "My mom teaches at the community college level in Virginia, so I know you all have your areas."

She smiled. It was nice to hear a man talk about his mother with such pride. "I teach beginning composition and reading comprehension."

He said nothing for a few long seconds. "You like you job."

"No. I love it. It was what I wanted to do from the time I started college."

He gave her a full smile. Every drop of moisture dried up in her mouth. *Damn.*

"That's all that is important."

She nodded but wanted to move on. "What is it like having three older brothers?"

"It was horrible. They hated me because they're all ugly and stupid."

She laughed enjoying him. "Yeah, so are my sisters. Are your brothers in the Air Force too?"

He shook his had. "We all went for different services. Leo is in the Army. Marco is Navy and old man Vince is in the Marines—which is what our father was."

"Ah. So you're all brats."

"And damned proud of it."

"And you jump. And you're leaving tomorrow?"

He nodded as he finished chewing a bite of his malasada. He rubbed his hands to get rid of the sugar from his sweet treat. She could just imagine sucking one of those sugar-covered fingers.

Dammit.

"What are you doing today, Kianna?"

It took her a second to dispel the fantasy she'd just conjured in her head. She shrugged. "I was going to grade some papers."

"How about spending the day with me?"

She didn't answer right away. "Why?"

"I told you. I wanted to spend my last day here with a pretty Georgia woman."

"This isn't some kind of incident that will have me ending up on a show on Discovery ID, is it?"

"What?"

"This isn't some kind of date from hell where you lock me in a basement and leave me for two months?"

He put his hand over his heart. "I promise."

His expression was solemn but his eyes were dancing with amusement.

"Just hang out?" she asked.

"Yeah."

Normally she would say no. Men like Gianni usually didn't flirt with her and generally didn't ask her out—not unless there was something they wanted from her. But he was leaving in the morning. And, he was sitting there giving her the most beautiful smile. She couldn't say no.

"Okay."

His smile widened and she felt her heart turn over. What the hell had she just gotten herself into?

* * * *

By the end of the night, Gianni was completely charmed. They'd spent the day all over Valdosta, including the Wild Adventures Theme Park. It had taken his mind completely off the worry of his deployment.

"I had a great time, Gianni." She barely flirted, but those cute little smiles of hers had his head spinning.

"Thank you for spending the day with me."

"It's the least I can do," she said.

"Well, there is one more thing you could do."

"Yes?"

"A kiss to remember you by."

She blinked. "Uh…"

"What?"

"Sorry, just…never mind."

She leaned forward and gave him a kiss on the cheek. When she pulled back he was amazed she didn't pat him on the head. That was just not going to do.

"That wasn't a kiss, Kianna."

God, he loved her name. It rolled off his tongue every time he said it. He could imagine what it sounded like when he groaned it.

Whoa, boy, slow down. He had an o dark thirty appointment with a plane. He just thanked his mother for her early training. He was packed and ready to go, so it made it easy for him to spend the entire day with Kianna.

"It wasn't?" She shook her head. "Then what was it?"

"A peck."

She frowned. "Funny, I thought it was a kiss."

He shook his head. "No. This is a kiss."

He slipped his hand to the small of her back and stepped closer. Leaning down, he slammed his mouth over hers. She tasted sweet as he thought she would. Tempting, sugary…a decadent treat he wanted to gorge himself on. By the time he pulled himself back, they were both breathing heavily and he was busy convincing his body that there would be no reward tonight.

"Thank you for the wonderful day, Kianna."

He gave her another brush of his mouth over hers. "I have your email. I hope you don't mind a few emails from me."

She smiled. "I wouldn't have given you my card if I did."

He opened her car door and waited for her to slide in before shutting it. "Drive safely."

She nodded. "Be safe, Gianni."

He watched her drive away, her taillights fading into the night before he walked to his truck. Just like every other military man, he was always looking forward to the homecoming even before he left..

He licked his lips and he could still taste her there. Now he had something more to look forward to when he returned.

CHAPTER TWO

I love my family, but there are times they can be overbearing. Being Joey Santini's baby is a blessing and a curse. —Gee

Gee folded his last shirt and placed it in the suitcase. Ten days in Virginia was enough for him.

"I made all your favorites," Joey Santini said studying him. He would sigh, but he knew it would hurt his mother's feelings. She'd apparently been a wreck since his parents had gotten the call two weeks earlier. Vince had said the once indestructible Joey Santini had come undone. Gee hadn't seen it, but just knowing made him feel guilty.

"Mom, you really don't have to do that. I know you and Dad are busy."

She crossed her arms and leaned against the doorjamb. "You're injured."

"No, I'm not. I had a concussion because of an accident so they sent me back. I'm right as rain. You heard the doctor."

That had been the worst of it. His mother had insisted on driving him to his appointment at Bethesda. It had been beyond embarrassing to have his mother questioning the doctor as if Gee was five. Of course, he didn't tell her that the accident came under heavy fire and they had to set the copter down hard. She probably would have been even worse.

"Vince did say I was overreacting."

"He's right, Mom." He gave her a kiss on the cheek as he slipped past her into the hallway.

She followed him to the kitchen. His father was reading the news on his tablet while he finished his morning coffee. With a sigh, she grabbed the coffee pot to top off his mug. "I wish you wouldn't leave so soon."

"I need to get back to Georgia."

And back to Kianna. They hadn't done more than email over the last two months, but it had kept him going while he was over there. He lived for each and every email. She had even sent him a box of brownies. He'd talked to her a few times since he'd returned. Okay, every day since he returned. Each time the connection he felt with her seemed to strengthen.

His mother wasn't done trying her best to keep him close. "I think you should stay here."

"You think all the boys should stay here, Joe. Quit fussing," his father said. He glanced at Gee. "Can you walk and talk?"

"Yes, sir."

Papa as he was called—because only soon-to-be-dead men called him by his given name of Stewart—peered at his mother over the top of his glasses. "Then, he's fine."

She shot his father a look that usually spelled trouble for any Santini man but Vince saved him. "I have to get Gee to Dulles if he's going to make that flight."

His mother frowned but she nodded. She gave him a hard hug. "You get hurt again, I will beat the hell out of you."

He laughed. His mother had a twisted sense of humor and he loved her more for it.

"I'll make sure to remember that."

It took him more than ten minutes to get out the door. By the time they were heading down I-66 to the airport, Gee was exhausted.

"You're lucky Mom doesn't have direct access to reports."

He glanced at his brother. "I take it you do."

Vince nodded. "How bad was it?"

"To tell you the truth, I'm not sure. I remember the distress call, then flashes after it." He shrugged as some of the memories washed over him. "I woke up in the hospital."

Vince whistled. "Damned glad Mom can't read those things. She would freak."

"Did you ever tell her you broke your leg in three places?"

Vince snorted. "What am I, crazy?"

He chuckled. "No more than any other Santini."

"That's true. Glad you made it back in time for the wedding. We have a month to plan a bachelor party."

He rolled his eyes. "You know Marco won't do anything like that. Hell, Leo's was sad and pathetic."

"That's true." He took the exit for Dulles but said nothing for a few minutes. Gee knew there was something coming up. You just never knew when it came to Vince.

"So, you gonna tell me who she is?"

He shouldn't be surprised his brother figured out his reasons for rushing back to Moody. Still, it didn't mean he had to give into the questioning. "She?"

"The woman you want to get to see back in Valdosta."

He sighed. Close to ten years separated them, but Vince was the same with all the brothers. Hell, Leo and Vince were less than two years apart and Vince did the same thing to him.

"Just a woman I met the last day before I left."

Vince's eyebrows rose. "Oh?"

"Not like that. I met her at that sweet shop I go to. We hit it off and we spent the day together. We've been emailing."

"Name."

Gee smiled amused at the command. "Is this an inquisition?"

"I just want to know what to call my future sister-in-law."

Gianni rolled his eyes. "We barely kissed."

"Gee Santini, who never lasts more than two months with a woman has been pining for one for almost three. And you haven't even slept with her. Damn, I am going to be the last Santini standing."

"Yeah, old man, why is that?" he asked with a chuckle.

"I'm smart."

Gee grunted but said nothing else.

"And, you're not talking about her. That tells me more." He shook his head as he took the final exit for Dulles. "Last Santini standing."

Gee smiled but said nothing else. All he cared about was getting back home. Once he saw Kianna, everything would be right in his world.

Kianna was nervous. She always was before a date, but this was worse. It was like they had dated for months on end, over the Internet. Still, it was different that she was going to see him face to face. He knew things about her that she hadn't shared with other people.

At first, it had been just a few little funny emails, then...they had changed. It had progressed to something she looked forward to every day. Until she didn't hear from him for two days. She closed her eyes trying to ignore the panic when she got the email from him saying he had been injured. They had sent him home, well to Virginia. But he had only five days before he left and his replacement was already there, so he assured her it wasn't anything big.

Her doorbell rang and her body lit with fear and excitement. It made her slightly sick to her stomach.

She walked to the door, trying to calm her nerves and dragged in a deep breath and opened the door. Suddenly, she felt lightheaded. Damn, he hadn't changed a bit other than the small bandage on his forehead.

"Hey," she said. She couldn't come up with another greeting. Her brain had shut down. Majorly shut down. Like not allowing her basic things like communication to work.

"Yeah, hey."

Stepping through the door he pulled her into his arms and kissed her. It was like the one they had the night before he left. Hot and wet. He traced the seam of her lips with his tongue and she willingly opened her mouth.

His mouth slanted over hers again and again. He pulled her against his body. His fingers danced down her spine, then cupped her ass. There was no ignoring the erection she felt, or the way he moaned when she slipped her tongue into his mouth to tangle with his.

He pulled back, then hesitantly let her go. "We have to go or I'm going to tear your clothes off."

She shivered.

"Oh, good God, don't do that."

She smiled. "Sorry."

"No problem. Well, there is a problem, but I can deal with that. Are you ready to go out?"

"I made you dinner."

He blinked. "What?"

"I made dinner. I thought you would appreciate some home cooked food."

"Uh, not to be rude, but it would be bad to stay here."

"Naw, come on," she said delighted with him. She had never made a man that crazy in her life and she was thankful for it. It made her feel much younger than her thirty-three years.

"Now, you have a seat. You want a beer?"

He nodded.

"I've got to check on the lasagna, then I'll be back."

He smiled. "I'll be here waiting."

She hurried off to the kitchen, grabbing a beer before checking on the meal. She took it out of the oven and set it on the counter to cool for a few minutes. The need to see him, to keep her eyes on him battled with her embarrassment. She hadn't been this hung up on a man since her husband... and that was saying a lot.

Charley had been the sweetest man on the face of the earth. He'd teased her, charmed her, and she'd fallen hard. A three-month courtship and a wedding at the courthouse had been crazy and romantic. Being left a police-man's widow less than two years later hadn't been—or the last few weeks as his wife. His job had started wearing on their relationship. It was one reason she rarely dated men in uniform...any kind of uniform. But, here she was doing it again.

She shook away those thoughts. Brooding over her past life wasn't going to give Gianni a good welcome home.

* * * *

Gianni tried his best to control his need as he waited for his beer. He had meant to take things slowly, but the moment she'd opened the door, he had lost it. The need had been basic and primal and it had taken over him. He had to keep it under control. They hadn't been dating for two months. They had been exchanging emails and that was completely different.

"I hope it compares to your mother's," she said as she brought the pan out from the kitchen. His mouth watered for the woman and the food. She grabbed a beer off the counter then brought her own glass of water.

"No drinking for you, professor?"

She smiled as she sat, then he followed suit. "No. I don't drink much."

"But you had beer in your fridge."

"Well you were coming over, so I figured you might like it. If you didn't, I would give it to my sister Zoe. It's the brand she likes."

"Your sister has great taste."

She snorted as she cut the lasagna, serving him and then herself. "Well, maybe in beer. Not in men."

"Oh, so the older sister judges."

She blushed prettily. Damn, she was a delight. He knew her, knew about her family and she knew about his. It was as if they had been dating months.

When he realized he was making justifications to push things along, he decided to step back from those ideas. Vince had been right on one thing. This wasn't one of his normal quick and crazy romances.

"No. It's just she always dates losers."

"Meaning?"

"Guys who don't feel the need to work, or dress for the day. Or bathe. She had one guy she dated who apparently was on some kind of water strike. My father would have shot him where he stood if he had ever met him."

"So, he wasn't a high earner."

She blinked. "Money isn't important, but respect is. She doesn't seem to find men who respect her much. I want her to be happy and none of them seem to even try to accomplish that."

He couldn't help the way his heart jerked at that. She was sweet as peach nectar. "And Etta?"

Kianna rolled her eyes. "She dates men who are more interested in what she can do for their careers than anything else. No respect."

"And that is important to you?"

She nodded. "My parents didn't raise us to be mistreated. I can't say I've always chosen wisely...but maybe it's because I'm in my thirties. Zoe is only twenty three."

"And Etta?"

"She's more focused on her career so she pretends it doesn't hurt." Then she took a bite of food. "Oh, that was kind of personal. All that was."

"I don't mind."

"It's weird, but it's like I've known you longer and this is only our second date."

He smiled. "Yeah, I was just thinking the same thing."

"Are you going to taste my lasagna?"

He looked down at his plate then back up at her worried expression. Apparently, she was worried he wouldn't like it.

"Of course."

He took a bite and hummed. Tomato, basil, melted fresh mozzarella, and the hint of hot Italian sausage danced over his taste buds.

"So you like?" she asked, a shy smile curving her lips. Damn, he wanted to say forget dinner and move straight to dessert.

"No, I love. Thank you."

She grinned and returned to her own plate. Right then, he felt like he owned the entire world. Just because she grinned at him.

At the end of the night, Kianna was ready to scream. Her hormones were screeching for relief. She had told herself that Gianni had kept up with her because he needed it while he had been gone. It was hard not to get excited that she was the first person he had called when he got back to Valdosta.

Still, she shouldn't expect much. He was military and goodness, six years younger than she was.

He stopped at the opened door and asked, "So, what are you doing tomorrow?"

"I'm not sure. I have some papers to grade."

"How about we go to breakfast at Anna's?"

"That sounds good. She might even bring the baby in tomorrow."

She was holding the door open and he leaned in for a kiss. She felt everything in her flutter then explode. Her nipples tightened and heat danced over her nerve endings.

He pulled back then rested his forehead against hers. "I really should go."

She sighed, regret heavy in her chest. "Yeah."

Another kiss, this one quick but just as tempting. "I don't want to."

Her heart jumped. "Really?"

He gave her another heated kiss. "I really want to take you back to your bedroom and touch every inch of your flesh."

She really should say no. It was too fast, too much. But, instead, she threw caution to the wind and slammed the door shut.

"Sounds good to me."

CHAPTER THREE

Sometimes I think I think too much for my own good. —Kianna

Relief coursed through Gianni as he pulled her against his body. He cupped her face and leaned in slowly to kiss her. Part of him wanted to rush…gorge himself on her. He fought those urges. He wanted this to last, to be the one thing that they both remembered for decades to come. He swept inside, taking in the taste of the tiramisu she had made. Was there anything as delicious as that? He needed to see her skin, touch her flesh. He walked her back as he tried pulling up her shirt. It took a few tries to get the shirt up and over her head. He threw it somewhere on the floor behind him as they kissed their way into her bedroom. It was dark but he did his best to get her to the bed. They fell onto the bed and bounced up together. She was still laughing when he kissed her. He swallowed her joy, lapped it up. He had never met a person with so much love for life.

He kissed his way down her body, pausing long enough to undo her bra then continuing on. By the time he had her naked, he was barely able to think of anything but her. He pulled himself up to his knees and looked down at her.

Thank the good lord for curvy women.

"Gianni?"

"Sorry," he said trying to shake his head to get his brain to work.

He didn't want to wait. He wanted to dive into her, feel those muscles wrap around him and lose himself in the wonder of being inside of her. But, he knew better than to rush it. It had been a while for him—because of the deployment and before it. He'd been preoccupied with things…and hadn't met anyone worth the effort.

Until Kianna.

He leaned down and kissed her belly, then slipped down between her legs. He kissed each one of her thighs. With each lick, he inched closer to his goal. When he finally settled himself between her legs, he drew in a deep breath. Her arousal mixed with her unique scent drifting over him…teasing him…tempting him.

Gianni didn't hesitate. He placed his mouth on her sex. The first taste of her danced over his tongue. Decadently delicious. Her fingers slipped through his hair as he teased her clit, tugging on it with his teeth. She shivered, telling Gianni that she was close.…very close.

He pulled back and she moaned. When he rose to his knees again, she was frowning at him. He wanted to laugh, but he figured Kianna wouldn't be any happier with him.

"What's the matter?" he asked, teasing her.

"I'm naked and you're not."

He looked up at her. She was leaning back on her elbows as she looked at him. Just like that first day, she stole his breath away.

"That is something I can definitely rectify."

He pulled his shirt over his head, but when he tried to undo his buckle, he was embarrassed to find his hands shaking.

He slipped out of bed and tried again, but she was already there to help. She slid to the edge of the bed, grabbed hold of the waistband of his jeans and tugged him closer.

"I can help you with that," she said, her voice husky with her own need. She undid the buckle then unbuttoned and unzipped his jeans. Within moments, he was naked and she had her clever hands running over him. She teased his cock, sliding the tip of her finger from the base to the tip, then, she followed it with her tongue. Damn.

He usually had better control, but the action had his body raring to go. He thought she would stop but instead, she took him into her mouth.

He leaned his head back and groaned. She tormented him for only a few moments before he called a stop to it.

"That's not very fair," she said pouting.

He smiled. "I'll let you be as bad as you want to later. Right now, I just want you."

Then, he realized he hadn't come prepared. The man who prided himself on always being ready, came without his safety equipment.

"Gianni? What's the matter?"

"I forgot to bring a condom."

She laughed. "Is that it?" Slipping out of bed to open her nightstand, she grabbed a condom.

"I wanted to make sure if there was a chance, that I was prepared."

He laughed and took the condom. He cupped her face and kissed her. He expected it to be quick, but it turned into something else. Keeping his eyes open, he deepened the kiss, stealing inside, letting her taste herself on his tongue. She closed her eyes and hummed. He felt it all the way to the soles of his feet.

They fell on the bed again. He didn't waste any time. Ripping open the package, he got the condom out and rolled it on. He slipped his hands beneath her ass and pulled her up, entering her in one hard thrust.

Damn.

She had been prepared, and oh, damned, so fucking wet, but she still gasped at the intrusion. He knew he should apologize, but he couldn't seem to bring himself to do it. It felt so fucking good to be inside her.

He pulled himself up to his hands and started to move. Immediately, she picked up his rhythm. Soon, she was coming undone as she screamed his name. Her muscles pulled him deeper into her causing him to almost come. But he didn't want to. He wanted to see her lose herself in pleasure and be there right with her when it happened. He rose to his knees, and tugged her up so that they were face to face.

"Gianni," she said, her voice deepened with her release. It sent a spike of heat coursing through his veins.

He kissed her, open mouth, hot, wet…then said, "Come again for me, Kianna."

He felt it slam into her, saw her eyes go blurry with her pleasure as they shut and she leaned her head back with a moan. He was helpless then, watching her release, feeling all those little muscles clamp down on his cock. He followed her, shouting her name.

* * * *

"Okay, I might be dead," Gianni said.

Kianna laughed. "Yeah?"

"Tell my mother I loved her and it was worth it."

Her body was still warm and she hadn't gotten her breath back and he was teasing her. She loved a man with a good sense of humor.

"I will, although she will wonder who I am."

"Vince will know who you are."

That was interesting. "Yeah? So can I have his number?"

He rose up to look at her. He was frowning at her but his eyes danced with amusement. Not for the first time, Kianna thought she might be able to eat him up with a spoon.

"No. I am not giving Vince a chance to even get close to you."

She let one eyebrow rise. "And why is that?"

"He'd make a play for you."

She shrugged, enjoying him, enjoying the moment. "But you're dead, so it wouldn't matter.

"I would come back from the dead to haunt both of you."

She smiled at him. "Then you might get an eye full."

He rolled over on top of her. "Reports of my death might have been exaggerated."

He pressed himself inside her. He was already hardening again and she shivered.

Then he cursed. "I need a condom."

He pulled out of her, grabbed a fresh condom and had it on pretty fast. She expected him to cover her again but instead, he reversed their positions and she found herself on top of him.

"Take me in, Kianna."

She trembled just from the sound of her name on his lips. It spoke to something in her soul, something she was afraid to even think about. Brushing those thoughts aside, she wrapped her fingers around him and slowly slid down his length.

His fingers dug into her hips as she started to move, gyrating her hips every few times. Each time she did, she pulled a groan from his lips. She was still wet from their last time but she felt herself grow wetter by the minute. Seeing the power she had over him, just this little bit, sent a surge of arousal through her. It jolted her to her core but it also made her so damn hot. He leaned up and she thought he would take back control. Instead, he wrapped his arms around her and took her nipple into his mouth. She had never been someone with very sensitive breasts, but each time his teeth scrapped across the tip of it, heat danced over every nerve ending in her body.

Soon, though, his teasing, the feel of his breath on her flesh, and the sensation of being filled with him got to be too much. She bent her head down to kiss him as her orgasm rushed through her. Kianna was barely through with her last orgasm when a second slammed into her. This time, Gianni leaned his head back, and groaned her name as he came.

It was possibly one of the most beautiful sights she'd ever witnessed.

Moments later, they collapsed. Kianna was sticky with perspiration and she was going to be sore in so many places.

And it felt so good.

"Okay, I might be dead too this time. We better leave a note," she said.

He laughed, wrapping his arms around her, kissing the side of her neck. "Thank you for the best homecoming ever."

Kianna snuggled closer, enjoying the feel of him beneath her. Within moments she was drifting off to sleep to the beat of his heart.

CHAPTER FOUR

One of the things I miss the most while I'm deployed is lazy Sunday mornings. —Gee

Kianna woke to the smell of something sweet and savory cooking. Keeping her eyes closed, she drew in a deep breath. If her dream smelled that good, she didn't want to wake up. She wanted to sleep in, then mosey her way down to Anna's for something decadent for breakfast. Something with cream and sugar she could lick off her fingers.

She frowned realizing that she hadn't been dreaming it. She was awake. Opening her eyes slowly. The memory of the night before washed over her, through her. She smiled and reached for Gianni only to find his side of the bed empty.

She sat up, the sheet falling to her waist. She gasped when she realized she was still naked. Pulling the sheet up to cover her breasts, she sighed. It had been a really long time since she'd slept naked. It had been since she and Charley had first married. She was a lot younger and definitely not as curvy at that point of her life. She vaguely remembered getting up to throw on a nightshirt at some point, but Gianni had told her it was a waste of time to get dressed.

She pulled her legs up and rested her head on her knees. Damn the man had her head spinning. She couldn't get all tangled up in the idea that they were going to be involved for a long time. He was Air Force and would be moving on soon. Plus, he was younger. He wasn't interested in settling down. But, she couldn't resist the fantasy of having the man in her bed every night.

"Daydreaming, professor?" he said breaking into her thoughts.

She lifted her head and found him leaning against the doorjamb. Was there ever a more beautiful man who'd been in her bed? She didn't think so. Luck was rarely on her side, but it seemed for right now, she had her share and she wasn't going to waste it. "No, not really. Just thinking how much fun last night was."

It wasn't a big lie. It was part of what she had been thinking about.

"Fun?"

She nodded.

He gave her a brilliant smile and she felt her heart lodge in her throat. No one, man or woman, should be that pretty in the morning.

"I would call it one of the best nights of my life," he said.

Then he walked into the room and leaned over her. He brushed his lips over hers. "Good morning, Kianna."

"Good morning, Gianni."

He shuddered. "Damn, I love the way you say my name. That southern accent of yours makes me so fucking hot."

She slipped her arms around his neck to pull him into bed. "Then come back to bed."

He shook his head and untangled himself. "No, I will resist you because I have made you breakfast. Get dressed and I'll set the table."

She frowned.

"Oh, don't look that way. I promise you will be rewarded."

He gave her another intense kiss then left her alone. She sighed. It wasn't as if they hadn't had enough time together in bed. She lost count the number of times they made love. She grabbed her kimono and slipped it on as she stood and made her way to the bathroom. It had been a long time since a man slept over. She hadn't had many lovers. Timing and well…she was selective. Respect was as important to her as passion. Gianni had that in spades.

She rinsed off her face realizing she knew more about him than she did men she dated for months. Their emails had started out as simple back and forth's.

But in those few weeks he was gone, they had grown closer and she had learned so much about the man.

As she brushed her teeth, she thought about why she was so attracted. Well, except for zero percent body fat and that gorgeous face. He was so pretty—but it was more than that. She could tell he was kind, he loved his mama and the rest of his family, and he liked curvy woman.

There definitely was a God she thought with a chuckle.

"You better hurry up in there, Kianna or I'm going to eat this all myself."

Happy with him, with spending the day with him, she decided to heed his warning. She definitely would need some food to keep up with him.

* * * *

Gianni was setting the plates on the table when his phone rang with Leo's ring tone. "Shouldn't you be busy with that cute wife of yours?"

Leo chuckled. "Right now, Maryanne isn't in the mood for anything in the mornings."

"Ah," he said immediately understanding the situation. Maryanne was in her second trimester and the morning sickness had been pretty bad.

"So, what are you calling me for?" he asked.

"Just checking on you. No vision problems?"

He rolled his eyes at the question. "Leo, I'm a PJ and I have medic training just like you do."

"I know you have the training." Gianni heard Maryanne's voice in the background. "My wife just pointed out that Santini men are notorious for ignoring an illness."

"Yeah, well, I'm fine. Better than fine." It was then he realized he was smiling. He had the same goofy smile on his face all morning.

There was a beat of silence. "Damn. I owe Vince money."

"What do you mean you owe Vince money?"

"He said you wouldn't last twenty four hours. You're not even in your apartment are you?"

If there was a way to lie and make both his brothers lose money on the bet, it would be worth it, but Gianni didn't see a way. "No, I'm not."

Something caught the corner of his eye and he turned to look at Kianna. Right then, the air backed up in his lungs as every thought seemed to dissolve. She was fresh faced but her eyes were still sleepy. Her hair was still a springy mess, as usual. The emerald green kimono made her skin glow.

How did he get so fucking lucky?

"I hate that he's going to win," Leo said, breaking into Gianni's thoughts.

There was more from Maryanne. "I know you told me not to take the bet, but I thought Gianni had more resistance."

Without thinking, speaking from his heart, Gianni asked, "How long would it have taken if it had been you and Maryanne?"

"Ah, so that's the way of it."

"I think. But, see, I made a wonderful breakfast for my lovely lady, so I am going to go eat and enjoy the morning with her."

"Damn, you made that custard French toast didn't you? Oh, shit. Gotta go," he said not waiting for Gianni to sign off.

"That was one of your brothers?"

"Yeah, Leo. Maryanne still has morning sickness."

He was staring at her again but he couldn't seem to help it. She mesmerized him. It had taken all of his control not to wake her up earlier. They had been up most of the night making love, so he felt a little guilty. Okay, not a whole lot—but he wasn't an animal. Maybe.

"What?" she asked.

"Nothing."

She shifted her weight from one foot to the other. "You keep staring at me."

"I like you."

"Really? I could never tell."

He chuckled and walked to her. He had to kiss her again, had to reassure himself it wasn't all a dream. He cupped her face and did just that.

He pulled back before he lost control. "So, I hope you like custard French toast."

"I don't know if I've ever had it."

"Well, you are in for a treat."

He led her to a dining chair and waited for her to sit.

"Coffee?" he asked.

"I can get that."

He waved her back in her seat. "No, you sit, relax. You cooked last night."

He grabbed a mug, filled it then grabbed the cream and sugar. It was odd that he knew more about her than he'd known about most of his girlfriends in the past. When someone is your lifeline, the one person you can be honest with during a deployment, you get to know that person really well.

He shook away any deep thoughts today. It had been a long two months and he planned on making up time. He grabbed the plate of French toast and brought it to the table.

"Prepare to be wowed."

She laughed. "You would have to do a lot to top last night."

He smiled. Sunday morning, French toast and a sexy woman to share both with. Life just couldn't get much better.

CHAPTER FIVE

I have three downfalls: Sugar mixed with cinnamon, antique jewelry and books. Actually, I could probably do without the first two if I had an unlimited supply of books. –Kianna

Kianna sighed as she slipped another bite into her mouth. Cinnamon, sugar, hazelnuts and maple syrup danced over her taste buds. She moaned on the second bite.

"Oh, Lord, and I was ready to be nice about it. I mean, men always think they can cook, and it turns out that they can't. But, there is no reason for lies on this one. That was magnificent."

Gianni glanced down at her plate. "You didn't finish it."

"You gave me enough for five people."

"I gave you about half of what I ate."

She frowned. "You're younger and you're a man. What do you have, zero percent body fat?"

He shook his head smiling. "Of course, I did work up an appetite last night."

She wanted to tease, but she wasn't ever really good at it. Besides, he was making her uncomfortable the way he was watching her. He had been doing that since she'd joined him in the kitchen. He looked like he wanted to just eat her up.

"I don't think I can eat anymore."

"But you liked it?"

"No, it was horrible. I gagged on each piece."

He laughed. Every time he did, it tripped her heart up just a little.

"So, did your mother teach you how to cook breakfast like that?"

"First, my mother would point out that is sexist, but since Dad is useless with anything but a grill and chili, she would give you a pass. We all know how to cook. Mom thought it was important that we know how to fend for ourselves. She jokes around that my father was living off junk food and canned meats when she met him."

"I bet you're the best. I don't know if any of them could make something that good."

"I would like to say I am but Vince is the best cook. He really loves to spend time in the kitchen."

"The Marine?"

He nodded.

"Hard to think of a Marine in the kitchen cooking. But I guess that would be a case of me stereotyping."

"I have to say even after meeting him you would think the same thing. We are more than the rank and the uniform."

"I think you proved that last night, PJ." Then she felt her face heat.

He threw his head back and laughed. The happy sound bounced off the walls of the kitchen. God, he was so damned pretty, so wonderful.

Stop it, girl. He's not going to stay around. He's younger and military. She needed to remember she had rules about men in uniform. Especially this. For the first time in her life, she was going to have an affair with a man just to have the affair. Don't worry about what happens next, just live in the now.

She sighed and looked over the table. "I guess it's my job to clean up."

He shook his head and took her hand. Without a word, she knew what he had in mind.

"Gianni, I need to clean up the kitchen."

"I need to taste you. I think my needs come first…at least in this case."

He pulled her up out of the chair and lifted her into his arms.

"Gianni," she said with a squeal.

"What?"

She rolled her eyes. "I know I'm not an easy load to carry."

He stopped at the doorway of her bedroom. "Now that's just silly. Of course, you are a handful, but that's what I like in a woman. And seeing that I'm trained to carry men who weight a lot more than you do, you're nothing for me to pick up."

He walked into the room, and set her on her feet.

"I've always been kind of big for my age."

She snorted. "Definitely."

He laughed again, that wonderful sound that filled her bedroom. She would never be in her bedroom without being able to think of that.

"I was just always tall, more muscled, comes with trying to keep up with all my brothers. Little women make me nervous. I don't trust a woman who deprives herself of food because other people tell her she should."

"Oh...wow."

"I know, I sound like a freaking commercial, but I like you the way you are. Here," he said walking her to the full-length mirror. He slipped behind her.

"Do you see what I see?" he asked, his breath feathering against her flesh.

She barely noticed that he'd slipped his hands to the sash of her robe. It parted revealing some of her skin. She had been a little lazy and only pulled on a pair of panties. Kianna thought he would pull it all off. Men usually went for all or nothing. Instead, he let it hang showing a hint of her breasts and belly.

"Do you?" he whispered. "Do you see what I see when I look at you? Women rarely do."

She shook her head, her gaze still on his hands. His fingers were long and tanned, skimming over her flesh.

"I see a beautiful woman, in spirit and in deed. That makes the beauty on the outside more stunning."

He trailed one finger down her stomach all the way to her sex.

"I couldn't think of anything but getting back here to touch you."

He nibbled on her earlobe, his tongue darting out over it before he bit down. "Taste you."

She closed her eyes and leaned her head back.

"No, keep your eyes open. Watch." He said. His voice had grown rougher each time he spoke.

She complied and watched as he slipped his hand beneath the waistband of her panties.

"And here…so sexy. So beautiful."

He slid one finger inside of her and her knees almost buckled. Just that small touch had her ready to come.

He kissed her neck, grazing his teeth over her pulse—which scrambled. "So wet."

Before she was ready, he was removing his hand. He spun her around and cupped her face with both hands before taking her mouth in a hard, wet, wonderful kiss. She knew he had meant to tease her, but in the end, he had been overwhelmed.

Wrapping her arms around him, she returned the kiss with everything she had. Her body was hot, her mind spinning and her heart melting.

"Take your robe off, babe," he said, as he kneeled in front of her. Kianna did as ordered even as he started to pull her panties down. He helped her out of them.

Gianni didn't hesitate, but he also didn't hurry. He kissed first one knee, then the other.

"I feel like I could feast on all this flesh." He smiled up at her. "That's a bit literary, isn't it?"

She chuckled then moaned when he kissed her mons.

"I have a feeling that it's the last time I'm going to be able to make sense for awhile."

"Oh, I don't know about that," she said pulling in a quick deep breath as he slipped his tongue inside of her. "God."

Every thought in her mind dissolved as he thrust into her over and over. She was shaking by the time he moved up to kiss her belly. He teased her, kissing and licking his way up her body. When he finally stood, she couldn't even remember her first name, let alone her last.

He cupped her face with one massive hand then slid his free hand down her back. He kissed her, teasingly, nipping at her bottom lip, then diving in. She could taste her arousal.

When he pulled back, he said, "See what I mean? How wonderful you taste?"

She opened her eyes and found him watching her, his eyelids half closed, but the intensity of his gaze no less powerful.

"You don't see just how tempting are, do you? God."

He kissed her again, this one not so gentle. When he pressed against her, she felt his erection. A shudder slid through his body.

She thought he would take her to bed; instead, he lifted her then turned to settle her on top of her dresser. He apparently had no time to wait and pulled down his jeans. She sighed in appreciation. It seemed Gee Santini went commando on Sundays. He grabbed a condom from her bedside table and returned. He pulled it out and she took it from him.

Kianna settled it on the tip of his penis and unrolled it slowly, keeping her gaze on his face. He leaned his head back and moaned. It was probably one of the sexiest things she'd seen. Well, since the night before. The man knew how to take control, but he also knew when to let her take the lead.

How could she not want him?

When she finally had the condom on, Gianni opened his eyes. "That was close, Ki. You almost pushed me over the edge."

He tangled his fingers through her hair and drew her closer to kiss her. He slanted his mouth over hers again and again as he urged her to scoot to the edge of the dresser. Then, he pulled back from the kiss. She was so into him, so lost, she didn't think she would ever get enough.

He eased himself inside. She was sore from the night before, but she didn't care. It was worth a little to feel this connection, to escape into the erotic web he created.

He thrust into her again and again as he leaned her back so he could tease her with that dangerous mouth. Kianna rushed to the pinnacle, her orgasm jolting through her. Gianni didn't give her time to recover. He took her there again, and again, and again. She lost count how many times she orgasmed. The last time, Gianni pulled her back up and thrust into her hard and kissed her as her release swept over her. He shuddered, groaning her name against her mouth as he followed her into bliss.

CHAPTER SIX

Mom always said to make sure you enjoy where you live. No place is as great as your last assignment or as exciting as your next, but she said you should make sure you make memories of the present. —Gee

Gianni didn't really want to spend Friday night with his buddies. Well, his buddies and Kianna. He'd been back a month and he had yet to introduce any of them to her. There was a reason. He wanted to keep her all to himself.

"I don't think I've been here in two years," Kianna said as she walked with him to front door of Lucky's.

"Is that a good thing or a bad thing?" he asked.

She shrugged. "Neither, really. It's a big college hang out, though. Didn't know that many guys from the base hung out here."

"There aren't that many places around and this is where the coeds hang out."

She nodded as they stepped into the noise. It was crazy, even for five on a Friday. He had insisted on meeting early before the massive Friday crowd. He wanted to be out of there before the band started up.

Part of the problem was the way she was dressed. She'd worn a knee length dress that normally he probably would call demure. But, the fabric clung to her curves, highlighting every single one of them. She had opted for heels tonight, not normal for her, so she was just an inch or so shorter than he was. And, lord have mercy, she smelled divine.

His fingers were already itching to peel her dress off her and lose himself.

A shout from the bar pulled him out of his fantasy. "Dr. Jones."

She turned, smiled and waved at a group of students then continued on to the patio. Gianni just thanked God it was warm enough to sit outside. He couldn't handle all that noise. When they stepped out, he saw his friends immediately. They had grabbed a table and made sure there were two extra chairs.

Sam Andrews waved them over. When they got there, all three men stood. Dammit, they were attempting to impress her.

"Kianna, this is Sam Andrews, Mike Henry and Colbie Jackson. Guys, this is Dr. Kianna Jones."

They exchanged pleasantries and took their seats. The waitress bounced up. After taking their orders, she flounced away and Kianna chuckled.

"So, do y'all always get that kind of attention?"

Andrews smiled. "Most of the time. I figure they are drawn to my animal magnetism."

Without missing a beat, Kianna said, "I'm sure."

It was said with just enough humor the guys laughed.

"She's got your number, Andrews," Jackson said.

Gianni didn't realize how nervous he'd been about her meeting his friends until he started to relax as she got to know the guys. If she could fit in with them, she wouldn't have a problem with his family.

* * * *

Kianna smiled at Mike as he was relating some story about their last training mission. It was nice to see Gianni with his friends. It was a different side of him she assumed his family saw, but not everyone. She understood the camaraderie in the military, especially with a group like these men.

"So, Kianna, what do you teach?" Mike asked. He was a nice man, tall and thin, a year or two older than Gianni. The freckles on his face along with the red hair and guileless blue eyes made him look younger, though.

"I mainly teach freshmen entry classes. I do a few literature classes but I tend to like the grammar classes."

"Ugh," Sam said. "That is one class I always had a problem with."

"Of course you do, Andrews. It's your mother tongue," Mike joked.

Sam opened his mouth to say something then slanted her a look. She laughed. "You don't have to behave around me."

"Be right back," Gianni said as he kissed her cheek then gave the rest of the group a nasty look.

When he stepped into the bar, his friends started laughing. "Oh, man, that was the Santini Death Stare," Colbie said. A Texan by birth, it was easy to hear in his voice. He was the oldest of the group, and it showed on his face. He had seen the most action. He was dark, some kind of Mediterranean in his blood, she guessed. He had the most amazing green eyes, which were framed by long lashes. From the predatory looks he got from a lot of the women, she assumed he never lacked for companionship. Heck most of them probably didn't. They all were built like Gianni—she knew it was required for the job—and they exuded a level of confidence that drew women in.

"Death stare?" she asked.

"Well, yeah, we've met a few of the brothers and they are all the same. Very territorial," Sam said. The youngest of the bunch, he was the fair one. With his blond hair and blue eyes, he resembled a Viking.

"Are you telling me I'm territory?" she asked, pretending to be irritated.

His smile faded and he swallowed. "Uh…"

"Oh, shit, she's screwing with you, Andrews. Don't mess with him, Kianna. A pretty woman like you messes up his head," Colbie said with a smile.

She leaned forward. "Want to know a secret?" she asked.

Colbie nodded.

"I knew that and you spoiled my fun."

He looked nonplused for a second then threw back his head and laughed.

"So, tell us, Kianna, will you give us any dirt on Santini?" Mike asked.

She smiled and realized that she really liked Gianni's friends. They had accepted her as if they had known her for years. She had heard military folk were like that, but she hadn't experienced it.

"Sure what do you want to know?"

* * * *

Gianni was on his way back from the bathroom when he ran into Jackson. "You better make sure you keep that lady happy."

He frowned. "What do you mean by that?"

The older man shrugged. "She's a charmer and if something happens, she will probably have at least three PJs knocking on her door."

"Ah, I would hate to have to kill you, Jackson."

He said it with a little humor but Jackson apparently picked up on the under-lying threat. "Just saying you better keep her happy. Not all women are so easy with a horde of military guys, especially when she didn't grow up in the military. She's a keeper."

After giving Gianni a clap on the shoulder he walked off in the direction of the head. The band started up again and Gianni winced. Damn, time to head back home…Kianna's. It hadn't been that long but he spent more time over at her place than he did at his own.

He stepped out on the patio. She was laughing with his friends, her head thrown back as her laughter drifted toward him. Even over the sound of the band and the people around him, he could hear it. There was something so damn alluring about Kianna all the time, but she was irresistible when she was happy.

Andrews leaned forward and said something to her and she turned and waved at him. His friends started laughing. Okay, that was enough of that.

When he reached them, Kianna was already standing up.

"Do you have to leave just yet?" Henry asked. "I don't mind if Santini leaves, but we'd love to have you stick around."

"I don't think y'all need me around cramping your style. The coeds will be here soon, so you might want to clear the table, so to speak."

"It was nice meeting you," Henry said as he rose and gave her a peck on the cheek. Andrews followed suit. She was blushing by the time Jackson made it back to the table.

"Already leaving," he said with a frown.

"We tried to get Santini to leave but he wouldn't leave her with us," Andrews said.

"Of course not. He's afraid one of us might steal her," Jackson said with a slanted look in Gianni's direction.

Then, testing Gianni's temper, Jackson gave Kianna a kiss on the cheek, but he took a fraction or two longer than the others had. He figured Jackson and he would be having a long talk about Kianna and how he would get a punch to the throat if he tried that shit again.

By the time they were in his truck on the way to her house, Kianna relaxed. "I like your friends. They're nice."

"Yeah, and I almost had a fight with Jackson."

"Whatever for?"

"He told me he would make a play for you."

She patted his leg. "He's just messing with you. And like he would have a chance."

He laughed and leaned over and kissed her on the neck.

"You do know how to make a man feel good."

She leaned up against him. "Just wait until we get home."

* * * *

A week later, Kianna was finishing up her lecture when she saw Gianni in the doorway. She faltered for a second, heat instantly zinging through her blood. He gave her an apologetic look, then stepped out of view. It took her a second or two to get back to the discussion.

"Dr. Jones?"

She shook her head to clear it, and smiled. "Make sure to bring your advertising examples for the next class." She glanced at the clock. "That's it for tonight. Have a good weekend."

As soon as she dismissed them, Gianni slipped into the room. Several of her female students threw him interested glances, but he ignored them.

"Sorry for interrupting."

She shook her head. "Just finishing up."

"Dr. Jones." Gregory, one of her military students said.

"Yes, what do you need?"

"I've got night duty next week. I should be off, but they switched things up."

She nodded. "Tell you what. Email me your assignment for tonight, and I'll let you know the assignments for the next couple of classes."

"Thank you," then he left them alone.

"Well, seems you have groupies."

She started gathering her materials up. "What are you talking about?"

"That kid there."

"That kid is probably older than you are, and he's military."

He frowned. "Yeah?"

"What?"

He shook his head. "I'll look him up."

"Whatever for?"

"I have to check him out, make sure he's on the up and up. He's trying to move in on my woman."

She shouldn't like that term. There was something so wrong with it but part of her liked it.

"He's harmless and married."

"Still."

"Gianni, if you do that, I will have to dump you."

"That's not nice."

"I never said I was." She started to walk past him, but he grabbed her by the wrist and pulled her closer.

"You *are* sweet. Particular parts of you are amazingly sweet."

She shivered as he gave her a kiss.

"I have to drop some things off at my office, then we can head out."

He smiled and gave her a quick peck on the tip of her nose. "Cool, I want to see where you work."

She pulled away to gather up her books. "Why?"

"It's part of you."

When she glanced at him, she realized he was being serious. Unless she worked with the man, most didn't want to know about her work, but Gianni did. In fact, he took as much pleasure as she did in his work.

She unlocked the door and stepped into the cramped space. "Sorry, it's always a mess."

He laughed. "No worries. This is actually what I expected a professor's office to look like."

"You've never been to a professor's office? I thought your mother was a teacher."

"Art teachers don't usually get something like this. For myself, I've taken a few classes but they were all online for now. Getting the basics out of the way. I want to get a Bachelor's to back up my Medic training, but not in a hurry right now."

She nodded as she slipped her files into the cabinet then locked it. "I'm ready."

"Yeah, I am too."

Something in his tone stopped her. "What does that mean?"

He smiled as he approached her. She had to fight the urge to back up.

"Uh, Gianni, what are you doing?"

"I have this fantasy of being very naughty in the professor's office."

She laughed and slipped away. "No."

"You are saying no, but your body is saying yes," he said slipping behind her. He nuzzled her neck, his teeth grazing the sensitive flesh. "God, woman you drive me crazy."

She was seriously thinking of accepting the offer he had just made, when she heard her baby sister's voice.

"Am I interrupting?"

CHAPTER SEVEN

Sometimes, it's hard to remember how not to be the big sister. —Kianna

Gianni bit back a growl when he saw the petite woman leaning against the doorjamb. He knew she was the youngest of the three sisters and possibly the most needy. One thing he had learned about Kianna was that she was more of a control freak about her younger siblings than Vince had ever been. But, then again, her parents were gone and as the oldest she probably saw it as her duty to take care of them.

"What are you doing here?" he asked.

Okay that was a little rude, but he was still trying to pull his head out of the fantasy of office sex.

"Zoe," Kianna said. "This is Gianni. Gianni, this is my baby sister Zoe."

She nodded in his direction but said nothing else.

"So, are you going to tell you me what you're doing here?"

She shrugged. The petulant look on her face told Gianni she wasn't happy finding a man with her sister. It was hard to believe they were sisters to begin with. Kianna was all rounded curves and soft smiles. Zoe was a little bit shorter, smaller boned. Her waist length braided hair was purple. Her jeans had seen better days, as had the shirt she wore.

"I thought I would come over for the weekend to see you." She gave Gianni a measuring look. "Not a student?"

Before he could answer her, and he was pretty sure she wouldn't like Gianni's answer, Kianna did. "No. Gianni is a PJ here at the base."

"Hmm."

Her sister wasn't impressed apparently.

"We were just leaving," Kianna said.

"Is that what they call it now?"

He had to fight the chuckle. Apparently Kianna didn't get caught fooling around that often and her younger sister probably loved turning the tables.

"Yeah, we were going to go out for a late supper and some drinks if you're up to it," he said.

Kianna gave him a surprised look.

"Sure," Zoe said, but her expression told Gianni he was in for a long night.

* * * *

The place he picked was close to the I-95 but quiet being a Thursday night. He could almost feel Kianna's relief.

"So, how long have you been sleeping with my sister?"

Kianna choked on a drink. She patted the moisture away from her lips then frowned at her younger sister. "Zoe."

"I think I have the right to know."

Before she could answer her though, Gianni took over the conversation. "I think you do too, but I think you should show your sister a little more respect."

Kianna gave him a curious glance. She'd never heard that tone from Gianni before. The frown told her Gianni wasn't happy with her sister.

Zoe frowned right back at him. This was definitely not going to be the fun and happy night she had planned.

"How's work going?" she asked.

Her sister shrugged. "It's going. I'm hoping to have enough for a show by early next year."

"That would be wonderful. We'll have to have a huge party in Savannah."

"A show?"

"You know Zoe paints. She's working to have enough on hand to have a show."

She beamed at her sister and Zoe smiled. "I said I was hoping."

"You'll do it." She glanced at Gianni who seemed to relax a little bit more now. "You like the picture she painted of Savannah's waterfront for me."

"Oh, you mean the one that hangs over your bed?" Zoe asked, but she was smiling. "My sister is very traditional, but I couldn't resist it. And I knew she would love it."

She patted Zoe's hand. "The ribs are amazing here. You should try them Zoe."

She tried to keep the conversation flowing. There was one thing that she knew and that was Zoe didn't just show up out of the blue for nothing. Something was wrong, very wrong, for her sister to pop up out of the blue.

She just hoped it wasn't anything too terrible.

* * * *

Gianni understood being the youngest. It wasn't the easiest thing in the world. You were always taking shit from your siblings and you had to prove you were just as good as them to the rest of the world. Being mean to embarrass Kianna wasn't right. It was bratty.

By the time they reached the house, he had made up his mind. He would have a talk with Zoe. Kianna gave him a chance the moment they walked in the door. She was tired, he could tell, and not in the mood for her sister's antics.

"I need to change." She sighed and looked at them. "You two, just whatever."

She left them alone in the living room.

"You've upset your sister."

Zoe shrugged. Oh, damn, she must have been a handful in high school. Part of him wondered at that. Zoe wasn't that much younger than he was, but he felt like he was old enough to be her father when he was with her.

"If your sister is upset, I am."

She cut him a look out of the corner of her eye. "Is that so?"

He crossed his arms. "Other people might like the bratty side of you, but I don't. It's cute, but it gets old since you are apparently doing it to upset your sister. That I find unacceptable."

One eyebrow rose and he wanted to laugh. It was so apparently Kianna but he figured neither sister would be happy to hear that.

"Really?"

"Yes."

"And you think it's your job to see to this?"

"It's my job to make sure she's happy. You are not helping."

She snorted and walked around the room. "You think that she's so nice?"

"No, but I know that while she might not be happy with people's life choices, she accepts you and the men you date. You should show her the same respect."

Before she could respond, Kianna joined them back in the living room. He was pretty sure she was going to try and push him out the door, but that wasn't going to happen. He knew that Kianna was used to rearranging people and for once she was going to have to understand where he fit in her life.

"Did you want to watch something?" Kianna asked.

Zoe looked from him then back to Kianna. "Sure."

* * * *

"What did you do with my sister?" she asked as he shut the door behind him.

He smiled. "I have no idea what you are talking about."

She gave him a suspicious look, but he didn't give her a chance to argue anymore. He knew she had wanted to send him home. Not because she didn't want him there, but he knew that her sister wasn't happy he was there. He would give them their time, but he was busy making up for the two months he had fallen for her through emails. He wasn't about to give up even one night, especially when nights with the woman you loved weren't easy to come by.

For a second, he stopped. *Love.* Shit, he was in love with her. He looked at her and she was studying him as if he was sick.

"Are you alright?"

He shook his head and smiled. "Nope, but that's okay."

He took her hand and pulled her to him.

He kissed her then, fast, quick and wet. Damn, the woman had a mouth on her.

"Gianni, my sister's just down the hall."

"I'll be quiet...but not sure you can be."

"Really?"

"Yeah."

She cocked her head to the side and studied him. Humor danced in her eyes. Of course he loved her. How could he not? She was made for him.

"I accept that challenge."

He picked her up and threw her on the bed. She gasped then giggled as she bounced.

"I aim to win that," he said.

Moments later, he called truce as he captured her moans with his mouth as they road the crest together. He figured it was totally worth it.

* * * *

The next morning, Kianna watched her sister breathe in the aroma of her coffee.

"Did you sleep okay last night?" she asked and almost winced at the banality of it. She didn't know how to act the morning after she'd had hot sex just a couple rooms away from her baby sister. It had been different when she had been married. Not really, but for some reason it just seemed different.

"Sure, you know I can sleep anywhere." She didn't open her eyes when she answered. Zoe was definitely not a morning person, had never been. From the moment she had come home from the hospital, Zoe had always been a night owl.

"I remember when we lived in that house in Athens, remember that? You slept through the tornado siren."

"Well, a lot of people do that. That's why they have those weather radio thingies now."

"The siren was right by our house. It was less than a block away."

She smiled and opened her eyes. "So, you want to tell me what's going on with you and fly boy up there?"

She shrugged. "Not sure. Want to tell me why you're here?"

Her sister smirked. "Not sure."

She sighed and stared. "Zoe."

Her smile faded. "Just had to get out of town. I'm kind of over my head right now."

"Did you and Adam break up?"

She shrugged.

"What does that mean?" Kianna asked, even though she was afraid of the answer.

"That means I don't know where the hell he is."

Kianna heard the tears in her sister's voice. "Oh, baby, I'm sorry."

She stood up and pulled Zoe into her arms as she started to sob. "I don't know what happened, Kiki."

The use of Zoe's nickname for her was a worry. She rarely used it these days so she knew there was a problem. "Did he take anything, steal anything?"

She shook her head and pulled back. "That's just it. All his stuff is still there. He just vanished off the face of the earth. No one has seen him. It isn't like him at all."

Kianna wanted to roll her eyes but didn't. Zoe seemed like a pain in the ass to most people, but the truth was she had a soft heart for bad boys. Kianna just wished some day Zoe would meet a good guy. And like him.

"Have you talked to the police?"

She nodded. "Nothing. I filed a missing person's report, but that isn't going to go anywhere." She sighed. "I feel better now. Thanks for letting me vent. I haven't told anyone really."

Kianna kissed her forehead. "Remember that I'm always here to talk to."

"I think that's why I wanted to come see you. I knew you would do something about it. So, what is going on with you and the younger man?"

"He's not that much younger."

"Okay, but not your usual type. Uniform types…you've avoided them since you were married."

She nodded. "Yeah. But, well, we started emailing while he was deployed."

"Just be careful and remember to be happy." The sound of the front door had Zoe making a face. "He went to work out this early?"

Kianna laughed. "He is military."

* * * *

Gianni stepped into the house and heard laughter. He couldn't help smiling in response. He noticed the bag sitting on the floor by the sofa. Gianni hated to admit it but he was kind of happy to see her go. Granted, once she started to behave, she was pretty cool, but he wanted time alone with Kianna. His revelation from the night before was too new. He wanted to work it out.

Zoe stepped into the living room. "You are disgusting."

"Well, good morning to you too."

She chuckled. "I never understand the reasons for getting up so early."

"You can't get much done sleeping the day away."

"Yeah, but you're asleep by the time it gets fun."

He laughed. "Okay, you got me there."

Her smiled faded. "So, fly boy, I figure you're probably going to be here when I come back next time."

"Probably, unless I'm deployed."

She rolled her eyes. "You military types are way too happy about order to suit me."

He laughed. "I take it you avoid us at all costs."

"Yeah. You know what it's like to be the youngest. Kianna might seem sweet to you, but as an older sister, she wasn't when I was a kid."

"She loves you," he said, enjoying Zoe but feeling the need to defend Kianna.

"And I love her. I also know her better than anyone but Etta. If I listen to the vibes around here, I'm going to have to get used to you. I just want you to know that if you hurt her, I will come back here and make you disappear. They won't be able to find enough pieces to identify you. Understood?"

"Yeah, but I won't hurt her, not on purpose."

"God, you two were made for each other. Just be sure to make her understand you're in for the long haul. Kianna doesn't have a good track record with men, although she's the only one of us who has been married."

He said nothing to that. His brain was trying to wrap around the idea that Kianna had been married at one time. She had never said a thing. It had been three months...if he counted their time together in emails and she never mentioned it. Before he could sort out his feelings, Zoe was calling her sister in.

"Okay, Kianna, I need to head out now. I heard there was a storm moving in.

Kianna came out of the kitchen with a bag. "Here, eat something on your way back."

Zoe smiled and he could see the love right there. She might have been acting like a brat the night before, but there was no doubt she loved her sister.

"Thank you," Zoe said, giving Kianna a hug. "I'll call or text when I get home."

"No texting on the road," Kianna warned.

"Of course not. You two behave yourselves now."

She danced down the porch steps to her little car. As she backed up, Kianna sighed and settled her head against his shoulder. Something settled in his chest... something that should scare the hell out of him. Being a Santini, he knew better than to fight it.

It was going to be hard enough fighting for the woman he loved. Fighting himself just seemed stupid and a waste of energy.

CHAPTER EIGHT

As a born and bred Santini, I believe in fate and listening to signs. —Gee

A couple weeks later, Gee came to an abrupt stop in front of an antique store. There in the front display was a ring. Not just any ring. This one was gold, and from the looks of it, about a hundred years old. A simple solitaire sparkled in the late afternoon sunlight.

"Damn, Santini," Andrews said as he ran into him.

"Sorry. Hey, I need to go in here and look for something."

Andrews gave him a look that told him he knew what was going on. The entire flight had been giving him shit over Kianna since he got back. He'd missed every poker night and there had been a lot of moaning when he skipped a trip to Pensacola for a weekend. He didn't really want to waste time with the guys when time was so precious in the military.

"Antiques?"

"That ring," he said taking a step closer.

He looked at the ring and rolled his eyes. "Aw, damn, you're gonna get married."

"When you find the woman…that's it."

Andrews sighed. "I have to get to City Hall."

"Just a peek," he said and hurried into the small store before Andrews could say anything else. When he heard the little tinkle of the bell, he knew his friend had followed him in.

A little man shuffled out from the back. "Can I help you young gentlemen?"

"Yes, sir. I would like to look at the ring in the window. The diamond solitaire."

He nodded as he shuffled over to pull it out of the display. "A beautiful ring. Circa 1920 with a flawless diamond."

The old man's hand shook as he handed it to Gee. The moment he touched the ring he felt a little jolt.

"How much?"

The man named a price that had Andrews whistling. "Better make sure you love her, Santini."

He slipped the ring back between the red velvet but didn't respond. He had figured out he loved Kianna several weeks ago, but he hadn't had the nerve to say it. It made him a bit of a coward, but part of it had to do with Kianna. She was still wary of him, and when he talked of more permanent things, she would change the subject. If he had told her he loved her, she probably wouldn't believe him.

"I can afford it." Just barely. He would have to dip into his savings, but he had it. He had finally gotten his hazardous duty pay all worked out and finance had gotten it to him just a few days ago. So…it was possible.

"I also offer a ten percent discount to military. So take that off the top."

Gee glanced up at the man. "Yeah?"

He nodded, a proud smile curving his lips. "I was Army once upon a time. I have two sons who are retired Air Force, and a granddaughter who is in the Reserves."

"I'll take it."

"God, I hope you know what you're doing," Andrews said. "I'm going to walk down to City Hall."

"Okay. Catch up with you."

Once Andrews left, Gee watched the old man package up the ring. "Do you know what you're doing, young man?"

Gee grinned. "Nope. But that's not always important. I know I need to be with her. That's all."

He nodded. "You're one young man with your head on straight."

Now he just hoped Kianna thought the same thing.

* * * *

Kianna hated the politics of her job. She loved teaching, loved the fact that she actually helped people become better English students, but she hated smoozing around. She had always thought of it as a necessity of the job. She wanted to make tenure. Or had wanted it at one time. Lately, though, she started to think of other things, of possibly not always teaching in Valdosta. It was silly of her, but just being around Gianni made her think of other things.

She had been trying her best to inch out of the President's monthly get together for the last hour. Every time she made it close to the door, she seemed to get caught by someone. Gianni was supposed to be picking her up soon and she wanted to be back in the office before he made it to campus.

Right before she made her escape, she was caught.

"Hey, Kianna, why are you here so late?"

She glanced up at her colleague, Dr. Brenda Hollison. The daughter of two other tenured professors on campus, it was pretty much a given that Brenda would make it. She was definitely the epitome of what a tenured business professor looked like. Sleek business suit, short business-like hair, and stilettos. Why did women who were already tall seemed to feel the need to wear those shoes from hell?

She smiled. "Not sure what you mean by that, Brenda."

They had both started at the university at the same time, but for some reason, Brenda thought she should be called by "Dr.". So, Kianna deliberately called her Brenda. Sure she was a bit younger than Kianna, but there was no reason to be such a bitch.

"I just thought you would be out with that boy toy of yours."

She said it loud enough that a few people turned their heads.

"Excuse me?"

"That young man you've been seeing."

"I haven't been seeing a young man. I've been dating a PJ."

"Oh." She took a sip of her martini and smiled. "I just wondered why you didn't invite him here. It seems that you don't want any of us to know about him."

She hadn't been hiding him really. Sort of—but not because of his age. Their relationship was so new and so special, she didn't want anyone but family knowing. She just wanted to keep him all to herself as long as she could. When Brenda glanced over Kianna's shoulder, her smile turned evil. Kianna turned to find Gianni waiting for her.

"Hey, Gianni," she said walking over to him.

"Hey." He gave her a kiss on the cheek and she tried not to get embarrassed. She wasn't a woman who liked huge displays of affection, especially in her work place.

"Are you going to introduce me?" Brenda asked.

"Of course. Gianni, this is Brenda Hollison. Brenda, this is Gianni Santini."

She held out her hand and Gianni shook it, then dropped it like she was poison. She wanted to smile, but didn't. Most men were enamored with a reed thin bleach blonde with perfect teeth and surgery perfect breasts. Gianni was different.

"Let's go, Gianni, I need to pick up some things at my office."

He nodded and followed her out. While she shut down her computer and locked up her office, she felt as if there was something wrong. Gianni said nothing, but there was a vibe she didn't like coming off of him. By the time they got to her place she was ready to scream.

"What?"

He looked at her and blinked. "What do you mean what?"

"What has you irritated?"

"Nothing."

God save her from stubborn men.

"Nothing?"

He just looked at her. This was not the laughing man she was in love with.

Her brain stopped working and her world tilted a bit.

Oh shit.

No. No. No. She was *not* in love with the man. No way. He was younger. This was an affair. And right now, she wanted to smack him upside the head. She could take him being mad but she couldn't take him shutting her out. It was something her mother had done as punishment to all of them. And she hated it.

"If you aren't going to talk to me, then why not leave?"

"I just want to know what functions I am allowed to attend."

What the hell was he talking about? Maybe she had been dropped down the rabbit hole, or maybe it was just because she just realized she was in love with the stupid man.

"Excuse me?"

He crossed his arms. The eyes that normally danced with humor now focused on her with an intensity that made her want to hide.

"It was clear you were uncomfortable with me being there tonight."

She could only stare at him in wonder. The man actually thought she was embarrassed of him. It was the opposite. Sure, she had kept him a bit of a secret, but it was mostly because she didn't want to share.

But before she could respond, he answered for her.

"Of course you were. You are ashamed of your younger…white…lover."

"What the hell are you talking about? It has nothing to do with race. My husband was white." Now she was getting irritated. She never in her life had ever been accused of being racist. She had been sure that Gianni would never assume that. From the look on his face, Kianna was wrong. "I like you so I didn't want to subject you to that scene. It is one of my least favorite things about my job."

"Ah, another thing you didn't tell me. You were *married.*"

It took her a second to realize that he had skipped over her explanation. "I told you I was married. Didn't I?" Then it hit her. She never did. It was so long ago and she had lived through it and survived.

"No. You didn't. Is there a reason why you wouldn't share that part of your life?"

"I…seriously, Gianni, I thought I did tell you." He didn't look convinced. There was something akin to hurt in his eyes and she didn't know what she had done.

It was as if there was a fire and she kept throwing oil on it. "He was a cop and was killed in the line of duty. I was only nineteen at the time. It seems like…I hate to say it…but a lifetime ago. I was a different person. And seriously I thought I told you."

Then it hit her that he hadn't been surprised. Just accusatory. She settled her hands on her hips.

"You knew."

"Zoe told me."

She wanted to kill her little sister, but she could wait. Right now, the man she loved was looking at her like she was some kind of freak. And then, another revelation hit her upside the head.

"You knew and you never said anything. What were you waiting for?"

"I was waiting for you to tell me."

"Yeah, right. You weren't waiting for that. You were going to lord it over me in a fight just like you did now. My husband used to do that and I hated it. It was one of the reasons we were headed for divorce when he was shot."

That stopped him. "Wait, what?"

"We were headed for divorce but my baby sister didn't know that. Didn't know that the job had changed him. He wasn't the man I loved anymore and I had put my foot down. He couldn't have cared less. But, wait, you never asked me. If you had, I would have told you."

"Now, wait, this isn't my fault."

"It isn't? Of course it isn't. It is never the man's fault, is it? Women are the secretive ones, the ones who don't tell you anything but then expect you to know things."

"Yeah, I would say so."

"Bullshit."

His eyes widened.

"Yeah, I am calling you on it. You have never discussed anything else with me. Not what is going to happen and you sure didn't ask me about Charley. You just waited until you could use it against me."

She didn't realize she had been backing him up until he hit the door.

"You know what. Go away. Go away and figure out if you can be a man in this relationship."

She knew she had hit a nerve when his face flushed. "What did you say?"

Okay, maybe she had pushed him a little too far. Gianni would never hurt her, but he was pissed.

He stepped up to her and grabbed her. Without a word he slammed his mouth down on hers for five long seconds. She felt his anger, his passion and something she couldn't quite figure out as he devastated her with the kiss. When he pulled back, he let her go and she stumbled back, almost falling down. Gianni would have normally helped her, or she thought he would have. This time, he didn't.

"Just so you know who is the man in this relationship."

Before she could respond, he was out the door. She stumbled over to the sofa, her body hot from the kiss and still vibrating with anger from the fight. Dammit, the man had her head all messed up. She closed her eyes and realized she was crying. Damn, she hadn't cried over a man since Charley.

What had gone wrong? One minute she was thinking about how happy she was, the next they were yelling at each other. Had she been holding back? Maybe. She just realized she loved the man. He had only been back a couple of months, but they had spent two months emailing several times a day. And all through that she never mentioned her marriage.

"Because I felt like a failure."

She whispered it as if it was a sin. And in her eyes, it was. She had never told a soul about the divorce. She was ashamed because her husband died in the line of duty, and when she had asked him to get help, he refused. The job had made him angry, mean and scary. It wasn't the laughing man who had teased her and tempted her into bed. He had been her first…and she had felt like a failure when he had chosen the job over her.

She wiped her eyes and went in search of her phone. She needed to get out of town, take a break. One person in the world would let her be herself, to just be.

She dialed the number. "Etta, I think I need to see you this weekend."

CHAPTER NINE

My mother always says that it's always the man's fault. My father always agrees, especially if he's within hitting distance. —Gianni

Gianni was trying to keep his temper in check, but it was hard. Kianna hadn't done a damn thing to dispel the idea that they were just having an affair. True, they had never talked about it. And she didn't really say it tonight.

He almost growled when his phone rang with Leo's ringtone.

"Hey, Gee, guess who is going to be in Valdosta tonight?" Leo asked.

"What do you mean?" He asked, still annoyed over his fight with Kianna. It wasn't even a fight. She just made assumptions and kicked him out of her house. Like he was one of her sisters.

"Your favorite brother."

"Marco made it from Hawaii?"

"Smart ass. We were just in Pensacola seeing Jesse and I suggested coming up there to see you."

Checking on him. Dammit. He expected this. It'd been a few months, but Leo had been the worst of them checking on him. Vince had classes and Marco was in Hawaii. Leo apparently was the only one of them with time off. And he didn't mind. It was just the wrong day for that to happen.

"You know how to get here?"

"About ten minutes away."

He hung up and tried to calm his anger. He knew he was wrong. Knew that part of it was his fault. She had been embarrassed by him and it had stuck in his craw. How many damned times did he get asked by women if he was an officer? Too many to count. He didn't realize until now how much that irritated him.

Gee was lucky that his family didn't care. Joey Santini always said she wanted her men happy and healthy. Everyone had accepted he would go into the Air Force to be a PJ. He would work on his degree now, but he wanted to be enlisted. But at bases with women looking for a date, there were some that just wanted nothing to do with enlisted guys. Tonight, when she had tried to rush him out of the room, he had felt used. For the first time since knowing her, he had been pissed with her actions.

And that had hurt. He struck out to hurt her the way she hurt him. He knew she wasn't racist and it had nothing to do with that. He felt like an ass for doing it, but saying she was embarrassed because she thought she was too smart for him hurt too much. Considering what the ring he had in his pocket set him back... and he had been ready to propose tonight. Okay, that might have been rushing it, but he had made the decision.

He was going to have to figure out how to put it all back together, but he wasn't going to be given a chance. He'd splash some water on his face and get ready for his brother. Gianni would make sure he would at least not make an ass out of himself in front of his sister-in-law.

* * * *

"Are you going to tell me why you're being such an ass, Gee?" Leo asked conversationally. They were sitting at his dinner table. "I would think with your new lady friend you would be all happy."

"How do you know I'm still seeing her?"

Leo rolled his eyes and swallowed a quick sip of beer. "Of course you are."

"Damn, there are no fucking secrets in this family."

MJ smiled. "You know better than that, Gee. Your brothers are meddling old women."

"You have the old part right. Why don't you run off with me, leave the old guy to die alone?"

She smiled. "I thought about it, but he's grown on me like a fungus really."

Gee laughed. Of all the women his brother could have fallen for, his Marine brat, tough nosed physical therapist was probably the only one of them who wouldn't put up with crap. She was cute as a button, with huge blue eyes and her long dark hair. As usual, it was up in a tail. So tiny and now glowing with her pregnancy.

"He's avoiding the conversation he needs to have," Leo said.

MJ rolled her eyes. "Good lord, you are as about as subtle as a soldier at a tea party."

"Leave it alone, Leo," Gee warned.

Leo opened his mouth, but thankfully MJ stepped in. "Listen, babe, do you think you can run to the store and get me a snickers?"

He looked from Gee to MJ then back to Gee. Gianni sensed his brother wanted to argue, but MJ gave him one of those brilliant smiles of hers. Leo melted like he always did for her.

"Sure."

Once Leo was gone, MJ rose to clear the dishes.

Gee shook his head. "No you will not clean up the dishes. You're pregnant."

She chuckled and settled back in the chair. "We need to have you talk to Leo. He seems to think I can do anything."

"It's because he loves you."

Her eyes softened. "Oh, Gee, what's wrong? Was she mean to you?"

"She told me to leave her."

She reached out and patted his hand. "Why?"

"Well, she didn't tell me she had been married and I got pissed. I mean I love her and she didn't tell me. Plus, she won't introduce me to people she works with. She did, but well…it was implied I was just her boy toy."

MJ choked. "Her what?"

Now that he said it out loud, it sounded silly. "One of her friends at work called me that and Kianna said nothing. Then when I asked her about it, she backed off."

MJ studied him for a few moments. "And she knows you love her. You told her?"

He shook his head. "Not really." He had wanted to, had wanted to start talking of more serious things, but that stupid little fight had pushed him away.

"Okay. But she should know, right?"

He smiled. "See, that's why we should be together."

"I love you, Gee, just like one of my brothers."

"I love you too, MJ."

"So, I am going to do this out of love."

"What?"

She leaned forward and smacked him upside the back of his head.

"Damn, MJ."

She sat back and shrugged. "If you would get your head out of your butt, I wouldn't have to do that."

"Why did you do that?"

"Because you're being an idiot. That woman you say you love tells you to leave. Why?"

"I wanted to know why she hid it from me." He hadn't wanted to voice his real concerns. He thought she might have not wanted him there because of his education. That would have been worse than anything, in his mind.

"Granted, I know that she should have told you, but there might be a part of you that makes her scared to tell you."

"Why?"

"Why did they break it off?"

He sighed. "Apparently, they didn't. He was killed in the line of duty. He was a cop."

She nodded. "And, telling you might have been too scary. And I have a feeling from what you have told me about her tonight, she isn't someone who likes to show that side of herself. She's tough."

"She's not. She's soft and sweet."

"And practically raised her sisters by herself and survived losing a husband. She's tough."

"I—"

"What you need to do is go apologize to her."

He frowned. "Why should I apologize?"

"I will take a page out of Joey Santini's book on men. Go apologize because it's your fault because you are the man. If you didn't get this wrong, you will get something else wrong."

He leaned forward and gave her a kiss.

"What was that for?"

"Making me understand. I'm going to go see if I can find her. I'll be back."

He hurried out the door ready to make amends. Twenty minutes later, he was pissed. She was gone. Sure it was Friday night, but she wasn't anywhere to be found. Dammit, she had left town without telling him. Well, her next-door neighbor had been happy to tell her she had gone to see a friend somewhere. Worse, after he called five times in five minutes, he realized she was not going to answer the phone.

He parked his truck and frowned. He had to go back in and make nice with his brother and MJ. Thankfully they were staying at a hotel. His tiny apartment couldn't accommodate them and he wasn't in the mood to be around the happy couple.

And he needed time alone. Time to figure out what the hell he was going to tell the woman he loved.

That is, if she ever talked to him again.

* * * *

Kianna was in one bitch of a mood. Nothing, not even her favorite malasada was helping.

"You know, just because you hate sweets doesn't mean you need to give that malasada the stink eye."

Kianna slanted a look at Max Chandler. "If you aren't nice, I'll tell Anna all the mean jokes you told behind her back about her not being able to see her feet a few months ago."

He shook his head. "Mean woman. I am surrounded by so many of you. Tell me why you're mean today."

She sighed. "Men, you suck."

"Is this a general feeling, or more of a one guy kind of thing?"

"Both."

He studied her for a second and she looked at him.

"What?" she asked.

"So, the PJ's been mean to you?"

She sniffed. "Yes. I don't ever want to see him again."

"I think you might have to deal with him sooner rather than later."

"Why?"

"Because he's walking in the shop."

She turned on the stool and realized that Max was telling the truth. Her heart leapt into her throat and then splattered on the floor.

Damn the man. He had two people with him, like he needed an audience or something. She recognized them from pictures he had shown her. Great, now his brother and sister-in-law could report back to the family. Just what she needed.

Max tsked. "Oh, and he doesn't look happy with you."

She gave him a dirty look but she wasn't given the chance to respond. Gianni had other plans.

"Kianna Mechelle Jones, just where the hell have you been?"

There was a stunned silence. She could understand why. The few regulars in shop knew Gianni and had never seen him mad. She hadn't really seen him mad either, before the other night.

Then, she realized he was waiting for an answer. In fact, he looked like he was getting madder by the moment. How dare he embarrass her?

She slipped off her stool and settled her hands on her hips. "What right do you have to know?"

"I have every right to know."

She saw his brother roll his eyes and his sister-in-law stepped around him. She gave Kianna a smile. She was so small, she just couldn't believe this was the MJ that Gianni had told her about.

"You must be Kianna."

She nodded but Gianni's brother took over.

"I think everyone knows who she is now, love," Leo said. "I'm Leo, the idiot's brother and this is my wife, Maryanne."

"I haven't been able to find you," Gianni said ignoring his brother and Maryanne. "You didn't answer my calls."

Of course he hadn't. She had slipped out of town. More like ran out of town to Atlanta for a weekend. It really hadn't been because she was avoiding him.

"I went to see Etta."

"Ran away."

She almost stepped back and apologized, but something out of the corner of her eye caught her attention. Maryanne was shaking her head and Kianna realized that she shouldn't back down.

"I went to see my sister. I figured she wanted to spend time with me and I wasn't in the mood to put up with a whiny little shell of a man."

There was a whistle and she didn't know if it was Leo or Max but it told her she might have taken a step too far. Gianni's eyes narrowed.

"You really know how to push my buttons, woman."

She didn't know what he meant by that until he stepped forward and bent at the waist. The next moment, her world tilted as he lifted her up and over his shoulder.

"Gianni put me down!"

"No."

"Maryanne," she screeched but when she looked in her direction, Maryanne was waving goodbye.

He set her down on her feet and backed her back up against his truck.

"What was that for?" she asked.

"I wanted a little privacy for what I want to say to you."

She glanced to the window and he followed her line of vision. Most of the customers and all of the staff were watching. Gianni cursed.

"I wanted them out of earshot at least."

She crossed her arms. "So say it, PJ. I don't have all damned day."

He looked at her then laughed. "I swear, Zoe was right about you. You aren't as sweet as everything thinks you are. Damned pain in my ass. I try and tell a woman I love her and she throws me out of her house and disappears."

Her throat closed up and she tried to swallow. "You love me?"

"Of course I do. God, I can't think of anyone but you." He cupped her face. "I'm sorry I was such an ass. I didn't mean to do that. I shouldn't have said those horrible things."

Just hearing him say it had tears burning the backs of her eyes. When she blinked a few of them escaped.

"Don't cry, baby. I can't stand seeing you sad."

She shook her head. "No, not sad. I should have told you about Charley. It's just…well I have a lot to tell you about that part of my life. But I never have been ashamed of you. Are you kidding me? Hell, I want to flaunt you around on campus."

He chuckled. "I'm not sure how I feel about that."

"It was exactly what I said. I hate that part of my work. I only go because… well I feel I have an obligation. I would hate to make you do that kind of thing."

He kissed her then, slowly, deeply. "I love you, Kianna."

"I love you too, Gianni."

He smiled that pretty smile of his and she couldn't help but laugh and hug him closer. "I really do love you, even if you are my boy toy."

He laughed, then sobered and reached into the pocket of his jeans.

"I know you were married before and it wasn't going the way you wanted it to before Charley was killed." He opened the box. In the center of the red satin sat an engagement ring. Not something new. It was antique, a simple solitaire. It sparkled in the bright sunlight.

"I found it in an antique shop the other day and I bought it."

She couldn't take her gaze away from it. "The other day?"

"I wasn't sure why, but for some reason, I felt the need to buy it."

She glanced up at him. "Yeah?"

He nodded and for the first time since meeting him, he looked...well...nervous. "It's beautiful."

"It's just the thing I thought you would like. Its circa 1920." When she didn't say anything he sighed. "I'm asking you to marry me, Kianna."

Her vision wavered.

"I know it's a lot to ask for and you might be hoping to make tenure and having to move will hurt any chances of that."

She shook her head. "That's not important."

"No? Are you sure?"

"I've only cared about teaching. I love the job. Tenure was just something I thought I wanted."

"So, is that a yes?"

She drew in a deep breath and nodded.

"Are you sure? It isn't the easiest of lives."

"When you left the other day, I thought we were through. I thought that I would never see you again. That was worse than anything else I have ever been through."

He smiled.

"Yes, Gianni, I'll marry you."

He took out the ring and put it on her finger. The fit was almost perfect. He hugged her close and kissed her neck. "You've made me the happiest man in Georgia."

He pulled back and kissed her.

"Hey, Gee, get that woman in here," Leo yelled.

They pulled back and realized the whole shop had been watching them. She blushed.

"Get used to it, Kianna," MJ said. "Santinis always like an audience."

She laughed as she and Gianni walked hand in hand into the sweet shop.

EPILOGUE

"I hope you don't mind going to Virginia for the weekend," Gianni said, as they waited at the airport.

Kianna smiled at him. "Of course not. What woman in her right mind would complain about get a private jet ride?"

Gianni chuckled. "It's hard to think of Alana of being that rich, but I guess she is."

"So, she's not snobby?"

"First, none of the Santinis would want to deal with a snob. Secondly, Alana is the antithesis of snobbery."

She smiled but it faded. "I'm still worried about how your family will take me?"

"I told you. Mom is kind of a hippy child. Your radical political views are no problem."

She snorted and Gianni couldn't help but smile. Three weeks since they had gotten engaged and he was ready to tie the knot right now. His mother would have freaked if he'd called to say they'd eloped though. And there was one thing every Santini understood: Don't upset Joey Santini.

"I wasn't asking about that. I'm worried about my age. I am a bit older than you."

"Yeah, you're a year or two away from AARP membership and social security benefits."

"I'm serious, Gianni. I'm not so sure most Mamas would be happy about their sons marrying someone so much older."

He studied her and realized that she was serious. Damn, he hadn't realized she'd been worrying about this. He pulled her into his arms.

"Mom is going to love you. She's so happy with more women in the family, she doesn't care. But, she will love you not only because I love you, but for all the reasons I do. You're sweet, smart, and beautiful, inside and out."

She gave him a small smile, "Yeah?"

He nodded and gave her a kiss. "Yeah."

"Is that the plane?" Kianna asked looking over his shoulder.

He turned and saw the plane taxiing up to the hanger. "Probably. Not many private jets fly into Valdosta."

It took a few seconds and they watched together, his arms wrapped around her as she stood in front of her.

"You know I love you, don't you?" she asked.

He did, and every time she said it made him feel twenty feet tall. "Yeah, I do." He kissed the side of her neck as the door to the jet opened and the stairs descended. "Come on, you have some Santinis to meet."

VICENTE

Melissa Schroeder

A NOTE FROM MEL

Virginia. It is where we are headed in just a few months. It was our favorite assignment for location, but I worst for seeing the Man we live with. Our first fall there was magical. We lived through the first Snowmaggeden and lived near the city of much crime, according to NCIS. Being a history geek, I loved to go into DC and walk around the monuments. And of course, for those of you who know me well, I fell in love with Wegmans grocery store. This fall, we will make our way back to those soft rolling hills of Northern Virginia for the next chapter of our life. I cannot wait to settle down and have a place that is our home base.

CHAPTER ONE

Vince Santini fell in love for the first and only time in his life thanks to getting hit in the face with a locker door. He didn't even remember where he was going or what he was doing. He just remembered turning to hurry out of school and walking straight into steel. He fell back, smacking his head on the tiled floor. When he opened his eyes, his world was spinning.

"Oh, I'm so sorry," a girl said. She was leaning over him, her dark brown eyes filled with worry, her red curls tumbling over her shoulder. "I didn't see you coming."

He shook his head trying to clear it and found himself face to face with a titian-haired goddess. And she kept putting her hands on him. Jesus. If she didn't stop, he was going to embarrass himself. He could smell her. Some kind of mixture of baby powder and lust. Although, the lust might have been on his part.

Then she stopped. "Vince? Vince Santini?"

He nodded then winced. "Damn."

She laughed and offered him a hand. "You don't remember me. It's Julianna Andrews, from Twenty-nine Palms. You know, the seventh grade, Mrs. Gillepse's Algebra?"

Then it clicked—the gangly girl, taller than most, so skinny…always with a smile. "Yeah, Jules." It had been more than three years since he'd seen her and Jules had definitely filled out. He let her help him up and shook his head trying to clear it.

"You live here now?"

She nodded. "Dad's an instructor. We moved in a month ago."

"Julianna, I see you met my best friend, Vince," Mike Callahan said as he walked up and slipped his arm around her shoulders. "I told you about Julianna, didn't I, Vince?"

He nodded. "I didn't make the connection. We were at Twenty-nine Palms together. Of course, I called her Jules."

"Yeah, well, Mike doesn't like that." She bent down to help him pick up the books he'd dropped. "I thought it might be you he talked about. I mean how many Santini families are there, especially with four boys, but you never know."

Once he had all his books and papers in his arms, Mike smiled. "We were going to get a burger, you up for it?"

He shook his head. "Naw, you go ahead. I've got some studying to do."

Mike chuckled. "Vince is kind of an egghead, but then, he'll probably get into Annapolis. See ya, later."

They turned to walk away and Jules smiled back over her shoulder at him. "It was great to see you again."

He watched as his best friend walked out of the school with the girl of his dreams.

Almost 18 years later.

"Vicente, are you there?" his mother asked him. He was sitting in the back of his parents SUV daydreaming.

Great instincts, Marine.

"Yeah, just sort of dozed off back here."

She sighed. "I thought you two would help me. You will help me pick flowers, both of you."

His father gave his mother an indulgent smile and followed her out of the SUV. That's the way it was for Santinis. Hard as nails military men, always done in by a woman. And he was about to come face to face with the one who always tied him in knots for the first time in fifteen years.

* * * *

Jules wanted to scream. Worse, she wanted to do harm to an inanimate object. The one thing about running her nursery was that she had a lot of freedom. Unfortunately, she also had to handle the computer work.

There was a knock at the door and through the glass she saw Joey Santini waving at her. Immediately, Jules' heart lightened. Since starting her business six months earlier, Mrs. Santini had been a godsend, suggesting her to friends and even giving her advice about advertising.

She waved the older woman into her office and stood. "Mrs. Santini, I didn't know you were coming by today."

She hugged her and it felt good. With her parents back in California, Jules was pretty much on her own. Mrs. Santini had taken her under her wing and had checked on her from time to time.

"Well, the whole family's coming in. Marco is bringing Alana for us to meet, since we've only talked on the phone, and that skypy thing. I wanted to get some arrangements and flowers for the house. Oh, and Gee just got engaged."

"Oh, my. Little Gee is getting married? Now I do feel old."

"You? I'm about to be a grandmother."

She looked at the woman she had known for over twenty years. "You haven't aged a bit, Mrs. Santini."

"I told you to call me Joey."

"Babe, did you say you wanted tulips? They're a little expensive," Mr. Santini said from behind her.

"Yes, I think we can afford some tulips. They are Kianna's favorite from what Gee says and I want to give them to her."

He grumbled something but went off to do her bidding. It never failed to amaze her how all the Santini men did whatever Joey wanted. There was a healthy dose of fear among all of them.

"You're a rock star, you know that?"

She shook her head. "What do you mean?"

"That man will do anything to make you happy."

Joey laughed. "That's a Santini. I'm sure you'll see it all in action tomorrow night."

For a second, her brain didn't comprehend. "Wait. What?"

"I want you there. The boys would love to see you."

Only Joey Santini would call four hulking military men 'boys' and make them sound like they were sweet little innocents. Of course, in Joey's eyes, they were all sweet and innocent.

"That's really sweet of you, but I have a lot of work to do."

"I didn't say what time and I doubt you have work to do on a Saturday night."

Jules narrowed her eyes. "Joey, quit trying to be all innocent like you don't know what you're doing."

Joey made a face. "I want you there. Can't you do it for me?"

She shook her head. "You should be ashamed of yourself."

"There is nothing shameful about this. I would like you to see the boys and they would like to see you. In fact, Vince is with us today. Vince."

And true to her word, Vince walked across her nursery. Okay, walk was too simple of a word. Striding…marching…something because Vicente Santini just didn't walk. And seeing him among the flats of flowers was kind of surreal.

"Hey, Jules."

Just like they hadn't talked in years, as if there was no strain between them. "Hey, Vince. How're doing?"

"Pretty good."

Jules didn't miss the eye roll his mother gave him. "I was telling Jules she needed to come by tomorrow night. I know the girls would like to meet someone from your childhood."

Something like alarm moved over his features before it dissolved. "They would probably like that. Of course, I don't know if we can leave her alone with MJ."

"You leave Maryanne out of this. You be nice to my daughter-in-law."

"You are all sweet on her because she's giving you a grandbaby."

"Exactly. I have no problem admitting that."

He laughed and now that he was paying no attention to Jules, it was easy to study him. He was even more attractive than he had been in school. He'd always been well muscled, but now he'd filled out. The extra lines around his blue eyes made him even more attractive. Another of those unfair things women had to deal with.

"So, it's settled."

"What?" she asked when she looked at Joey.

"You will come. Seven o'clock. Unless you have a date or something," Joey said smiling.

A date? She couldn't remember the last time she'd even entertained that idea. She was usually so tired by Saturday she would only plan for spending all day at home on Sunday. Rufus expected it.

"Okay."

"You know the address? Wait, wouldn't it make sense for you and Vince to come together? He lives over here in your neck of the woods."

Alarm shot through her again. Vince and her. Alone. They hadn't done that until the day before her wedding.

"Sure," Vince said.

"Write down your address for Vince and he'll pick you up. See you tomorrow, Jules."

Joey turned and left them alone.

"Just go with the flow. It is always best to let her have her way on the little things."

She blinked and looked at Vince. "I don't even know what to wear."

"It's a Santini family get together. Casual always works. Plus, Mom is gonna be cooking all day, so nothing too fancy just in case you drop red sauce."

She chuckled. "Of course you remember what a klutz I am."

She wrote down her home address on a sticky note and handed it to him. "What time?"

He blinked. He still had all those wonderful dark lashes around his deep blue eyes. It was almost hypnotic to look into them. "What?"

"What time will you be picking me up?"

"How about six-thirty?"

"Okay."

He didn't leave. He just kept standing there staring at her as if he expected her to say something. She didn't know what to say to him. Other than go away and that seemed rude.

"Vicente, I have a house to clean, let's go," his mother bellowed across the nursery.

Vince gave her a smile and she felt her heart take a tumble. "What she really means is she making Dad clean the house."

"I heard that."

"Ears like a bat. See you tomorrow, Jules."

Then he walked out. She watched the family pile into their car together feeling a little homesick. Not that she had a home since she was a brat but it was where her parents were, which was Modesto, California. She sighed. She'd been happy when Joey had started to come around. They had even started to do lunch every now and then.

"Who was that hunk?" Angela asked as she walked down the aisle to Jules. She was only ten years younger than Jules, but Angela made her feel as if she were a hundred.

"That was Vincente Santini, Joey's oldest baby boy, as she calls him when he's not around."

"Well, he is hot. I wanted to take a big bite out of that perfect ass."

Jules smiled at the younger woman. She had been a great find in a sea of applicants. A military brat working her way through college with a head for numbers and a personal gift for selling, Angela made the long hours all that more enjoyable with her unrestrained commentary. "It is kind of perfect. All the girls in high school were in agreement with that."

She rolled her eyes. "Oh, lord, you went to high school with that?"

"No. He looks better today than he did then. Which is why men suck."

Angela laughed. "Well, he was mighty interested in you."

She shook her head. "No, he isn't."

"Yeah, he is. He kept looking back there when his Mom was talking to you. He's got a thing for you."

"Have you started drinking with breakfast? Besides, I doubt Vicente Santini spends any of his time thinking about me."

"I bet you ten bucks he does. A lot. I have a sense about these things."

"You mean like the sense you had about the UPS guy being a mob guy in witness protection?"

"Okay, so I was wrong about that, and UPS had no problem changing his route when it got uncomfortable."

"Yeah, he got sick of you trying to trick him into saying his real name. He didn't even look Italian."

"Not everyone who works for the Mafia is Italian and not all organized crime is Italian. But, that hot hunk of burning Marine blood is. I'm right about him. Bet ya."

"I'll take that bet, because I know for a fact he doesn't like me."

Especially not after *the* kiss. She could remember like it was yesterday. They were alone in her parents' backyard and were supposed to be getting ready for the wedding and he had kissed her. Right there with the cherry blossoms blooming overhead. And, he told her he loved her.

They had been the last words he had spoken to her until today.

CHAPTER TWO

MJ leaned back in the easy chair and smiled at Leo. As always, Leo melted.

"I want a pickle."

Leo sighed and Vince fought a chuckle. MJ had been a handful before the pregnancy but these last few months apparently had been a strain. Leo hadn't said that much, but just observing them made Vince realize just how much work she had become. Considering she was huge, he didn't blame her for being cranky.

Leo did her bidding and she smiled. Oh, how the mighty had fallen, Vince thought. Of course, he knew the curse of the Santinis. Still, since he was the only real bachelor left, he would happily give each and every one of them shit.

"So, do you have a bell you ring for him? I think that would work well," Vince said with a smirk.

MJ gave him an evil smile. "Oh, I like that idea."

"You do that and I'm wearing earplugs," Leo yelled out from the kitchen.

"Be nice to your wife, Leonardo. She's eating for two," his mother said smiling. Vince had a feeling that his mother would allow MJ to shoot Leo if it meant getting her hands on the first Santini grandbaby.

"About that. We had a sonogram the other day," Leo said as he walked back in the room with a big dill pickle.

MJ smiled and grabbed it from him. "Thank you."

"Nothing's wrong is it?" his mother asked, alarm easy to hear in her voice. "You're entering the last trimester. I knew you shouldn't come up here. We should have come down there."

"Joey, calm down. Everything's fine." MJ shook her head. "What's wrong with you Santini? You don't say things like that." She smiled at his mother. "We're having twins."

There was a moment of stunned silence then everyone started talking at once.

"We are going to have to get a drink out tonight. The Santinis out on the town," Gee said smiling. Of course, Vince noticed he received the go ahead nod from Kianna before he said it.

"Sounds like a plan. Leo drives because he's pregnant," Vince said.

Leo shook his head. "Damn. I should have seen that coming."

* * * *

Jules looked at herself in the mirror and thought about changing her clothes—for the fourth time. Three times was okay. Four times moved her into the crazy category. She glanced at Rufus who was watching her from her bed. The lazy dog was no help.

"What do you think?"

He snuffled and buried under the covers more. Oh, great. Now her dog was doing his version of an eye roll. A girl sunk to a new low when her dog judged her behavior and found it lacking.

"He said casual." The reminder didn't help her decide.

She tilted her head from one side to the next. Jules was embarrassed to admit that making decisions like this was still hard. Other parts of her life she had triumphed. Moving back to a place she liked, opening a business she loved…even going out occasionally with Angela or with Joey, those had all been small victories. She always thought she was completely over the nightmare of her marriage, until she had to pick out something special to wear. Jules assumed that it was because Mike had often belittled her fashion sense.

She shook those thoughts away and ran her hands through her hair. Three years and she was still beholden to the memories. Tonight was about fun. She couldn't wait to meet the wives…to see happy marriages. And the Santinis were always fun.

In her opinion, she looked good. Healthy. She'd gained back fifteen pounds and was finally filled out again. The soft purple shirt, her favorite pair of jeans along with boots might be too casual but when she heard the doorbell ring, she realized she didn't have a choice.

She hurried to the door and opened it. Instead of finding just Vince, Leo was with him.

"Jules Andrews." He said and just like always, he pulled her into a huge hug. He was like a big bear and such a sweetie.

"You're going to suffocate her, Leo," Vince said, not sounding happy at all.

"Oh, yeah, sure." He set her on her feet. "But I can bring you back to life since I'm a medic."

She laughed and swatted him. "Did you bring your wife with you?"

He shook his head. "I left her at mom's earlier. She needed rest."

"Come on in, I need to grab my jacket."

Belatedly, Rufus barked as he shuffled into the living room.

"What is that?" Leo asked looking at him.

Jules smiled at her faithful companion. "That's Rufus."

"What's a Rufus?" he asked.

She wanted to laugh, but she couldn't do that to her baby. He was a bit scrappy looking. No matter how much she spent to have his hair groomed, it grew back unevenly. "He's a rescue from the shelter."

Leo didn't look convinced. "If you say so."

She settled her hands on her hips. "Leonardo Santini. I'll tell your mom."

"Good lord, does every woman we meet threaten to tell our mother on us?" he asked Vince.

"Not sure." Vince looked about as happy as a man about to get a prostate exam.

She shook her head. "Rufus, you ignore the Santini brothers. You are beautiful." He gave her a lick then shuffled off to his bed in the living room.

"Let's go. I'm ready for some Joey food."

And maybe by then, Vince wouldn't be giving her the death stare.

* * * *

It was easy to see Jules there with his family. Well, not easy for him, but she had always fit with them. His brothers had always treated her as part of the family, like a sister or a cousin. He wished he could see her that way. Even now, two hours later, his palms were sweating.

They had gathered around the kitchen table as his parents had drifted away. Joey and Papa Santini knew they needed time to hang out, to just be...well it used to be brothers. Now there were spouses and fiancés and lord, kids.

"So, Leo the Lion is going to be a daddy. It's hard to believe," Jules said.

She was sitting next to Alana who had been watching her. Alana was the perfect match for Marco. They both seemed to study things with the same kind of intensity.

"Yeah, but then, I am kind of fantastic, so it was inevitable," Leo said.

"Oh, gawd, could you all leave now? This is a woman thing," MJ announced.

Leo frowned. "No. You are not going to hound Jules for information about us."

"As if," MJ said with a laugh. "You're all standing around here as if you're protecting us from intruders. We're fine. Go away."

Leo glanced in his direction. He knew his brother picked up on his feelings for Jules years ago. "I think we should stay."

MJ sighed. "Joey, Leo says maybe we shouldn't try for a base stateside next."

"Leonardo Santini!"

He groaned. "That was cruel."

She smiled. "That's why you love me."

He leaned down and whispered something in her ear. She blushed prettily and smacked him the arm. Soon they were in the living room with his folks and his mother was irritated. Her frown was enough to make any grown Santini man to run for the hills.

Vince clapped a hand on Leo's shoulder. "You really should have let me date MJ, because that woman is nothing but trouble for you."

Before Leo could answer their mother stepped closer and gave Leo a narrowed look. "So what the hell is this about going overseas?"

* * * *

"So, there's all this shouting down by the riverbank. None of us know what's going on, but we knew the Santinis were down there."

"You never know with those four. I caught them arguing in my front yard," Alana said laughing.

"Yeah, and Joey's had to use the hose on them before out back," MJ said.

Jules laughed. "That's the way Santinis are. Anyway, Gee's just a little guy and he comes running up like there is some demon of hell on his tail."

"Oh, no, what was it?" Kianna asked.

"First, you have to know Gee has an armful of clothes and he can barely see over them. Behind him, in all their glorious nudity, the three older Santinis are running like a determined pack of well…Santinis."

The table erupted into laughter. Jules joined in enjoying herself for the first time in a really long time.

"So, Vince is calling him names that his Mama would box his ears for when he realizes there are at least forty girls standing at the top of the ridge."

"Oh, my." MJ was laughing so hard there were tears pouring out of her eyes. "What did you all do?"

"We protected Gee of course, because he was so little, and well, all of us were pretty happy to get a peek at those guys in the birthday suits."

Kianna was laughing the hardest. "That man is insane. And I can see him doing it."

It was easy to see why these women had caught the eye of a Santini. None of them were similar in looks, but they all seemed to have personalities that fit their husband's perfectly.

Kianna had skin the color of cocoa, laughing golden brown eyes, and a head full of springy curls.

"He is such a sweetie though," Alana said. "He asked me to marry him when I first met him."

The Hawaiian was soft spoken and had a gentle spirit that complimented Marco. Then there was MJ.

"They're all troublemakers, every last one of them. They're men. I know because I grew up in a household of them."

She was a gorgeous petite brunette who was enormous at the moment. She glowed with her pregnancy.

"So, tell us, you saw all of them naked except Gee…so any details?" MJ asked.

"MJ," Alana said. "Jules will think we're horrible."

MJ rolled her eyes. "Oh, please, you want to know too."

"Know?" Jules asked.

"Well, we want to know about the Alpha, Vicente. Fess up."

She didn't know what to say. The memory of Vince Santini completely and gloriously nude was something she could still conjure up in her mind. And damn, he had been barely a senior at the time. Now…

"Yeah, Jules, why don't you tell them about it?" Vince said from behind her.

CHAPTER THREE

Vince couldn't believe he'd caught Jules telling stories on the four of them. Of course, he shouldn't have been surprised. If there was a non-Santini who knew more stories about the Santinis it had to be Jules. She'd been there for most of the embarrassing moments of his life.

Now, though, she was turning pink from embarrassment and he couldn't help but be mesmerized by it. Being a red head, she had skin that showed every little blush, and he was enchanted.

"We water boarded her, Vince," MJ said already taking defense of the Jules. The other three apparently caught her mortification and frowned at him. Jesus, they looked ready to beat him up.

Jules shook her head. "It's not like everyone around here doesn't know that story. I am sure more than one woman has recounted the tale of the naked Santinis."

All the women started laughing and Jules grinned. "That's what we all called them after that. Or *The River Incident*." She looked at Vince. "I mean, you have to admit that was pretty damned funny."

He crossed his arms and frowned at her. She bit her lip and he realized she was trying to keep from laughing.

"Oh, suck it up, Santini. Not like you have anything here that any of us haven't seen before," MJ said, standing and stretching her back.

"Are you okay?" Jules asked her, immediately concern darkening her eyes.

"We're fine. I've got to get up and move every now and then. Plus, of course, the bathroom is my best friend lately. After all that laughing, I'm lucky I haven't already embarrassed myself."

Jules didn't look convinced but MJ ignored the concerned look. "Vince, help me down the hall."

He knew that tone. He had heard it every day of his life. There was a reason Leo fell so hard for MJ. She had the temperament of their mother.

"Sure."

"I'll be right back for more stories. I need some ammunition because apparently those idiot brothers of mine have been telling Leo things."

He walked down the hall with her feeling kind of odd. MJ didn't need any more help than a bulldozer needed with a molehill. When they were out of earshot, MJ said, "Be nice to Jules. She hasn't had a good time of it."

"What's that supposed to mean?" he asked. There was more than a little heat in his voice and he realized he was still upset with her rejection years ago.

MJ stopped in front of the bathroom. "Listen, Vince, I know y'all are kind of hardheaded but you can learn. That marriage of hers wasn't good, and I've never seen a woman jump so easily that didn't have memories of a bad relationship."

He frowned. "She's the one who sought the divorce."

And that had been hard for him to accept. She had rejected him just a few years earlier, then she divorced Mike. Before Vince had made it back from his deployment, Mike was dead.

"There are always two sides to every story. Just remember that. Now, I really need to get in here before I embarrass myself.

Vince didn't say anything as he watched the bathroom door close. It wasn't like MJ knew what went on all those years earlier, and she really had no idea about what went on in Jules' marriage.

"You're gonna have to leave, Vince. I can't pee with you standing guard at the door."

He smiled and turned to walk back down the hall. He ran into Leo. "Where's Maryanne?"

"She's in the bathroom."

He nodded. "I think Jules is ready to go. I can take her home if you don't want to."

Great, now his brothers were treating him like he was some kind of coward. If Jules could take it, Vince could.

"No. I'll take her back. I didn't think she'd want to go so soon."

Leo shrugged. "I think she wants to get back to Rufus. Kind of insistent on it."

"Okay. When you heading back to Texas?"

"Day after tomorrow."

"Sounds good."

But he still didn't leave. He hated to admit it but he was a little unnerved about spending forty minutes in the car alone with Jules. Not scared. Just...uncomfortable.

"Vince?"

Leo was frowning at him.

"I'll be back tomorrow morning."

Then he walked down the hall. The noise level rose as he neared the living room.

"Gianni Santini put me down," Jules said between squeals.

"You said I couldn't pick you up, Jules. I had to prove you wrong."

Then, he heard that laugh again. It had always been one of his favorite sounds in the world. She had never been a girl who held back her happiness. She belted it out for everyone in the world to share.

"Gee, put her down now," his mother ordered. "You're going to break something. I swear you boys will never grow up." His mother said with the usual combination of disgust and love.

He did and Jules was laughing when she looked at Vince. His heart just about stopped right there and then. Then it sunk when her smile faded when she noticed him watching her.

"Leo said you wanted to go home."

"Yeah. I don't like leaving Rufus long."

He nodded but said nothing else. "Let me grab my keys and my coat."

With that he hurried to the kitchen to get the hell out of the house. The sooner he got her home and out of his vicinity, he'd breathe easier.

* * * *

The ride home was uneventful, but almost silent. It was a bit nerve racking after being in the Santini household. Although she'd come from a pretty quiet family, she always enjoyed the fun at the Santinis. Kids congregated there after school and weekends because there was always a good time.

As the silence grew, her skin started to itch. From the inside out. Silence was always one of Mike's worst weapons against her and he had used it many times.

"How do you like teaching?" she asked.

"I like it. It's different. Plus, it keeps me from being deployed. With all these weddings and babies, I'd miss out on a lot of it."

She nodded but said nothing as he pulled into her driveway. "Well, thanks for the ride. I could have done it, but your mom is always looking out for me."

He glanced at her. "I was surprised that you didn't move to California."

She shrugged. "That's home for them. Not me." There were too many memories there for her. It had been where she had gone to recover...to forget even for a little while.

"Must be hard for them to have their only child across the country from them."

She glanced at him wondering at the tone. It was almost as if he was accusing of her of something.

"Yeah, but they understood."

He nodded but said nothing else.

"Okay, well thanks again."

Before she could open the door, he asked, "Why did you do it?"

She glanced back him. "Do it? I thought I explained."

"No. Why did you marry Mike and then just divorce him a few years later?"

She sighed. She had waited for this conversation for years, but it had never come. Until now.

"There are things about my marriage to Mike well…it just wasn't good."

"Wasn't good?"

She didn't want to have this conversation. Mike had been a bastard. His dishonorable discharge had turned him into a stranger. She might not love him, but she did have feelings for Vincente still and she knew he had loved Mike like a brother.

"It just wasn't good after he got out of the Marines. He changed and it ruined our marriage."

He nodded. "He never told me why he got out of the military."

She sighed. She didn't want to fight about it, or even tell him horrible things about a man he had treated as one of his own brothers. But, she couldn't lie.

"Mike didn't get out. He got kicked out."

Vince's head whipped around and she was caught in that ice blue gaze of his. "What do you mean? The only hint he gave me was that you didn't like being a Marine wife."

How like Mike to blame her. It was her fault he'd been kicked out. It was her fault he hit her. It was his fault he'd been arrested for the last assault. The man never accepted he was a world-class fuck up.

"No. He was dishonorably discharged. If you don't believe me, look it up. I really need to get in. Rufus has probably made it to the front door by now."

He smiled. "Okay. Night, Jules."

"Night, Vince."

Jules slipped out of the car, ready to get away from the questions. She wouldn't lie to Vince, but she didn't want to be the one to tell him about Mike. She opened the door and found Rufus waiting for her. She led him to the backyard, let him do his business and hurried to get ready for bed.

All the while she pushed the thoughts of Vince to the back of her mind. She didn't have time for romantic fantasies about a man who apparently despised her.

She'd just pulled on her nightshirt when the front doorbell rang. She frowned as she walked to the front door. When she peered through the peephole, she frowned again. It was Vince.

She opened the door. "Vince?"

He didn't say anything. He just kept staring at her.

"Vince?" she asked worried now.

"Oh, sorry, you forgot your jacket in my car."

He held it out and she took it.

"I'm sorry if I was rude in the car. I realized that I didn't know everything... well, I have no idea what Mike did after you got married. I was always worried."

"Worried?"

"I...I thought you might have told him."

For half a second, she didn't know what he was talking about. Then, it hit her. The kiss.

"No. No, I didn't see a reason to."

And seeing what Mike turned into, that could have been another weapon he would have used against her.

"Oh."

Then nothing. He kept staring at her as if she were...well, like she was naked. Instead of being uncomfortable, it made her hot.

"Was there anything else?"

Something changed in his eyes that made her want to take a step back, but before she could he answered.

"Yeah."

Then, he grabbed her and slammed his mouth down hers.

CHAPTER FOUR

Years after that first kiss, Vince felt himself falling again. Jules hesitated, not responding right away. He dragged his tongue over her lips and she opened them. He delved inside and lost himself.

She tasted the same, but different. He slanted his mouth over hers, deepening the kiss. She moaned against his mouth and he wanted to take her right there. At that moment, he wanted her in bed, beneath him, moaning his name.

But in the next instant, he felt a hand grab him by the collar and pull him back. He turned around, his arm raised to elbow the attacker. The man fell down, his head hitting the pavement hard. Jules made a desperate sound behind him, but he said nothing and stepped in front of her to face the intruder.

"Fuck," the man said. The voice was vaguely familiar as was the dark hair, strong jaw and the mean blue eyes.

"Jesse?"

He glanced up at Vince then groaned. "Shit, a Santini."

Vince looked down at MJ's oldest brother wondering just what sweet hell he had dropped into. There was no way he would keep his damned trap shut about this. He held out his hand and Vince helped him up. "What the hell are you doing?"

Jules stepped around him. "Did Vince hurt you, Jesse?"

Jesse's frown softened. "Hey, Jules. I'm sorry, I thought…well, I thought it was something different."

"So you two know each other?" Vince asked.

She didn't say anything for a second or two, but then said. "Yeah. Jesse worked with Mike."

He looked between the two of them, trying to figure out the relationship. Was this the man Mike had claimed she was interested in? But that would make no sense at all. Mike had said she wanted him out of the military and the one thing Jesse Johnson was not going to do was get out of the military.

Apparently, Jules had enough of the stare down. She made an exasperated sound before saying, "Oh, come in the house you two. It's silly to be standing out here."

They both stepped through the door after her. Vince picked up the jacket she had dropped on the floor and handed it to her. He realized she was standing in full view of Jesse with only a nightshirt on.

"You might want to get a robe," Vince said.

She frowned then looked down at what she was wearing. Her face turned pink and she said, "Be right back."

The only sound in the living room was the sound of the clock ticking. Vince looked around the room and found so much of Jules there. He recognized her love of soft colors and cool tones, along with some of the memories of her Marine brat childhood. German knickknacks littered most surfaces. Family pictures decorated the walls.

When she returned, Vince could tell she was embarrassed. He gave Jesse a hard look. The major just returned his look with a bland one of his own. Then, slowly, Jesse's lips curved and an evil light filled his gaze.

Shit. MJ would hear about this and damn sure his brothers would hear after that.

"So, I understand you're coming to brunch tomorrow," Jesse said, sitting down at the breakfast bar as if he was making himself at home. "I didn't know you knew Jules."

"We went to school together at Quantico."

"Oh." Jules said looking at Jesse. "You're related to the Santinis?"

When Jesse looked at her, his expression softened. Vince couldn't put his finger on it, but there was something there. It was enough to have his irritation bubbling. He'd never been so damned possessive of a woman, especially one that had never been his to begin with.

"I guess you met MJ tonight. She's my sister."

She blinked as she study Jesse, then Vince saw recognition light her eyes. "Oh. Yeah, now I can see it. I didn't make the connection."

"Mom was kind of disappointed you and the General couldn't make it tonight," Vince said. MJ and Jesse's father was a three-star at the Pentagon, so most nights he was on call and at work.

"Not sure what dad had going on, but I wasn't supposed to be in until late tonight. I got an earlier flight so I would make sure not to miss MJ."

He might be pissed at Leo's brother-in-law, but he was family in a round about way. "She's huge."

Jules gasped. "Vicente Santini, that's not nice."

Jesse ignored Jules. "From the pic I just saw, it might not be nice, but it's pretty true. I can't believe they're having twins."

Vince laughed. "It's going to be so interesting with a set of Santini twins running around."

"Yeah, between her and Leo, those kids are going to be a handful."

Then silence.

"Was there something you wanted, Jesse?"

He shook his head. "No. Just stopped by to check on you."

"She's fine."

Jesse shook his head and smiled. "Settle down, Santini. I get the hint. I'll see you tomorrow."

He stood and gave Jules a kiss on the cheek. Something dark slid through Vince blood and he had to bite back a growl. Jules gave him a narrowed look, but he said nothing.

When she shut the door, she turned to face him. "Really, Vince. You should be nicer to Jesse."

"He's an officer and you call him by his first name."

Mike had been enlisted and while not everyone went by the rules, Vince knew Jesse well enough to know he would expect a proper address from an enlisted wife. It was…odd.

"I'm not in the military. And, I know I have a lot of customers are in the military and I call many of them by their first names. I call you by your first name."

"I've known you forever."

She cocked her head to the side. "Not really."

"What's that supposed to mean?"

"Once Mike and I got married, you disappeared."

"I didn't disappear."

She shrugged.

"What do you mean by *that?*" he asked, getting aggravated now.

She threaded her fingers through her hair. It was done in agitation, but he found it mesmerizing. And arousing. He wanted to do the same, but she didn't look like she would welcome that right now.

"Oh, good lord, Vince, could you just go?"

"No. I think we need to talk about what happened."

"That you acted like an ass in front of Jesse?"

"Before that." Then he realized what she said. "Wait, I didn't act like an ass."

"You did. And there's nothing to discuss."

"Really?" He crossed his arms.

"Yes. It was just a kiss. No biggie."

He let one eyebrow rise. "I think we were five minutes from you being naked."

"And I think you are overestimating my attraction to you."

"Why don't we test that theory," he said and started walking toward her.

Panic filled her face and he stopped. This wasn't something normal, there was another level to the expression on her face that seemed…over the top.

"Look, Vince, I think you should go."

"I'll go, but we are going to talk about this."

"Why do we need to talk about it? Let's just let it go, pretend it never happened. Like you have for over fifteen years."

"What?" It was a stupid question for him to ask because he knew. When she had told him she had no choice than to marry Mike, he had walked away.

"I think it's best to forget it again."

Forget it? Is that what she did? She had no idea that he had compared every woman to her. They had never made love, but he remembered the feel of her mouth beneath his, the way she clutched at the lapels of his tux, and the scent of jasmine that surrounded them.

He took a step closer until he was only a few inches away. He could smell it now, that intoxicating scent. It was on her skin. He could imagine lying in bed, having it on his sheets.

He gently cupped her face. "I never forgot. I wanted to, but I never could do it. Now…I refuse. I won't push you tonight, but I don't plan on ignoring this. I've always wanted you, from the moment you hit me with that damned locker door."

He settled his free hand on the door behind her and leaned closer. Without closing his eyes, he brushed his mouth gently over hers. He watched the flare of arousal darken her eyes before her eyelids slowly shut. He lost himself in her.

Vince slipped his tongue inside her mouth and drew her closer. She shuddered against him. He slipped the tie of her robe loose and slid his hand up to her breast. He brushed his thumb over her nipple and it hardened. He deepened the kiss and pressed against her. Vince knew without a doubt that she could feel his arousal. She moaned against his tongue and he felt his control slipping. He wanted—needed—her now. Right now. But he knew if he pushed her tonight, it wouldn't be good. With regret, he pulled back.

"I have to go now, or I won't make it out the door. I just want you to know that I will be back."

She opened her mouth, probably to argue, but he settled his fingers on her mouth.

"No. Don't. I'll give you time, Jules, but I won't give up."

She sighed and nodded. He dropped his hand.

"Why not come to brunch tomorrow?"

She shook her head. "No. Tomorrow will be busy at work. With spring approaching, its kind of crazy at the shop."

He nodded. They both needed space. "Okay. How about dinner Monday night?"

She chuckled. "Not waiting this time, Santini?"

He gave her a quick hard kiss. "Nope. So how about it?"

She sighed. "Can you call me tomorrow and get my answer?"

"Playing games?" he asked.

Jules shook her head. "No. I want to make sure I don't let my hormones get in the way."

"Okay." He kissed her nose. "Sleep tight, Jules."

She slipped out of the way and opened the door.

"Night, Vince."

It took all of his control to walk out of that door. He waited until she closed it and locked it before walking down the steps to his car.

He was on his way home when he realized what he'd just started. When it came to Jules, he never seemed to have any control. A guy just didn't kiss his best friend's fiancé the morning of their wedding if he had control.

He sighed as he turned onto Highway 1. Vince knew that if he started something up with Jules it wasn't an affair. She was the one woman he had always loved and getting tangled up with her would be serious. Get married and have kids kind of serious.

Vince waited for the panic to set in. It always hit him about this time when he thought of marriage, but it didn't. Instead, a feeling of rightness settled in his gut. He wanted Jules. He wanted her forever.

He sighed. Now, he had to figure out a way to convince Jules.

CHAPTER FIVE

Jules was helping Mrs. Markinson pick out some annual flowers when she felt the fine hairs stir on the back of her neck. She looked out over the hundreds of flowers filling the greenhouse and saw Vince Santini pretending to shop. She wanted to be irritated because she wasn't too sure how she felt about the kiss or last night. She didn't like pushy men, and that was one thing Vince was. Well, he was in a way. When they'd been in high school, he'd been a bit of a nerdy jock...and so sweet.

"Jules, dear, did you hear me? I said, I'll take another flat of marigolds."

She shook herself back to the present. "Of course, I'm sorry, Mrs. Markinson."

She helped the retired schoolteacher to the check out then went in search of Vince. She found him in the fountains. God, why was he here? He had apparently stopped by the shop without going home after brunch. He was wearing a polo shirt tucked into a pair of casual dress pants.

He must have felt her watching him because he asked, "Why would someone want one of these in their yard?"

"It brings birds to the yard that will eat bugs, adds another level of decoration to your garden, and flowing water helps reduce outside noise."

He looked at her then back at the fountain. "No, why would someone want a naked little boy in their yard?"

She looked at the fountain and laughed. It was one of the Cupid fountains. "That's Cupid. He's not a little boy. Considering the stories your mother has told me about you, you should not be judgmental. Oh, and don't forget *The River Incident.*"

He looked out of the side of his eye at her. "I can't believe you told the women that story."

She raised one eyebrow and crossed her arms. "The women?"

"They're now a group. A scary group."

She laughed. "Your father always said there was nothing that scared a Santini man more than his woman."

"I hope you didn't tell Mom that."

"No. What are you doing here?"

He shoved his hands in his pockets. "I was driving by and thought I would stop."

"Ah." She looked at the fountain again. "So, you're not here to buy things for your garden. Your mother said it needed a lot of work."

He rolled his eyes. "That woman. She's been after me since I moved in last fall."

"It will add value to your house."

He smiled. "Indeed?"

"Yes. If you're just here to flirt with me, I don't have time. Plus, you kind of suck at it. I mean, asking me about fountains? Really, I expected more out of a Santini."

At first, he looked stunned, then slowly, his mouth curved.

Oh, my. Her heart did a little jig and she had to draw in a deep breath to calm it.

"Is that so?"

"Yes."

"So what do you expect me to do about it?" he asked.

His voice had deepened and brushed over her nerve endings. Heat threaded through her blood. Oh, this was not good. He was just smiling at her and she was losing control. The man was lethal to a girl's libido.

"Well," she said inching closer. "What do you want?"

For a second, he only stared at her. Then he swallowed.

"What do you mean?" he asked, his voice a little deeper, and God, it sounded good. She could just imagine hearing him whisper in her ear as he woke her up in the morning.

Damn.

"Well, do you want something that lasts just a little while or are you looking for something longer?"

His eyes widened and then darkened. "Huh?"

She crossed her arms. "Do you want annuals or perennials?"

For a moment or two, he said nothing. Then, he threw back his head and laughed.

"I forgot what a warped sense of humor you have."

And Vince had always appreciated it. Mike never had. Now that she looked back, she realized it was probably because Mike didn't get her jokes. Vince always did.

"Hey, it's hard not to be warped when you're raised in the military, right?"

He continued to smile at her and she felt her heart bump up against her chest. Oh, lordy, not good.

"Maybe you should come by and look at the mess of a yard I have, then you can help me pick what I need."

"You're serious?" she asked.

"Yeah. Mom's right but I don't know where to start and I trust you not to make it look too flowery."

She laughed. "Trust a Santini to make that kind of statement."

"What?"

"You're asking me to come by and decide on flowers, but don't want it to be too flowery."

"You still didn't answer my question."

She sighed. "Okay. When do you want me to come over?"

"How about tonight?"

"Hmmm. I have a lot—"

"I can close up," Angela said from behind her. She looked back over her shoulder at the younger woman.

"See," he said with a smile. "I'm on my bike if you want a ride."

She knew she shouldn't. Riding on the back of a bike was not something Jules Andrews did. Not anymore. And she had Rufus at the shop with her today.

"No. I need about thirty minutes to close out some things on the computer."

He looked like he wanted to argue, but he apparently accepted her excuse. "Okay. You know where I live?"

"Yeah, your mother told me."

"Of course she did. I'll see you in a few."

He turned and walked out.

"Lord love a duck, that is one fine man. And seriously, I couldn't let you ignore an invitation like that."

"I should though. Santinis are never easy."

"Who wants easy when they can have a Santini?" She shook her head. "Wait, there are more?"

"All taken, sorry."

Angela sighed. "And you have the last one in here drooling all over you."

"He was not drooling on me."

"He was. He watched you for awhile with Mrs. Markinson."

She didn't know how she felt about that. "Either way, not really sure I'm going to do anything about it."

She opened her mouth to argue, but Jules stopped her. "Don't. You know I have my reasons."

She hadn't told Angela about her marriage. Jules assumed that she picked up on things, but she didn't really tell anyone about it. Her therapist said it wasn't healthy, but Jules figured that she could only take one step at a time.

"Yeah, but you need to get out there. Have some fun. That Santini dude looks like he would be a lot of fun."

"That might be the problem," she said more for herself than for Angela. There was no reason to question her decisions right now. She had said she would go out to his house so she would. "Okay, I'm going to shut down my computer and head out."

"Quit making it sound like a death sentence. Of course, if there was a way to die I wouldn't mind dying in bed with a man like that."

"Good lord. Does your mother know you talk like this?"

"Where do you think I learned to talk like I do? And, there's Rick."

"What's your brother doing here?"

"When Major Hunkmeister came in, I called him. I had a feeling I was going to close up alone, so I told him he had to come up here."

"Only you would order a Marine around."

She laughed. "Of course. Now, go."

Jules shook her head. "Okay."

As Jules shut down her computer, she formulated a plan. Taking Rufus worked because he could be a buffer. He wasn't enamored with men to begin with. In fact, the first few times Jesse came over, he peed on his shoes. So, he might ward off Vince at least for tonight. Jules knew he wanted more, wanted to at least take her to bed. If she had any doubts, that kiss last night had blown those to bits. She closed her eyes as she thought about the way it felt to have his mouth on hers again.

He had been a good kisser years ago, but now…he knocked her socks off. Okay not her socks, but she wasn't that far from offering her body up in exchange for more kisses like that one.

Sadly, sex wasn't something she had ever really enjoyed. She had only been with one man and from her point of view, Mike had been a very selfish lover. She had thought it would get better with time, but Mike…well, he didn't get any better.

Sighing she looked down at Rufus. "I have a feeling that Vince wouldn't be the same…but he might just be worse."

She was very nearly in love with the man. She had been years ago but thought him out of her league. Now, though, he was determined to get her in his bed.

She knew Santini men and their belief in home and family. It wasn't in her to get serious about a man again and it would kill her when he walked away.

She pushed that thought to the back of her mind. As she walked Rufus out to her car, she convinced herself she was just going to talk to him about those flowers and nothing else.

And if anyone believed that, she had some oceanfront property in Arizona to sell to them.

* * * *

Vince kept it light as they talked about his shrubs. Jules was very knowledgeable but he expected nothing less. She had always been a go-getter in high school. But, it was kind of hard to be too serious with her. The distressed noise she made when she saw his shrubs and flowerbed was well, cute. He couldn't think of another word. Okay, sexy. Good lord, the woman was sexy. Crap, she was asking him a question.

"What?"

"I asked how long have you ignored this?"

The accusatory tone in her voice surprised him.

"I moved in this fall. There wasn't much I could do."

She snorted and crossed her arms. Damn, he just wanted to eat her up. Now that he had decided to go after her, he couldn't think of anything else. He wanted to have her in his bed. And his shower. And damn, he would love to take her in every room of the house.

"Santini if you aren't going to pay attention to me, I'm leaving."

"Sorry. I was thinking about something else."

She gave him a look that told him she wasn't buying that. "There is always something you can be doing in the garden. All year."

Vince smiled. He had her now. When Jules was passionate about something, there was no stopping her. She had been so involved in high school. Drama, choir, and student council had filled her time. Now, all he had to do was get her passionate about him and everything would work out fine.

"That's why I need your help. I've never owned a home before. Actually, I've only lived in apartments until now."

"Why would you do that?" she asked, frowning at him.

"Special forces don't spend a lot of time at home. It was usually safer to have an apartment than a house sitting there for weeks or months at a time without an occupant. But, when I got this assignment, I decided to take the plunge. Truth is, I'll probably end up retiring here some day."

"Hmm." He could see she was working things out in her head. Probably calculating how much money she was going to charge him. He didn't care. If it meant she was going to be at his house on a regular basis that was fine by him. Sad to admit, but true.

"Why don't we have something to drink and you can tell me what I need to do?"

She gave him a skeptical look but she nodded. He held the door open for her, then shut it behind her. Rufus gave a huff, and laid his head back down. He'd wondered when she showed up at his house with her dog, but the animal just made himself at home.

"I can't believe he's so calm," Jules said.

"What do you mean?"

"He doesn't like change and he really doesn't like men."

He glanced at her. "Is that why you brought him?"

Her face flushed. "Not really. He was mad I left him for so long yesterday, so I brought him to the shop with me. He was very agitated last night."

Vince looked at the old dog that was already snoring then looked back at Jules. "He has the energy to get agitated?"

"He does. I swear. He has a particular distaste for Jesse."

He smiled. "I might have to buy that dog a steak."

She rolled her eyes. "Where is this drink you promised?"

He nodded and headed to the kitchen. The sound of the wooden floor beneath is feet was one of Vince's favorite sounds. He could have bought a newer house, but he wanted something old, something he could put his own stamp on.

"Wow," she said walking into the kitchen. He couldn't help but feel a small sense of pride. He'd worked hard at getting the kitchen redone the last three months.

"Thanks."

"You did this?"

"Some of it. I had to hire contractors for most of the wiring and plumbing. If you think the garden is a mess, you should have seen this."

"It's nice. Not too big, but I love the granite countertops. Oh and a gas stove. I have an electric. It sucks."

"So, want a beer."

She shook her head. "No. I have to drive and I'm not much of a drinker. I'll take some ice water though."

As he went about getting her drink, she walked around the kitchen. He had started on the kitchen first because to him, it was the heart of the house. Plus, he loved to cook.

He handed her the glass of water then got one of his own. He watched her while she drank, unable to do anything else. She looked good in his kitchen, in his house. It was like it was made for her. She had a love of antiques and history. The house was built at the turn of the last century with a large wrap around porch. It was one of her real loves.

They were the same age, but he felt older, and he knew he looked older. Jules looked the same. That alabaster skin was as sooth as it was in high school. And he adored those freckles across the bridge of her nose.

"Stop."

He blinked. "What?"

"Stop staring at me like that."

"Like what?"

"Like you're the big bad wolf and I'm your next meal."

The minute she said it, the air between them grew heavy. He did want to eat her up. Damn, if she didn't get that right. He set his drink down on the island and walked toward her.

"Now, Vince…"

He didn't give her time to finish. He grabbed her glass and set it down, then grabbed her.

"This isn't smart," she said, but she was breathless as he pressed his body into hers.

"Nope, but it feels good."

She hesitated for a second, and for that small amount of time, he was sure she would say no. Then, her resistance faded and she slipped her arms over his shoulders.

"You're right, Vince. It does."

His arousal soared, his head spun. He bent his head.

"And it's about to feel whole lot better."

He bent his head, crushing his mouth against hers, determined to prove it.

CHAPTER SIX

Vince lifted her off her feet and into his arms as he continued to kiss her. Her world spun as he walked down the hall.

"Wait," she said, though it sounded weak even to her. Maybe that was because she was weak.

He stopped at the entrance to his bedroom. "What? Are you going to tell me no now? You want me. I want you. Don't play games. If you don't want to do this, I can still walk away right now."

Jules knew she should say no. She had never been one for casual affairs, and there was nothing casual about Vince Santini. She couldn't remember wanting something this badly in her life. So, for once in her life, instead of doing what she knew she should, Jules did the opposite.

"Yes. I want this as much as you do. Just know…"

How did you tell someone you weren't any good in bed? It was something that had been a problem in her marriage. It was one of the things that Mike had thrown in her face when she caught him cheating. She was lacking in bed so he had to go elsewhere. It had hurt at the time, and she had believed him.

Since he'd been her only lover, she didn't have any other opinions on the matter.

He kissed her then, slowly, sweetly. It wasn't as carnal as his other kisses, but it moved her even more. When he pulled back her body was humming and her heart was melting.

"Don't worry about anything, Jules," he said walking into the bedroom and laying her on the massive California king bed. "You let me worry about it and you just enjoy."

She sighed as he covered her body with his. He kissed her, not on the mouth, but on her neck. It sent a wave of heat rushing over her flesh. He tugged on her earlobe. She shivered.

"Ahh, you like that?"

She couldn't speak because he was already slipping his hand under her t-shirt and cupping her breast. She'd always felt she was lacking in that department, as did Mike.

She banished that thought. She would not let bad memories cloud this one. Mike was a bastard and this...this was special. Instead, she did just as Vince told her to do and enjoyed.

He worked her shirt up and off her and easily undid her bra with one hand.

"Wow," she said impressed.

He smiled down at her and the air backed up in her lungs. He looked so young, so carefree, so like the boy she knew all those years ago.

"Hey, I've gotta have some moves. I *am* a Santini."

She started to chuckle, then gasped as he pulled her bra away and took a nipple into his mouth. Slowly, he teased her with his mouth, his hands...there wasn't anywhere he didn't touch her. Before she realized it, she was naked.

He worked his way down her body between her legs. She opened her mouth to say something—she didn't remember what—but he set his mouth on her sex. The feel of his wicked mouth on her wiped out any and all thoughts. Her need grew as he slipped his tongue inside her. She went from hot to screaming in just a minute. Waves of ecstasy pummeled at her as he slid his hands beneath her ass and continued his assault on her.

Just as the first orgasm was fading another hit her, this time more intense. She screamed his name as she came this time, shuddering against his mouth. Little bursts of pleasure sparked through her as he slipped out of bed. By the time she opened her eyes he was already gloriously naked.

Good God. The man was all sinewy muscle and beautiful flesh. She sat up, resting her weight on her elbows.

"I take that expression as a good sign," he said.

She glanced up at him. Joking in bed wasn't something she was used to, but apparently Vince was. He was grinning down at her and she smiled.

"It is."

He grabbed a condom out of the bedside table drawer. He ripped open the foil package and pulled out the condom. She watched, mesmerized by his large hands rolling it down his penis.

She licked her lips.

"Lord, don't do that, Jules. I'll never last."

She glanced up at him.

"I've been waiting for this for a really long time. I'm riding a hair trigger right now. One little move from you and it's over."

Instead of being embarrassed by his frank talk, she felt powerful. She had never had a man say those kinds of things to her before. There was enough light to see the humor in his eyes and she smiled and held out her hand. He took it, joining her back on the bed.

He kneeled between her legs, and entered her swiftly. She was prepared but not for his size. It had been years since she'd had sex and she was just not ready for the intrusion.

"I'm sorry, Jules." Apparently picking up on her discomfort, he gave her a long, wet kiss before he started moving again. With each thrust, she felt more and more relaxed. Soon she was moving in rhythm with him. He still had his hand in hers as he bent down to kiss her.

"Come with me, Jules. Come."

He whispered the words against her mouth and she could do nothing more than follow his orders. The orgasm burst through her, pushing her to the limits. She bucked up against him as he thrust one last time, her name on his lips as he followed her into bliss.

* * * *

Vince wrapped an arm around Jules and pulled her close to him. It hadn't been anything like he expected. It had been better.

She sighed and lifted herself up. "I guess I should get ready to go."

"Why?"

"Well…I don't know why. Isn't that what people do?"

He frowned at her. "You don't have a reason to go home, do you? Rufus is here."

"I just thought that maybe this…"

She didn't continue and he realized she seriously wanted to leave. Or thought she should leave. He leaned over and turned on the light. She blinked and that's when he got a full view of her.

Damn.

All those dark red curls were a tangled mess dripping over her shoulders. Her lips were swollen from his kisses.

He was never going to get enough of her.

"Tell me why you think you should leave."

She shrugged and sat up pulling the sheet up to her chin, unfortunately. His fingers itched to yank it from her grasp but she looked too vulnerable. Now was not the time to insist on nudity. But, damn, he wanted to.

"I just never did this before. I don't know how to handle it."

"You've had sex before." He was starting to get irritated. It was stupid and completely irrational but he had been blown away from their lovemaking. The fact that she was trying to skip out on him bothered him.

"Yes. It's just that there's only been Mike."

That had his anger fizzling. "You've never been with another man? You've been divorced for years."

She pulled her knees up as if to protect herself. She didn't look like the savvy business owner at the moment. Instead, she looked like the girl he left all those years ago. It tugged at his heart.

"I wasn't really in the mood to date after the divorce, then, the business took up all my time. I don't know how to have a casual relationship like this. I was a virgin when I got married."

Which hit him. Mike had lied to him about that. He'd claimed they'd been having sex for years. Then, he realized what she said. He opened his mouth to tell her there was nothing casual about what they had but knew she would freak. Her unsteady gaze told him that she was ready to leave as fast as she could. She might have enjoyed herself, but their connection was still fragile. Vicente didn't want to do anything to scare her away.

"We do what we want. There are no rules."

Her shoulders relaxed and she gave him a shy smile. "Yeah?"

She was naïve in so many ways and he laid the blame at Mike's feet. Jules wasn't that experienced, but she had been married. She should know more about her power over men if she'd been married to the right man.

Now that she seemed relaxed, he tugged on the sheet. She gasped, and giggled when he pulled her over on top of him. "Yeah."

He pulled her bottom lip between his teeth and she shivered against him. He couldn't stop his reaction any more than he could quit loving her. When his cock hardened against her, her face turned red. He laughed.

"I'm sorry, Jules, but I hate to tell you I'm in a state of almost constant arousal around you. Now that I have every gorgeous inch of you against me while we're both naked, it's gonna happen."

She smiled. "So everything was okay?"

"Okay?"

She rolled her eyes. "I don't have much experience so I don't have any idea."

"First, for most guys it doesn't take much. Seriously. But, you blew my mind."

And she had. He'd been confused about her reactions but now they made sense. There was an element of...innocence and when she had her first orgasm, she'd sounded surprised. He wanted to know what went on in her life and her marriage but he couldn't ask her now. He didn't feel he had a right. Besides, he was feeling too good to bring it down with questions. So, he kept it light.

"Now, what about me?" he asked with a smile.

"What?"

"Well, I said nice things to you. Now tell me how wonderful I am."

Jules settled her forearms on his chest. "You were wonderful?"

She tilted her head to the side as if giving the question great thought. Her silky tresses slipped over his skin.

"What did you exactly do?"

He leaned up and kissed her then swatted her on the ass. "I rocked your world. Three times if I counted correctly."

"You kept count?"

"All men keep count. At least the good ones."

"What do the bad men do?"

"They don't rock your world three times."

Then, she laughed. That Jules laugh he loved so much. Over the years, he would hear a woman laughing that almost sounded like Jules and he would search for her. Didn't matter where he was, he would think she was there. And now, she was lying on top of him, naked, and laughing. A man couldn't ask for much more.

When she noticed him watching her, her smile faded. "What?"

"Nothing. I just always liked your laugh."

"Yeah?"

"Yeah."

She wiggled and he groaned. "I'm sorry."

"No, don't be." He shifted and entered her, then cursed. He opened the drawer to grab another condom. He rolled it on and said, "Take me in, Jules."

She sat up, and rose to her knees. Inch by inch, she sank down on his cock. He was ready to come just from the sight of that. He'd left the light on and he was glad for it now. Smooth skin, all that red hair, and lord, she had the prettiest breasts. Not overly large, but the perfect size for his hands...or his mouth. She lifted up and sank down again. The woman was going to be the death of him. She was so damned tight.

Soon though, she sped up her rhythm. Watching her take control of her pleasure was probably one of the sexiest things he'd ever seen.

His control was slipping, but he didn't want to take over. He wanted this to be hers to give. But it didn't mean he couldn't help her along. He slipped his hand between her legs and pressed on her clit. A couple of strokes and she came apart. She shuddered with her release, arching her back and allowing her head to fall back. A sensual moan escaped from her throat.

Erotic, amazing and beautiful. He couldn't resist joining her a moment later as she still shivered from her release.

Moments later she collapsed on top of him and he wrapped his arms around her.

It was then that he knew there was no doubt. She was the woman he wanted in his bed, by his side, for the rest of his life.

CHAPTER SEVEN

Vince was looking over the course directive for the next session when there was a knock at his door. He welcomed the interruption. He wasn't getting anything done thanks to daydreaming about Jules.

"Come."

The door opened to reveal Jesse Johnson. He was in civilian clothes.

"Are you busy?" he asked.

"Not really, come on in. Have a seat."

Before MJ and Leo married, he knew Jesse by reputation and now he knew him just a bit better. Of the three brothers, he was the hardest to read. He was the oldest and reminded Vince of the General more than the others. There was already talk that he would make a star early and from everything Vince had seen, he was definitely on track to do it.

Jesse settled in a seat in front of Vince's desk. "I guess you're wondering what I'm doing here."

Vince nodded trying not to reveal his irritation. If the man thought he could warn him away from Jules, he better think twice. After the night he'd just had with her, he refused to let anyone get in the way, even if he was family in a round about way.

"I sort of feel responsible for Jules. I was the one who started the paperwork to kick Mike out of the service."

"He said he decided to get out."

Jesse shook his head. "No. He was lucky he lasted as long as he did. He had a lot of problems from the very first. He barely made it out of basic."

Vince didn't know what to say to that. They hadn't really talked after the wedding. Truth was, he dreaded each call. He didn't want to hear how happy Jules and Mike had been in their marriage. Vince wasn't too sure how he would have handled them having children.

And in that instant, he realized that's what he wanted. In his head, he had seen the two of them together, but now, he knew what he wanted for sure. He wanted that marriage, kids, the whole thing. And he only wanted it with Jules.

"Earth to Santini."

He shook his head and focused on Jesse. "So, you're saying he was a shit Marine."

Jesse shrugged. "I could handle it if he at least tried. He didn't though. He expected to succeed without trying."

The memories of high school came back to him: Mike quitting the basketball season, quitting his job, ditching school. Without the happy haze of high school friendship clouding his thought process, Vince realized his former friend hadn't been good at sticking it out.

"Yeah, he had a history of it."

Jesse nodded. "You know some guys. They're losers, can't get their shit together. They get in the military and it seems to all come together for them. Then they're the best in the unit. That didn't happen with Mike."

"So what happened?"

He shrugged. "Truthfully, he didn't give a fuck. As I said, he wanted the reward without even trying. Subsequently, when he failed, he blamed everyone else. Including Jules. And, well, I know after he got Article Fifteen, he just never recovered."

For a moment, he said nothing. "Are you telling me he was court martialed?"

He nodded looking confused. "Yeah. He'd had all kinds of issues. Insubordination, dereliction of duty. When he started drinking, he was lost to the Marines."

"He'd said he got out because of Jules."

And that had always bothered him. Not that he thought he had a chance with her, but the truth was, he had never met a woman more ready to be a Marine spouse than Jules was. She loved being a brat, loved the lifestyle. It had always niggled at him that Mike claimed she'd been a dismal failure. When she had told him Mike had been kicked out, it hadn't really registered. Mainly because he hated hearing anything about her time with Mike.

"Nope. In fact, he held it together longer thanks to her in my opinion. If you know Jules, you know that she's one for organizing anything and she did it for Mike, for a while at least. But, he started to resist. Then...the drinking and the women."

"Women?"

"Yeah, your friend was a real bastard. He couldn't keep it in his pants. I think that was what drove Jules completely away. She put up with a lot from the bastard, but when he started cheating on her...not to mention messing with their money, she walked away."

It was hard to think of Mike that way. Of course, Mike had had his faults just like anyone else. But these things...Vince would have never expected the cheating. Of course, he'd lied to him about sleeping with Jules when they were in high school, so now Vince wondered what else his friend lied about.

"I just wanted you to know there was a lot in their relationship and I want to make sure you don't hurt her. That's one woman who doesn't need any more pain."

"You aren't interested in her otherwise?"

Jesse shook his head. "Naw. I kind of see her as a sister. Of course, if Mike hadn't had that wreck, I probably would have killed him myself. Their marriage, in the end, was a living hell for Jules. There was more than one night I felt I failed protecting her."

At the moment he had much of the same feelings.

"And I'm assuming you're going out with her soon."

"In a way. We went out last night."

Which wasn't exactly a lie. He just didn't feel right outing their relationship in front of Jesse. Truth was that Vince wanted to keep it between them for the next little while. It was something he wanted to share with only her.

Jesse chuckled. "And here I thought you were committed to your title of Last Santini Standing."

He shrugged. "I guess we'll see."

He gave him a look that told Vince he didn't believe him.

"So, I take it you went out to see MJ again."

He smiled. Vince might not like the man sniffing around his business, but it was nice to see another military family as close as the Santinis, mainly because it prepared MJ for the intrusive life of a Santini.

"Lord, yeah. I think she's bigger today than she was last night."

"You didn't tell her that, did you?" Vince asked.

Jesse rolled his eyes. It was so like the same expression MJ had when she was irritated that Vince laughed.

"I'm not stupid." He sighed and stood. "I just wanted you to know there's nothing going on between Jules and me. And, know if you do anything to her, I will hunt you down and make you pay."

Vince studied him for a moment then nodded.

Once he was alone, Vince sat back and looked outside. He had been ready to live alone the rest of his life. He'd always thought that he'd never meet a woman like Jules. He didn't feel comfortable settling for someone who just didn't have his whole heart. It wasn't the Santini way. And, he couldn't do that to another woman.

She'd been back for a while and Vince knew that his mother had been spending time with her. He'd avoided the shop even though he drove by it at least once a week. Which did not make him a stalker. Really.

Okay, a little bit, but his mother had been so worried about her, Vince felt the need to make sure she was alright. Of course, he never stopped, but that didn't mean anything.

He scrubbed his face with both his hands. He had to ask Jules about her relationship, but he was worried about pushing her. Last night had been more than he ever expected. Waking up with her in his bed had been a memory he would never forget.

He needed to know what went on at some point, but he didn't want to lose her. Vince knew without a doubt, this was his last chance with her and he wasn't about to screw that up.

Now, if he could just remember that, he'd be fine.

* * * *

Jules was just stepping out of the shower when she heard the roar of a Harley. She dressed as fast as she could knowing that Vince would probably stop over. They hadn't made any plans, but she had a feeling he would want to stop by.

As she pulled her top on, she admitted that she had hoped he would stop by. Last night had proven that she wasn't a complete failure in the bedroom. And sadly, she had been daydreaming all day about another night with Vince. Being preoccupied with sex was something that she didn't have to deal with since her high school days.

Her doorbell rang and she rushed out, her hair still damp. She peeked out and saw Vince on her doorstep, a pizza box in his hands.

She opened the door smiling. "Hey, I was going to call you after I got out of the shower."

One eyebrow rose in typical Santini fashion. "Really? After? Why would you wait for that?"

For a second she didn't get his meaning, but it hit her and she felt her face heat. "Oh get in here."

He stepped through the door and Rufus came shuffling out. He gave a happy bark and moved over to Vince.

"I thought you said he didn't like men."

"He only likes you because you brought pizza. You know men just want to be fed."

He laughed and set the pizza on the table. He bent down and gave Rufus a scratch behind the ears. Vince straightened, grabbed her by the hand and in the next instant, he was kissing her breathless.

"I've been waiting to do that all day," he said giving her a little kiss on the nose.

"Yeah?" She couldn't stop the grin. Having someone preoccupied with her was a new feeling. "I had the same problem."

"Do you have any paper plates?" She nodded and retrieved them from the kitchen. When she returned, she found Vince pulling off a piece of his pizza slice and about to throw it to Rufus.

"Don't you even dare. That dog cannot handle pizza. Especially with pepperoni on it."

And then she realized it had pepperoni and mushrooms. Her favorite pizza. Well, half of it was. The other just had the pepperoni. She looked up at Vince.

"You remember my favorite pizza?"

He looked a little sheepish and nodded. How could she resist a man who remembered things like that? It was useless in her opinion.

"Why don't we eat this in the living room?"

He nodded and grabbed some napkins and followed her in. Rufus followed him as if he was his long lost father.

"You disgust me. I saved you, rescued you, and took care of you. And you abandon me for a man with pizza."

"Us guys have to stick together, right, Rufus? Even if she stole your manhood."

She chuckled. "That was gone before me."

"Jesse Johnson came by to my office today."

And just like that everything in her tensed. "Yeah?"

He nodded and played with the remote control trying to find something to watch. "He said that Mike was booted out."

She sighed. "He was. I told you that before."

Vince looked at her then, his gaze direct and his expression serious. "He said he was drinking and cheating on you."

She was going to have a talk with Jesse. A very loud talk with him. She knew he was just trying to look out for her, but this was stepping over the line.

Vince shook his head. "No, don't look like that. You have nothing to be ashamed of."

Jules set her pizza down. "I don't like talking about it."

"We don't have to. I just wanted you to know I knew about it. Of course, Mike was an asshole."

He took another bit and turned the channel to an old NCIS episode.

"You think your best friend was an asshole?"

He shook his head and swallowed. He faced her. "We weren't friends by then, Jules. You know that we drifted apart after your marriage. It started before that when he didn't make it into Annapolis and I did. You knew he blamed me for getting in."

She nodded remembering how bitter Mike had become. Even the mention of Vince's name would send him on a tirade about how the process was screwed up.

"Then, when you got married, it was just too hard. I couldn't see Mike with the woman I loved for the rest of my life. It had been bad enough in high school."

She blinked. "What did you say?"

"I love you, Jules. I don't see a reason to pretend I don't."

He took another bite of pizza and watched the show. He said it as if it was no big deal.

"Listen, Vince…"

He looked at her again. "I am not asking you to do anything about those feelings. I just thought I should tell you right off." He gave her a quick kiss. "So, are you an NCIS fan?"

She glanced at the TV then back at him. Suddenly, her heart felt lighter, her outlook cleared.

"Yeah. I have a bit of a crush on Gibbs."

He gave her a wink. "Of course you do. He's a Marine."

She laughed. "You are full of yourself."

"How can I not be? I have NCIS to watch, a pretty girl, pizza and an ugly dog. Pretty good night if you ask me."

She grabbed up her pizza and snuggled up against him. Vince was right. A pretty damned fine night.

CHAPTER EIGHT

A month later, Jules was still in a haze of happiness. There were moments she thought it was all a dream. She had never been this happy with anyone in her life.

"Why do I have to plant it?" Vince asked as she watched him pummel an impatient. They were in his backyard. Although there was still work to be done, the yard and flowerbeds were starting to look almost manageable. She had insisted that he help her with it because it had been fun to do. Until now. If he massacred any more flowers, she might have to hit him.

"Stop abusing the flower. And you have to do it because you'll value it more if you do it with your own hands."

He snorted and she had to fight a smile. He'd been bitching since she'd dragged him out into the backyard earlier. His idea had been to stay in bed and make love. Again. It had been tempting, but they needed to spend time out of bed. Although, now that she thought about it, she couldn't come up with a reason why.

"What's next?"

She glanced at the flower. It was barely alive, but at least he'd done the work. And he looked so damned hot doing it. He was wearing a pair of faded, holey jeans and no shirt. It was enough to make a girl lose her head.

"Jules?"

"Oh, sorry. They need water. Let me get the hose."

Not that they would survive his abuse, she thought, feeling safe to smile. She turned on the water and headed back to the flowerbed.

She had her head down and was messing with the nozzle. "What's wrong with this thing? You need a new one."

"I don't need a new one. This one works just fine."

He stepped in front of her and reached for the hose. She finally got it to work. The hard spray of water hit him smack in the chest. She didn't say anything for a moment or two. Then she started chuckling.

"I'm sorry."

He cocked his head to the side and frowned at her. "That's funny. You don't sound sorry."

The gleam in his eyes warned her he was after payback. She dropped the hose and ran, squealing. He chased her up the steps and into the house. She barely got in the door when he grabbed her. He slammed the door shut and crowded her up against it.

"Think you're funny, do you?"

She was giggling when she shook her head. "It was an accident."

"Yeah?"

She nodded, and another bubble of laughter escaped. He was frowning at her one instant, then the look changed. His eyes heated.

"Jules," he whispered. She barely heard it, but she felt it. He smoothed his hand over her face, brushing her hair out of her face. "I love you."

For him, it was that simple. He loved her and it was all he needed. In that instant she knew she didn't have to hide her feelings.

"I love you, Vince."

He crushed his mouth against hers. Saying the words freed her, and in that one moment, it was just the two of them. Vince pressed his body against hers and she felt his arousal. Her need soared.

"Now, I have to have you now, Jules."

The words thrilled her. The dark, dangerous voice had her head spinning.

I did this. That was all she could think. He tugged off her shirt and made a sound when he realized she hadn't worn a bra.

He said nothing as he tried to undo the snap on her jeans.

"Damn," he said, embarrassment coloring his voice.

"What?"

"My hands are shaking so bad, I can't do it."

She laughed and he looked up at. "Oh, you make me happy, Vince. I never thought I would inspire such lust in a man."

He smiled and she undid her jeans. Together they worked them down her legs. He didn't even do that much. He undid his pants then lifted her off the floor and thrust into her in one motion.

She gasped at the intrusion.

"Sorry, baby," he said, pressing his mouth against her throat.

Jules wrapped her legs around his waist. "Don't be."

He chuckled. "I should say I really am, but I'm not."

He started to move. Again and again, he thrust into her as he continued to kiss her throat. Power and need entwined within her, sent her body into overdrive. Every thought dissolved. It didn't take her long to reach orgasm. Vince thrust into her once more then groaned as he came.

Moments later, he said, "I'm sorry."

She cupped his face and looked at him. "Don't ever be sorry for doing that."

"I should have more control."

She shook her head. "I like it. No one has ever done things like that for me. It makes me feel wonderful."

Then, slowly, his lips curved. "Yeah?"

She nodded and kissed him. Then, he carried her into his bedroom, barely making it to the bed. He shucked off his jeans and crawled into bed beside her.

"I think I'm getting a handle on this gardening," he said yawning.

She chuckled.

"I'd say you were an expert."

She cuddled closer, happy to have a man she reduced to such animal instincts. It was definitely a banner day for her.

* * * *

Vince walked out of the bedroom the next morning, a stunned look on his face. "Jules, we didn't use a condom yesterday."

"Oh." It was all she could think of. "There's no worry. I'm on the pill."

"Ah." He kept staring at her. He was dressed for work, but he was going to be late if he kept standing there.

"You need to get going, yeah?"

He nodded. "Just so you know, if something happened, I'd insist on marriage."

Her heart almost stopped beating right then and there. Something close to fear gripped her. How did that happen so fast?

"Why would you do that?"

He blinked. "If you were pregnant, I would insist on it."

"I understood the statement. Why do we have to screw this up with marriage?"

"Where did you think this was going?" he asked.

"Not to marriage. I will not marry again." Now panic has set in. She had to fight to breathe evenly.

"Jules, I would never cheat on you like Mike. You know that. I love you."

Oh, damn, just hearing those words were the sweetest joy. It was also the worst temptation. She wanted to say yes. What woman wouldn't want to marry a god like Vince who said sweet things to her? She'd never known someone who could engage her on so many levels.

She just couldn't. Not again. "I do. I trust you Vince or I never would have gone to bed with you. You're the most trustworthy man I know. I just can't get married again."

Just saying the words had her head pounding. *Married.* Getting married just screwed everything up.

He frowned. "What are you not telling me?"

She looked at him then, and realized if she loved him like she said she did, she had to tell him the truth. She didn't want to tell the story. Her parents knew.

Jesse knew…and her therapist. Otherwise, she hadn't told anyone else. But this man who had made her feel so loved and wanted deserved the truth.

"Cheating wasn't the only thing Mike was good at." She sighed. "The first time he hit me was after he came home pretty drunk."

"He hit you?" he asked.

She nodded. "I let it go that first time. He'd never been violent with me."

"Never? He just hit you out of the blue?"

When she studied him, she realized Vince believed her. It took every ounce of courage she had in her to tell him. There would be no reconciling the stories she told him with the Mike. She understood just what she was doing. She had never gotten the chance to stand up to Mike and it still pissed her off.

"Yes. Of course, after a lot of therapy, I realized that Mike had been abusive in other ways. He didn't have to hit me to hurt me. He was a master at drawing blood with just his words."

Vince nodded. "Mike always did have a nasty temper and he liked to mouth off a lot. It was one of the things…"

"I know. You two were friends, but I know that you kept him in line a lot. The truth was he wouldn't have gotten anywhere without you in high school. You don't think I didn't know he had issues with his temper. When he got mad, he got mean."

And those memories would haunt her forever. Why didn't she see it? Why didn't she just walk away before they got married?

Because she had loved him and believed that he would grow out of it.

"What did you do after he hit you?"

She shrugged and looked out the window. "He apologized the next morning. And it didn't happen again for a few months. That honeymoon period they all talk about. It's just like they say. Brought me home flowers—which I ended up paying for. I look back now and wonder just how lost I was to accept that." She looked at Vince. "I must have been a sorry excuse of a woman to expect so little from the man I married."

She drew in a breath and let it out slowly. Her therapist had warned her about negative thoughts.

"But it happened again?" Vince asked softly.

She looked at him. He'd sat down at the table. He was so good, so...strong. Just thinking about his feelings for her made her happy.

"He came home so drunk I was amazed he could walk upright. I'd had enough. Worse, he smelled like cheap perfume. We were overdrawn in the bank and he was out drinking and whoring. I told him I was sick of his cheating."

She remembered the way his face had changed from petulant drunkard to angry abuser in the flash of an eye. She hadn't been prepared for the punch to her face.

"What happened?"

She swallowed. "This time it wasn't a slap. It was a beating. It was...well bad. He passed out later and I ran. I didn't know where to go, so I called Jesse."

She closed her eyes trying to forget the feel of Mike's fist against her flesh, but to this day, she would wake up thinking he was there again.

"That's why he kept in touch. Didn't you have any girlfriends to call?"

She shook her head and looked at him. When she saw that he was blurry she realized she'd been crying. "I had no friends by that point. Mike was already out of the Marines. Court martialed. Most of the other wives wanted nothing to do with me. Well, a few of them had slept with Mike. Another thing I didn't realize at the time was how much he'd alienated my friends. I didn't talk to my parents for months at a time. He'd chipped away at my circle of friends and family. I thought I had no one."

"So, you went to Jesse."

She nodded. It was better to just have it out in the open. "So, Jesse took me to the hospital."

"You had to go to the hospital? It was that bad?"

"Yeah. I had a couple cracked ribs and he broke my nose. They also had to take pictures of the injuries for the police report. Mike was arrested and I filed for divorce. I moved out of our apartment into a little studio. I thought I had made strides. I thought I was safe. I didn't find out until too late that Mike made bail. The first thing he did was hunt me down."

She stopped and took a few moments to compose herself. Going over the story always sounded odd, like it had happened to someone else. Vince said nothing but he rubbed her back. It was the best thing he could do for her. The silent show of support gave her the strength to finish the story.

"He broke into my apartment. It was all a blur after that. They tell me he had beaten me pretty bad. Of course, I know he did because I saw myself in the mirror when I woke up."

"Woke up?" he asked when she didn't go on.

"Yeah. Mike apparently had his hands wrapped around my throat when a neighbor heard the noise and came to investigate. If the man hadn't shown up, I'm positive I'd be dead right now."

"What happened?"

"Mike got away. The neighbor, Craig, was more worried about me. He saved my life. The worst part was the police couldn't find him. He'd disappeared and they thought he might have headed to Canada. Two days later, Mike had that wreck."

Vince said nothing for a few moments. "Jules..."

She finally turned her head. The stunned expression wasn't one she expected. "I'm sorry I didn't tell you. I haven't told a lot of people. Even some of my closest friends have no idea."

He shook his head and brushed the backs of his fingers over her cheek. "Don't. Don't ever feel you have to explain your reasons to me. I wish you had told me sooner, called me. I can't believe you had to go through that alone."

"My parents were there the next morning. Jesse had called them. It was one of the worst things seeing my mother break down in tears when she saw my face."

"Hurting our moms is worse than stabbing our fathers."

She laughed.

"That's good to hear."

"I went home with them and spent the next few months trying to figure out what to do. That's when I decided to move back here. It was where I had always wanted to settle one day."

He smiled. "And you opened your shop."

She nodded.

"But I don't understand why you can't get married."

It was so hard to explain it to him. She didn't truly understand it herself. "I love you, Vince. I do. I don't say things like that I don't mean."

"I feel a *but* coming here."

"I just can't do marriage again. I made such a mess of it before."

"That was Mike."

She shook her head. "Mostly, I agree. But there were two of us in that marriage. I should have never put up with his cheating or drinking. I should have walked away earlier. I'm not giving him an excuse. Now, though, I don't know if I can deal with marriage."

"So you won't marry me?"

"Are you asking?" When he didn't answer she said, "I'm not sure if I can. I love you, Vince."

"You don't want to have children?" he asked, his voice hoarse with emotion.

It was on the tip of her tongue to tell him yes. She would happily have his children, but she pushed that thought down. She couldn't allow herself to fall into that trap again. She had wanted to be a mother so badly when she and Mike married. He'd put her off and, in the end, she was glad of it. She didn't want to have a child see what a monster his father had become.

"Who says you have to be married to have kids?"

He shook his head. "You're not like that, Jules."

"At one time, maybe not. I'm not that girl anymore, Vince. Don't look at me like I'm lying to you. Marriage…I just wasn't made for it. I can't do it again."

He cupped her face. "You're wrong, Jules. That girl is still in there. I feel her every time I kiss you, every time I take you to bed. She's there. You just have to stop being scared."

"I'm not scared. Not of you. God, Vince, you make me feel safe just by being in the same room." *And complete.* She had never felt like that with Mike and that was sad. "I just don't know if I can accept marriage again. I don't know if I'm made to be a Marine wife."

"His failures had nothing to do with you." She opened her mouth, but he shook his head. "No. Don't argue with me now. I love you. I fell in love with you when I was seventeen and didn't know what the hell love was. You've always been the woman for me. You just accept I'm here for keeps. You don't have to marry me, but you have to give me the right to at least try and change your mind."

"You won't push me?"

He smiled and her heart squeezed tight. "I didn't say that. But, I will give you space. You can trust me."

"I told you I trust you. I just…I don't trust myself."

He nodded and brushed his thumb across her bottom lip. "Think about it, Jules. I'm here for the long haul even if you don't ever want to get married. Don't push me away because of what that bastard did to you. We both deserve better. I'll wait even if the day never comes."

He kissed her, just a quick peck then he stepped back and left her alone. She sat down at her kitchen table. Suddenly, she was crying again. She laid her head on the table and decided for once to give into the pity.

CHAPTER NINE

"There you are, Jules," Joey said. Jules would have groaned if she were alone. Which made no sense because she couldn't be alone and be discovered by Joey.

She looked up and found Vince's mother standing in the doorway. Monday did suck. It sucked bad.

"Here I am. Dealing with the books. Again. I need to hire someone."

"I agree. I think I should send Stewart over to help. He has an MBA."

It took a second for her to link Stewart with Mr. Santini. It was just hard to see him as anything but Papa Santini.

"Yeah. But isn't he retired?"

"Yes, and I'm glad for it, but he needs something to keep him busy. It's that or I might have to stab him. We need our space every now and then."

Then silence.

"Was there something you needed?" she asked, afraid of the answer. She knew Vince wouldn't tell tales. But if Joey sensed someone had hurt her baby boy, she might be mean. Jules didn't have it in her to fight his mother right now.

"Do you mind if I sit down?"

She shook her head. Joey shut the office door and settled in the chair in front of the desk.

"I never asked you about your marriage."

And she had been grateful for that. "No. You haven't."

She held up her hand. "I would never invade your privacy. I just know it wasn't good."

She said nothing. Everyone knew something horrible had happened so there was no need to deny it.

"I know a survivor of violence when I see one. Before I met Stewart I dealt with it."

"You? I find that hard to believe." And it was. Joey was a strong confident woman. She was terrifying in a good way.

"I was. In high school, I was kind of an art nerd." She chuckled. "I still am. Anyway, right after high school, that summer, the captain of the football team asked me out. I was thrilled. I didn't date much in high school because boys, well they rarely looked at me. So here was the most popular guy in school asking me out. It was so stereotypical that it almost hurts to think how I believed he really liked me." She sighed and for once, Jules saw the vulnerable woman beneath that steel surface. "It was horrible. There wasn't a name for it at the time, but today they call it date rape."

"Oh, I'm sorry."

"Don't be. You did nothing wrong. I did nothing wrong. It was that bastard." She smiled at Jules. "It took me a couple years of therapy to be able to say that and meant it. But, I couldn't stay close to home. Those days it was impossible to even think about going to the police about something like that. I lived in a small town and I would run into him every now and then."

"How horrible."

"I agree. That's how I ended up across the country waiting on tables instead of in college studying art."

"And you met Mr. Santini."

She chuckled. "I wanted nothing to do with men, but well, you know Santinis."

"Yeah. I do."

"I know you do."

"But, I wasn't raped."

"No. You weren't. But rape is violence. Someone has power over you. What you have to decide is if that is going to rule your life now?"

She didn't know what to say so she nodded.

"I think now if I hadn't met Stewart and he wasn't so hard headed, I wouldn't have had the most wonderful life. All my boys." She smiled. "I can't think of what life would be without them."

Jules smiled. "How did Mr. Santini snag you?"

Joey shook her head. "That's a story for another time. Just remember to have more faith in yourself."

"I do. To a point. It's hard."

The narrowed look Joey gave her was enough to scare her. "I love my boys. But believe me, I know what a pain in the ass each of them can be. Vince is so like his father it is scary. They get their head set on some task and they won't let it go. I know my baby boy and know he loves you. I know you love him. It's written all over your face. Still, don't put up with any of his crap. Swear to God every one of them think they know best. Also remember, whatever Vince does, he does out of love for you."

Jules blinked against the tears burning the backs of her eyes. "Thank you, Joey."

Joey gave her a blinding smile. She had seen it before. Whenever Joey flashed it at Mr. Santini, he melted like butter for her.

"Now, I like those little purple leaf things you put in Vince's backyard. I want some."

"You know you can just break off some of them from Vince's?"

Joey shook her head. "First, that's not good business. Second, he isn't answering my phone calls."

"Oh, but he and I…" then she trailed off realizing that Vince had been avoiding his mother but spending his time talking to Jules on the phone.

"That's fine, Jules. As long as he's talking to someone, I'm fine with that. For now. Well, for another day or two. After that, I'll send Stewart. Let's get some purple thingies."

She nodded pushing her concerns aside for the moment, but Joey had definitely given her a lot to think about.

* * * *

"So, you've decided to hide out here," his father said walking into his garage. Vince looked over his shoulder and stifled the sigh. He should have known his mother would send his father over to check on him.

"I've been busy the last few days."

He grabbed a cloth and rose, wiping the grease from his hands. He'd done just about anything to keep himself busy the last two days. He'd given Jules space, but they had talked the last couple nights. It had been almost as if they were in high school on the phone for hours at a time with nothing much to say. Hell, they had watched an episode of NCIS together on the phone.

"She's worried you and Jules had a fight."

Vince shook his head. "We had a difference of opinion, not a fight."

His father chuckled. "Yeah, your mother and I have those. She's a little more… expressive in her irritation than I think Jules would be."

His father had settled on the workbench, so Vince figured he was stuck talking to him. He was still a little too raw, but he knew better than tell his father to leave him alone. Instead, Vince opened the small refrigerator he kept in the garage and grabbed a couple of beers.

"Thanks," his father said, twisting off the top and taking a long drink. All the while he kept his gaze on Vince.

"You need to talk about it, son, or it's going to tear you up."

"Jules told me some pretty horrible things."

His father nodded. "About Mike I take it?"

"You knew?"

He shook his head. "No. Both your mother and I suspected and when her mother Margerie called your mother out of the blue and asked her to check on Jules, we knew something went on. When Jules first moved back, she was wounded.

It was easy to see. All we knew was that they were getting divorced then he was dead. Plus, she said things that were odd."

"Like what?"

"Your mother asked her how she liked living here and she said it was wonderful and she felt safe."

"So?"

"Safe isn't the first thing that comes to mind when talking about moving back. It was just an odd way of phrasing it." He shrugged. "Her mother's concern on top of that had your mother thinking she was hurt in some way."

He nodded. They had talked about it. He told her that he accepted it, accepted what she had been through.

"Jesse knows."

"Johnson? Interesting."

"Apparently, he's the one who took her to the hospital the first time."

His father shook his head. "And she lost count after that?"

"No, that's the worst part of the story. One slap, one beating, and she left. Filed charges, filed for divorce."

"Always said that girl had a good head on her shoulders. I never understood what she saw in Mike."

He glanced at his father. "What do you mean?"

Regret moved over his features. "Mike was a user. Always was. I know you were close friends with him, but there was something bad in him. He had a temper and let's face it, your friendship fell apart when you left for Annapolis."

"And he didn't get in."

"Yeah, he was pissed." He took another drink. "What happened?"

"What?"

"What else happened?'

He sighed. "Mike got out on bail and found her. He almost killed her."

"Damn shame he died in a wreck."

"Yeah, I would like to kill him all over again." He shook his head. "How is it I didn't know him at all?"

"You did. If you had wanted to stay friends with him, you would have known what was going on."

He shook his head. "That didn't have to do with Mike."

"No, it had to do with Jules." He glanced at his father who shrugged again. "We all know you were in hung up on her."

"I told her I loved her the day they got married."

His father chuckled. "Son, you have horrendous timing. If you weren't the spitting image of me, I would say you weren't a Santini."

He smiled. "Yeah. Well, she said nothing and that was the end of it."

"Until now. What are you doing moping around here?"

"She won't get married." It hurt to think about it, but it hurt to admit that she would marry Mike and not him.

"You asked her?"

"No. We tripped over the conversation. Then, she was telling me she wouldn't get married again and why."

Papa studied him for a second or two. "What are you going to do about it?"

"I've given her space. And I told her I would accept what she could give me."

His father sighed and shook his head. "What am I going to do with you and your brothers? Hell, MJ had to come here and get your brother."

"Mom called her."

"Well, that's true, but still. Go get that woman. She loves you. You love her. You make it work."

"But—"

"No buts. Go get her. You let her go once. Do you think you can deal with her getting involved with another man?"

"We're still seeing each other."

"Yeah. Well maybe she's gonna find a man who has a set of balls on him to go after her."

He frowned at his father.

"Exactly. Better get your house in order. Your mother will be thrilled."

He handed his bottle to Vince.

"And now I get lasagna for dinner."

"With meat and fresh mozzarella?"

"Yep. You're mother promised if I came over here to poke at you she'd make that and cannoli. If you want a bit of advice about your mother?"

"Not really."

His father smiled. "Don't ignore her calls. It doesn't work out well for anyone, especially for me."

He nodded. "Thanks, Dad."

"Just remember, Jules might be resistant to marriage, but then, she's never had to deal with a Santini before."

He waved as his father backed out and drove off. He was right. Vince had to deal with the problem head on. First though, he had some things to work out. Plus, he had a dog to kidnap.

CHAPTER TEN

Jules was tired. It was only four o'clock in the afternoon. She hadn't had a good night's sleep in five days. She'd grown accustomed to having Vince beside her in bed. Worse, Rufus had grown so attached to Vince that he howled every night for about an hour waiting for him to show up. It was endearing in a way, but she hadn't gotten any rest.

The talks they had over the phone had been good. The space had given her time to think. He wasn't punishing her, which she understood. But, she wasn't sure where they stood. At some point, they were going to have to deal with everything that came up.

She knew she hadn't had enough sleep when she thought she heard Rufus bark. She frowned and peered out the window of her office. There was a commotion at the front of the store. Worried what it could mean, she stepped out and started walking down the aisle. Then, she came to a dead stop.

Standing at the front of the store was Vince. He was in full mess dress complete with sword and gloves. Beside him at his feet was Rufus. The damned ornery dog was sitting there and she could swear he was smiling at her. He'd had a bath from the looks of it and he was wearing a red bow.

She looked back at Vince. He had no expression on his face.

"What are you doing here?"

Okay, that sounded rude. Really rude.

"I'm here for you."

She swore she heard all the woman in the shop sigh. She ignored it.

"You think I'm going to fall for that?"

"Yeah. Because I love you and I'm not going to let you deny us happiness because of past experience."

Her heart turned over and she blinked.

"You think you can't make a good wife? That you're not good at marriage? Rufus and I think you're wrong."

He stepped up and Rufus automatically followed. Both of them stopped right in front of her. Vince set a towel on the wet pavement then knelt.

"Julianna Erica Andrews, will you marry me?"

He opened the small ring case. In the white velvet sat an antique ring.

She said nothing. She couldn't. There was a lump in her throat. Joey was right. Was she going to let Mike ruin her life? One that would be full of Vince and babies, and God love them, Santinis.

"I can get you a new ring Jules. This was my grandmother's and I've had it for almost fifteen years."

When she looked up from the ring to his face she realized he'd had it that day. The day he'd kissed her so sweetly and told her he loved her. She was lost. There were hundreds of reasons not to get married again, especially to a man in the military. But none of them mattered because there was one important factor, the one thing that she could never replace.

Vince.

No one other than her parents had made her feel that good about herself. He made her believe in happy endings again…and she loved him. God help her, she was so damned in love with him. He had dressed himself in his mess dress, bathed her dog and proposed in public…in possibly the most romantic way. And with a ring he'd been carrying around for her for years.

Was there any way she could say no to a man who loved her so completely? The one man she was convinced was made for her?

"Oh, babe, don't cry."

She shook her head. "I just like the way you see me. You...ignore the things that I think are horrible and only see the good. It's been so long." She shook her head afraid she'd start balling in earnest. "Yes, Vicente, I'll marry you."

He rose to his feet and pulled her into his arms. With the flowers overhead again, he kissed her and she knew she had made the right decision this time around.

When he pulled back, she heard the howling. She glanced down at Rufus. "What did you do to my dog?"

"Nothing. He just isn't happy about that red bow."

She chuckled. "I don't blame him."

"You've made me happy, Jules." Then he smiled. "Now, do you want an ending like *An Officer and a Gentleman?*"

"Good lord, no."

He laughed pulled her up against him. "Angela, you can close tonight, right?"

"Wait, you don't run my shop."

"Ignore her, Vince. I can close up. Go," Angela said.

They walked down the aisle, the smell of roses in the air and a howling dog behind them.

There was one thing every woman knew: life with a Santini was never boring.

If you enjoyed The Santinis, you have another group of military men to fall in love with starting this August and a special edition for the holiday season.

You met two of MJ's brothers in The Santinis and now they are back in their own series!

SEMPER FI MARINES
The Johnson Brothers get their happily ever after!

A SANTINI CHRISTMAS
Mama Joey Santini won readers' hearts as she helped her boys find their way to true love. Now, read the story of how Papa (Stewart) and Joey first met and fell in love all those years ago. Coming this November!

Coming this month from Melissa Schroeder, the next exciting
book in the national bestselling HARMLESS series!

When this Dom falls hard, he will do anything to protect the woman he loves.

A Little Harmless Ride

Elias St John has lived a life most people wouldn't believe. An Aussie by birth, he has found his way to the Big Island working as the right hand man to Joe Kaheaku. When his boss dies and leaves the ranch to Eli and Joe's niece Crysta Miller, Eli finds himself more than a little attracted to her.

After finding her fiancé in bed with another woman and helping her father through his illness, Crysta is ready for a new start. The offer of the ranch far away from home is perfect. The only problem she has is with Eli who constantly tells her what to do. When an argument turns into a passionate kiss, both of them get more than they were expecting.

Eli finds himself completely enthralled with Crysta as his submissive. As seemingly simple accidents turn deadly, Eli realizes that someone is bent on destroying the ranch by any means possible—even murder.

WARNING, this book contains the following: A cynical Dom, a woman ready for adventure, Hawaiian cowboys-yeah they have them, horse rides, stunning sunsets and a new island for Addicts to cherish. Remember, it's Harmless so bring on the ice water and towels.

Eli stepped closer. She wished she could see him, but that would be admitting the need she had for him. The cocky Dom knew she wanted him, but it didn't mean she had to give him the satisfaction of acknowledging her attraction.

"So you think you can resist me?" he asked, his voice deepening. She felt his breath against her ear and she shivered.

"What you don't seem to understand is that I have control over my own desires. I'm not some little sub who is awed by the popular Dom."

"Hmm." It was all he said as he nibbled on her ear.

It took all her willpower to step away from him and the temptation he represented. Crysta turned then settled her hands on her hips trying to keep from reaching for him. Every fiber of her being wanted that…but she'd been truthful. She might be a sub, but she wasn't inexperienced.

"We have to run this ranch together for months. I don't think it's a good idea to get tangled up."

He wasn't happy, that was easy to see. His narrowed glare almost made her laugh. Had no one really ever rejected this man? Probably not. He was a Dom…a good one. The fact that he was a cowboy with a sexy Aussie accent was enough to make most women swoon.

Crysta was made of stronger stuff.

He moved forward and slipped his hand on her waist. Ignoring her protest, he pulled her closer and kissed her. It was a full frontal assault that had her senses reeling. She could smell the leather and sweet Hawaiian air on him as he thrust his tongue in her mouth. She resisted for a second, then surrendered to pleasure.

In the next instant he was gone. Eli released her then stepped back.

"If you want another taste it comes with a price," he said.

Both of them knew the charge would be her submission.

ABOUT THE AUTHOR

From an early age, Melissa loved to read. First, it was the books her mother read to her including her two favorites, *Winnie the Pooh* and the *Beatrix Potter* books. She cut her preteen teeth on *Trixie Belden* and read and reviewed *To Kill a Mockingbird* in middle school. It wasn't until she was in college that she tried to write her first stories, which were full of angst and pain, and really not that fun to read or write. After trying several different genres, she found romance in a Linda Howard book.

Since the publication of her first book in 2004, Melissa has had fifty romances published. She writes in genres from historical suspense to modern day erotic romance to futuristics and paranormals. Included in those releases is the bestselling Harmless series. In 2011, Melissa branched out into self-publishing with *A Little Harmless Submission* and the popular military spinoff, *Infatuation: A Little Harmless Military Romance.* Along the way she has garnered an epic nomination, a multitude of reviewer's recommended reads, over five Capa nods from TRS, three nominations for AAD Bookies and regularly tops the best seller lists on *Amazon and Barnes & Noble.*

Since she spent her childhood as a military brat, Melissa swore never to marry military. But, as we all know, Fate has her way with mortals. She is married to an AF major and is raising her own brats, both human and canine. She spends her days giving in to her addiction to Twitter, counting down the days until her hubby retires, and cursing the military for always sticking them in a location that is filled with bugs big enough to eat her children.

You can connect with Mel all over the web:

www.melissaschroeder.net

twitter.com/melschroeder

facebook.com/melissaschroederfanpage

www.facebook.com/groups/harmlesslovers

www.facebook.com/thesantinis

www.facebook.com/semperfimarinesseries

Or email her at: *Contact@MelissaSchroeder.net*

Other Books by Melissa Schroeder

Harmless

A Little Harmless Sex

A Little Harmless Pleasure

A Little Harmless Obsession

A Little Harmless Lie

A Little Harmless Addiction

A Little Harmless Submission

A Little Harmless Fascination

A Little Harmless Fantasy

A Little Harmless Ride

A Little Harmless Military Romance

Infatuation

Possession

Surrender

The Harmless Shorts

The Santinis

Leonardo

Marco

Gianni

Vicente

Once Upon An Accident

The Accidental Countess

Lessons in Seduction

The Spy Who Loved Me

Leather and Lace

The Seduction of Widow McEwan

Leather and Lace—Print anthology

Texas Temptations

Conquering India

Delilah's Downfall

Hawaiian Holidays

Mele Kalikimaka, Baby

Sex on the Beach

Getting Lei'd

Bounty Hunters, Inc

For Love or Honor

Sinner's Delight

The Sweet Shoppe

Her Wicked Warrior

Cowboy Up

Tempting Prudence

Connected Books

Seducing the Saint

Hunting Mila

Saints and Sinners—print of both books

The Hired Hand

Hands on Training

Cancer Anthology

Water—print

A Calculated Seduction

Going for Eight

Stand Alone Books

Grace Under Pressure

The Last Detail

Her Mother's Killer

Telepathic Cravings

Chasing Luck

Coming Soon

Semper Fi Marines

Tease Me

Tempt Me

Touch Me

Virgin Brewing

Only For Him: A Little Harmless Serial

The Santinis

A Santini Christmas

CPSIA information can be obtained at www.ICGtesting.com
Printed in the USA
LVOW12s2144300913

354769LV00001B/328/P